Seven Turns

Seven Turns

Bill Smith

Mojo Triangle Books™
An Imprint Of

SARTORIS
LITERARY
GROUP

A traditional publisher
with a non-traditional approach to publishing

Library of Congress Control Number
2015942124

A special thank you to Ms. Bernadette Kalteis
of the staff of Melk Abbey for her research
assistance in the preparation of this book.

SARTORIS LITERARY GROUP
Metro Jackson, Mississippi, USA
www.sartorisliterary.com

To Betty—I only wrote the
book. That was the easy
part. Betty did all of the things that
made it happen. That was the
hard part. And she did it willingly,
even encouraged me. That's the
wondrous part.

CHAPTER 1

Andrew looked like an average guy who followed the Pittsburgh Steelers on weekends, loved his wife and kids, had a mortgage on his house, and sold insurance for a living. But he wasn't typical at all. He lived in a 900-year-old stone building in Europe with one hundred other guys.

Andrew was a monk and he was about to discover something hugely important.

Surely Andrew was chosen by God to make the discovery that day. He was a careful and learned monk, but he almost missed the clues. They weren't big or obvious. Some clues tried to nestle affectionately with similar ones as if to hide, while others were made with color and easier to see, if one only noticed. It didn't happen right away, but later, near the end of his assignment that day in the quiet space of the ancient workroom above the monastery's great library.

And when Andrew made the discovery, he didn't know what he found.

* * *

The hour slipped into late afternoon at Austria's majestic 12th century Melk Abbey. Fewer than a dozen black-robed monks remained in the ornate Scriptorium, each one hunched over an ancient desk, immersed in a time honored task. They worked silently, slowly transcribing the gilded letters and words with care and precision from centuries old manuscripts to sheets of fine parchment. Tiny bottles of color ink, groups of quills and stems, and assorted writing aids were lined with precision across the front of each desk. The modern green shaded electric desk lamp seemed out of place, but it flooded their work area with shadowless light. A single traditional desk candle stationed on the left remained unlit.

Brother Andrew rubbed his eyes. He had been at his desk transcribing the word of God all day. He felt fulfilled as he neatly stacked four new hand-copied pages of parchment on the side of his wooden desk and carefully closed the six hundred year old book. His eyes fell casually on the worn cover. And then he saw it. It must have been there all the time, he just hadn't noticed it. Several lines of ink formed some type of a design.

It began with a four centimeter vertical line that ran downward along the spine of the cover then turned 90 degrees to the right and ran for another four centimeters parallel with the bottom of the cover. A separate line, this one heaver and marked in blue, ran along the opposite side of the cover. All lines were equal in length. He quickly reached for the enlarging glass and studied the marks from top to bottom. They were not part of the original book. They had been added.

The strange pattern of lines didn't register with him at first, but he quickly became disturbed when he determined that they were added for some unnecessary and perhaps mischievous reason.

He felt ashamed as anger swelled within him.

Who could have done such a terrible thing to this wonderful book? Surely it was not another monk. All of the brothers at Melk Abbey loved the wonderful collection of ancient books, no one would think of disfiguring a single one. Besides, such an action would violate the Holy Rule of Saint Benedict and the person would surely be expelled from the monastery. But if not another monk, who could it be?

But Andrew was only sent to make the discovery, not to understand it. He was the messenger. And what did he find? A group of lines and marks on a book held little meaning at the time. But that was only the beginning. There would be new and different clues and scores of discoveries, all of which would point to a mystery that begged to be solved. Sadly, Brother Andrew would never know that his find that evening was part of the most astonishing wartime discovery of the Twentieth Century.

CHAPTER 2

Wilhelm Gerhard paused in the lobby of one of Milan's stylish small office buildings and eyed the tenant directory.

Cavello & Sons...Suite Six.

He reached for the illuminated number six button, when a voice said:

"Not that elevator, sir. We take this one."

It was André Beau, his Swiss agent. They met a few years ago when André arranged for Gerhard to purchase a majestic chalet that overlooked Lake Lucerne. Now this trusted friend was about to conclude Gerhard's latest and possibly the most important assignment, the purchase of a private railcar. The two men greeted each other warmly as André explained they would not use the public building elevators in the front and would led Gerhard down a marble hall toward the rear of the building. The smell of cigar smoke increased as they reached a lone elevator at the end of the hall.

"This is Mr. Cavello's private elevator. It's used by clients who prefer to stay out of public view and opens directly into Mr. Cavello's reception suite."

Beau inserted a small key into the elevator lock and the door slid open immediately.

Gerhard's natural instants kicked in and he began to form a mental image of the attorney he had yet to meet. *I bet this guy is short and fat and smokes a sloppy cigar.*

Both men entered the small elevator and it began a slow assent. Gerhard was used to hearing elevator music of all types, but never anything like this. It was the sound of applause and cheering. It grew a little louder and more intense as the elevator went higher. His face twisted into an inquisitive frown as he looked over at Beau for an explanation.

"It's applause for Mr. Cavello. It was the applause he received for his performance during the 2009 Winter Olympics. He had it recorded and put into his elevator. Our attorney, Mister Alfonso Cavello, was one of two athletes to qualify from Italy for the World Figure Skating Championship."

Gerhard's jaw dropped at such unexpected news just as the elevator stopped and the door slid open to an elegant reception area. The secretary was on the phone, but she quickly interrupted her conversation.

"So nice to see you again, Mr. Beau. Mr. Cavello is ready for you." She gestured to a double pair of open French doors.

Cavello's office was old world, dark furniture, ferns, and heavy shutters. He wasn't short and fat at all, but medium in height, toned and trim, sported a large droopy mint green bow tie with a tailored gray suit, and appeared to be in his late twenties.

Gerhard thought he was too young to be a renowned attorney, but he certainly had the energy to be an ice skater. He almost bounded from behind his desk to greet his visitors as he led them to a conference table on the side of his office that was literally covered with legal papers—stacks of them, all neatly grouped according to subject.

The secretary closed the French doors and the men took seats in three comfortable chairs that were clustered in front of the table. Cavello served coffee from a small ornate gilded table near-by. Just three minutes of pleasant conversation passed and the attorney was ready to move ahead with business.

"These papers all reflect legal matters that relate to various aspects of the closing of the railroad car, which was in the estate of the deceased."

Now Gerhard felt Cavello sounded more like an attorney.

"As you know, all five heirs have accepted your offer of 500,000 euros and I have held your check in that amount. I'll make the disbursements according to the terms of the will and the conditions of the sales contract as identified in this addendum. Per your instructions, sir, the title is drawn in the name of RR Trust."

He continued with the legal explanation of the closing procedures and identified the purpose of each stack of papers on the conference table. Gerhard examined them all and was impressed with the thorough preparation of the documents.

He only had a few questions and Cavello answered every one. Then, he signed 'RR Trust' in the various spaces as instructed.

"Congratulations Mr. Gerhard," he said as he poured a bit of sherry into three small glasses. "You're now the proud owner of one damn nice private railcar. This occasion calls for something special."

They sipped the nectar as Mr. Cavello continued.

"I have two additional points that I'd like to mention. First, I've opened operational contracts in the name on your deed with every railroad company in Europe. Here is a list of those carriers and the contact person. Simply email or telephone the contact with your transportation instructions to store or move your car. I've found that on occasion it is both appropriate and beneficial for another person, such as your attorney, to initiate an order on your behalf. My firm will provide these services should you wish to take advantage of them. Your signature on this procedural paper will authorize us to act for you at any time you need us."

Gerhard thought about the idea for a moment. It offered some real third party advantages, so he signed the paper. He liked the way Cavello operated. He was sensible, articulate, and swift.

"Mr. Beau told me that you wish to move the car to Vienna as soon as possible. I've arranged for the car to leave Milan at 6 tomorrow morning. Would that be acceptable?"

Gerhard nodded that it was and Cavello told his

secretary to activate the release of Mr. Gerhard's move order.

"Second, the previous owner of the railcar traveled with a man who took care of the car for him. He knew how everything worked and became the owner's operational companion. I contacted him and asked that he stand by this afternoon to give you an orientation tour of your new car."

"That's a splendid and thoughtful idea." Gerhard turned to André. "Do you think we could have a bite of lunch and be at the rail yard in about two hours?"

André nodded that the timing would be fine and Mr. Cavello immediately punched a number into his cell phone.

"Hello Piccolo! It's Alfonso. The new owner will arrive at the car around two o'clock. Yes, I'll send it in a few minutes."

The meeting was over and Mr. Cavello escorted his guests to the elevator. The recorded applause and cheers started again as the elevator began its decent, but this time Gerhard's face broke into a broad grin.

"I like it. Very clever."

"I don't mean this as a pun," said André, "but Mr. Cavello told me the applause in the elevator gave him a 'lift.' It made him feel good. He listened to it every morning on the way up to his office and on the way down every evening as well."

"It's his applause. He earned it. Not everyone gets to perform in the Olympics. Did he win?"

"No. He didn't even place."

André stopped for lunch at a café that looked rather nice on the outside, but it was seedy on the inside. They had only coffee and a sandwich and quickly drove on to the railroad yard.

"I think you selected a good attorney for the closing," said Gerhard, as they drove through the Piazza della Repubblica. "I like him and I believe we can do business together in the future."

"I am glad to hear that. His father and grandfather were both in the National Assembly. The family is well known in Italy."

"Did Cavello ever hold political office?"

"No. He was too busy making money by helping other politicians avoid corruption charges and tax problems."

Gerhard smiled at the comment and watched the street scenes pass.

"Here we are."

Beau drove into the railroad complex and parked near the yard master's office. Gerhard could see his private railcar several tracks away. It stood alone, uncoupled to anything else and looked handsome; no, it looked flat-out intriguing. He felt good knowing it was his and he was anxious to go inside. Someone was sitting on a stool next to the rear platform.

That must be Mr. Piccolo.

They crossed the tracks to the railroad car. The man on the stool stood as they approached. He was quite short, perhaps only five feet tall. Beau mumbled something under his breath that Gerhard overheard.

"I think Piccolo means 'short' in Italian and he certainly is short."

"Hello. Are you Mr. Piccolo?"

"Yes," answered the little man.

"This is Mr. Wilhelm Gerhard, the new owner of the rail car."

"I am happy to meet you sir," he said as he extended his hand. "Mr. Cavello asked me to meet you and explain things about the car."

"He told me that you know everything about it. I'll listen to you carefully."

And so began Gerhard's introduction to something special, something unusual, and something few people own—a private railroad car. He hoped it would provide increased mobility, greater flexibility, and a level of security beyond that offered by a permanently fixed structure. Mr. Piccolo began his explanation in a slow and deliberate manner, careful not to cover items too briefly or too fast. It was surprising, but the two men seemed to have an immediate rapport with each other. Piccolo respected Gerhard as the new owner and Gerhard respected Piccolo for his knowledge of the car. One would never know by watching them that they had met for the first time just minutes ago.

Piccolo's practical explanation ranged from the simple to the complicated. He demonstrated how to kick loose the single metal step attached under the boarding stairs to reach the rear platform rather than carry around or store the portable wooden stool to climb aboard.

He reviewed the difference between 240 VAC and

480VAC and how they related to commercial power and onboard generated power, and how to convert each to gas and diesel power. Gerhard was amazed at the flexibility of his car and all of the interworking details that Piccolo had of it.

The onboard kitchen was small, but exceptionally convenient, with a cooking surface that used either electric or gas burners—and even diesel in an emergency. The refrigerator and freezer worked with the same flexibility.

Gerhard opened the freezer and found it full of steaks, chops, and sausage. The car even had a wine cooler complete with several bottles of Chardonnay. Piccolo explained that the previous owner wouldn't use the refrigerator for his white wine. It was too cold. "Fine wine required a cooler, not a refrigerator, and it should never be stored lower than 12 degrees Centigrade."

Gerhard was increasingly impressed with the little man's wide knowledge base and nodded in agreement about the storage temperature. Then he looked at André for an explanation about the presence of the meat and wine.

"Mr. Cavello sent the frozen meat and I sent the wine and bakery items in the pantry," he said with a big smile. "Call it a house warming gift."

Piccolo reviewed the operation and maintenance of the toilets, or 'heads' as he called them, where to fill the water supply, how the air conditioners and heaters worked, how to set the combination on both the fore and aft doors, and the ins and outs of the alarm system.

Piccolo was on a roll and he enjoyed explaining

everything immensely. Gerhard was exhausted. But the timing was right as every operational item had been explained. Or so it seemed.

"Three other items come with the car that are not on the construction plans that I gave you earlier," announced Piccolo. "The first one is back here." He led them to the closet in the master stateroom. "Press against the lower section of the paneling and slide it to the right."

Gerhard did so and it revealed a space about the size of a telephone book.

"This is a space to use in a private way," whispered Piccolo. "No one will know that it's here."

It was a secret compartment, one Gerhard felt he could put to good use.

"Now, two items remain for our attention," he said as he led Gerhard back to the spacious lounge area and stopped next to a piece of luggage that leaned against the wall and rested on a short riser or platform. He hadn't noticed it before, perhaps because it was black and nearly tucked out-of-sight.

"Is that your suitcase?" asked Gerhard.

"No, sir, it's yours. It's built into the railcar."

Gerhard looked confused.

"It's not really a piece of luggage, sir. The sides aren't leather but black marble. They came from a rare vein of black marble that was discovered in the hills outside of the famous Carrara marble quarries—the very one that Michelangelo used when he selected marble for his masterpiece, *David*. The wide center band is stainless steel with a top lock and center handle."

"It looks like an oversized marble briefcase to me. What would I do with that?"

"You would do this, sir. First slide the lock to the side. Then grasp the handle and pull it down firmly to the floor, like this. And surprise—a fireplace disguised as a briefcase."

"Absolutely ingenious!" responded Gerhard. "A tiny fireplace."

"Right," answered Piccolo in a mischievous voice. "A regular sized fireplace, even a small one, would consume lots of floor space and space was always at a premium on a railcar. But Mr. Pedretti still wanted one. He worked on lots of designs and settled on this one."

Gerhard kneeled on the floor next to the unusual fireplace to get a closer look.

"The narrow horizontal pipe in the back is connected to the railcar's main compressed gas supply. Just light it and you have a gas fireplace. Or you could pile small rounds of coal over it, and the gas will start a coal fire. The previous owner switched to charcoal briquettes because they were easier to find and burned much cleaner. The wall behind the fireplace was furred out slightly to allow fumes to vent through a flat chimney on the roof of the railcar. Mr. Pedretti and I spent many cold Italian winter nights around this warm little fireplace."

"Just amazing. I look forward to sitting here as well."

"The last item is over here."

Piccolo stepped to the side of the luxurious leather sofa.

"I always use the little metal upholstery tacks in the

armrest as my guide."

He sat down on the sofa and placed his arm on the armrest with his hand draped over the front.

"I find the center tack with my middle finger and carefully move it to either the three or nine o'clock position, depending on the side of the sofa that I'm sitting on."

They watched intently, mesmerized with what the amazing little man was doing.

I bet this is going to be another secret compartment.

It was secret, but what he was about to discover was nothing remotely close to what he was thinking.

"I take my finger to the outside edge and drop back 4 centimeters along the side like this. Now I have the spot. Use this procedure on either arm of the sofa and the arms of those two chairs. Simply press the spot, like this."

The entire lower front portion of the sofa slid into the drawing room as a large tray loaded with weapons. A huge wide-barreled gun almost two meters long complete with a sort of mounting device was first, followed by two black assault rifles, and two shotguns with walnut stocks, all neatly arranged in their sponged storage space on the tray.

Piccolo scampered to each chair and pushed its button. A tray of hand guns slid out of one chair followed by a tray of assorted ammunition from the second chair. He stood proudly, like a little kid showing off his toys, as he watched for a reaction from his guests.

At first, Gerhard and André just stood there with open mouths unable to comprehend what just happened. André spoke first. "My God, I haven't seen an arsenal like this since my days in the Swiss National Service."

Slowly the men walked around the display of weapons. They looked at one, and then ran a finger along another.

"Does all of this stuff come with the railcar?" asked Gerhard.

Piccolo rose to his tip toes.

"Yes sir. It's all yours. The previous owner, who died, told me that he needed these guns to protect him from hoodlums or thieves who might try to get him."

"Did an occasion occur when it was necessary to use them?" asked Beau.

"No sir. The guns have never been out of the holding tray, except to be examined, and they've never been fired. Of course, I took them out and cleaned and oiled them on occasion, but that was it."

Gerhard squatted next to the huge gun in the front of the tray and took hold of the tip of the wide barrel.

"What type of gun is this? It seems so big and heavy. How was it to be used?"

"Mr. Pedretti told me it was a cannon. It was too heavy for him to pick up and hold alone, so I had to help him. I'll show you where it goes if you'll help me carry it."

Piccolo instructed both men on exactly where to hold the cannon and all three of them lifted.

"Now what?" asked Beau.

"We walk slowly together out the back door onto the platform."

The three-man cannon procession moved carefully through the door without a problem, then out on the rear platform of the railroad car just as Piccolo instructed.

"That was much easier than when Mr. Pedretti and I moved the gun." Gerhard rolled his eyes and shook his head.

"I don't think this cannon thing is going work for me," said Gerhard as they balanced the big gun across the top of the platform railing.

"It was pretty big and awkward for Mr. Pedretti too. He was gonna trade it in on something smaller, like a rocket launcher."

Now it was André's turn to roll his eyes.

"How did you plan to support this thing and fire it at the same time?"

"Mr. Pedretti put this flag holder in the center of the top platform rail. The cannon has a stem on the bottom that supports the gun and lets it swivel. Just drop the gun stem into the flag holder like this."

Both Gerhard and Beau rushed to help the small man, who in his excitement nearly picked up the gun alone.

"And there you are. See how easily it swivels?"

Indeed, the cannon was stable and it moved effortlessly in about a 190 degree arc. And it tilted up and down as well. Any villain who tried to approach the rail car from the rear as it moved down the track would encounter an experience he would not soon forget.

"I think I like the rocket launcher idea a little better," mused Gerhard. "Let's put this thing back to bed."

The three men carried the gun back into the lounge

and carefully reset it into the sponged storage spot.

"How do I close up the furniture?"

"Just locate the same spot on each armrest and push."

Gerhard did, and each tray slid back into the furniture and disappeared. The room changed from a weapon arsenal back to a luxurious lounge at the push of a spot.

"I must admit that this is one fine way to hide something. Not in the usual wall or floor compartment, but in the upholstery."

They said goodbye to Mr. Piccolo. Gerhard thanked him with a one hundred euro note.

"Interesting person," he said as he watched the man step carefully across the row of tracks and head to a little red pick-up truck. "I think he's going to miss this railcar. He seemed so fond of it."

It was time for André to leave as well. He had to catch a plane back to Lucerne for a 10 o'clock appointment in the morning to show a farmhouse to a Canadian couple. Gerhard gave him a check for his services and fees that were not covered by the disbursement at the lawyer's office and walked him back to his rental car.

"Thank you again for your splendid assistance. You found a real beauty for me."

André drove away and Gerhard was alone. He turned to cross the tracks, but stopped as he caught sight of his new railcar. It glistened in the late afternoon sun and seemed to pulsate with energy. The car spoke to him. They were going to get along together just fine.

That was the feeling of the moment and it would be a lasting one, but there was no way for Gerhard to know the events of the future. An unimaginable adventure of a lifetime was already forming. It would transcend everything that happened to him previously. And it would start before he knew it. But for now, the future could wait a few hours. He needed time to explore the railcar, enjoy the steak and wine, and spend his first night aboard. Tomorrow would come soon enough.

CHAPTER 3

Wolf pushed the shopping cart from the grocery market to his car in the lot next door. It was a small store owned by a Vietnamese couple who were occasionally bullied by self-proclaimed neighborhood punks.

The couple had to keep the store open late to make ends meet, but shopping late was good for Wolf—fewer people, fewer police. He clicked his electronic car key holder and the trunk lid popped open just as he reached his black Jetta.

Without thinking about it, he switched the car keys to his prosthetic steel left hand and began unloading the cart with his right hand. First he shoved the tall bags to the rear of the trunk and then began to surround them with smaller bags with bottles and heavy cans to hold everything in place. He was meticulous about how his car trunk was packed.

"Hey goof ass!" said a sudden voice. "You don't need a nice car like this. Gimme the keys, goof ass!"

Wolf stopped short. He wasn't afraid. His three-fingered, steel power pack hand had killed people before and he also had his shoulder holstered revolver. The voice in the dark knew none of this. He slowly backed out from under the trunk lid, straightened up, and turned to face the voice.

It was an acid punk, two of them in fact, and each carried something in their hand. Both had pointy hair and red marks drawn down from their eyes, apparently to resemble blood. They looked ridiculous. Wolf tried to hold it back but he began to laugh in quick short bursts, which annoyed the acid punkers.

"I said gimme the keys, goof ass!"

The pointy hair raised a lead pipe and took a step toward Wolf.

An idea quickly shot into Wolf's mind. *This is going to be sooooo easy.*

"Okay, okay. You win. Here are the keys." He held the keys out in his steel hand, but it was too dark for the punkers to see the metal hand, only the car keys, free for the taking. The metal keys hung loose from the center point steel extension finger, the one with the copper ribbon of extra low resistance.

"That's a good little ass," mocked the punk.

All he has to do is touch it. Please, just touch it, pleaded Wolf to himself.

The punk grabbed the keys and Wolf instantly energized his power cell. His prosthetic finger became a discharging electrode and sent the punker to his knees. The second punker was confused by the sight and started to lunge at Wolf, but turned and ran when he witnessed his friend collapse completely on the parking lot pavement. It took all of five seconds. The electrocution was fast. The punker was dead.

CHAPTER 4

Gerhard bounded up the metal train steps and stood for a moment in the center of the rear platform of his very own private railcar. He sensed the energy of the car as he looked out across the railroad yard. He felt like the head of state ready to make a campaign speech to a cheering crowd, but there was no audience, just a couple of switch engines and some yard men moving freight cars around.

He was especially pleased with the design and engineering of the galley. It was super-efficient, much better than he had imagined and certainly more intelligently arranged then a regular house kitchen that was twice as large.

He didn't see the second wine cellar at first, perhaps because this one was covered with a red wool accent rug and was built into the floor of the galley. Surprised at the discovery, he opened the cellar and found it full of premium wine. He selected a bottle of French 2005 white burgundy. The stock was exquisite, but how did it get there?

A wine glass enclosure was built into the side of a galley cabinet. He chose a glass and began to pour the white burgundy when he noticed a crest etched on the glass. He held it up to the light and examined it more closely. It was the Papal Crest.

My God, could this have been used by the Pope? And why not? The Pope drinks wine! The glasses were probably brought on-board by the previous owner, but how did he get them?

The implication of the discovery was overwhelming.

Gerhard sipped the burgundy from the Pope's glass anyhow, but with dignity and very carefully.

A combination ice maker/freezer was tucked out of sight under the galley counter. Attorney Alfonso Cavello's house warming gift of six prime filet mignons was inside the freezer. He took one and looked for a frying pan only to discover a row of buttons. He pushed one marked grill.

The range cook top immediately flipped over, slid back into the wall, and a gas grill rose from below. He fired up the newly discovered grill, complete with a hefty down-draft exhaust to the track below.

And that's how the discovery of events moved along as Gerhard prepared his first dinner on board his private railcar—white burgundy and grilled filet mignon, rare. Asparagus would have added a lot to the meal, but he couldn't find any on board.

He went to bed that first night without thinking if it would be a good or a bad night. It was mostly a bad one. It was impossible to sleep with locomotives in the area.

Diesel engines passed his window repeatedly. Their steel wheels screeched against the steel rails as the noisy machines shuttled freight cars and assembled trains for the morning run. It went on for hours. *I'm never going to get used to this,* he thought. Then the switch engines moved to the other side of the railroad yard. Finally there was some quiet and he fell asleep instantly.

Eeeeeeeeeeeeeeeeeeee. Gerhard shot straight up in bed. A high-pitched electronic sound filled the car with ear piercing noise. *What's that?* he said to himself, still groggy and unsure where he was. The sound continued. He switched on the bedside lamp, but it wouldn't light up. *What's going on?* A quick glance at his wristwatch verified it was 5:20 AM. He grabbed his revolver, unable to decide which way to point it.

Rrrrrrrrrrrbbbbbbbbbbbllllllllllllll. The muffled sound of some sort of a motor started and the light on his bedside table suddenly went on. The high-pitched electronic sound stopped. Then, to his complete astonishment, the entire room swayed to the right. He hurried to the end of the car and threw open the door only to stare directly into a huge eye blinding headlight that was part of the front end of a giant locomotive just a meter from where he stood, its diesel engine rumbling to go.

"Morning sir," said a voce from the dark side of the track. "We got orders to connect you to that train over there for the run to Vienna. You leave at 6 o'clock."

The locomotive came to life with three short sonic blasts from its horn. *My God this is such a nosy place.* The hot diesel engine rived up and spit oil particles out of the stack as the locomotive moved in reverse. Gerhard's car again swayed, this time backward as the yard crew and the locomotive worked together and shuttled the car to another track where it was connected to the end of the train bound for Vienna. He went inside to the quiet drawing room, carefully sat in the leather chair over the stash of ammunition, and reviewed what just happened.

That was a most unusual wake-up call. It startled the hell out of me. That electronic sound was probably a no power alarm that activated when the car was disconnected from commercial power. The rumble sound was the generator that automatically started when the car lost power for a few seconds. Nice. I like that, but I'd better install some uninterruptible power systems for my computers or I'll lose all of my data when this happens the next time.

Gerhard was intrigued by this whole new process of life on a railroad car. Suddenly he heard a rumble in the distance. It crescendoed down the train ever closer until it included his car. Then movement. He was on his way to Vienna.

He scrambled a couple of eggs, pushed the button on the wall of the drawing room that raised the coffee table to dining height, and enjoyed breakfast. Italy zipped by. He was relaxed and comfortable. Just the quiet clickity-click and gentle sway. The lack of sleep last night caught up with him, his eyes flickered, and he nodded off.

The horn blast from a passing train snapped him back to life. He was awake, but groggy. His mind began to drift from subject to subject and stopped for some reason at diamonds—his diamonds in the safe deposit box at the Bank of China in Amsterdam. Five sacks of them he and Wolf stole from the preparation box in the armored car.

I think Nicole might be ready to enlarge her inventory of diamonds. Yes, I should call her. I bet she'd take half a sack, if not all of it. Besides, it would be so good to talk with her again.

Nicole Eversoll was totally vivacious—not only smart and fun to be with, but absolutely beautiful, tall and slender, with a gleaming swirl of brown hair. She was part of a large and tight-knit Swiss family that marketed an exquisite group of unusual merchandise.

Each family member had a specialty. Nicole concentrated on antique and estate jewelry with an emphasis in unmounted diamonds. A sister bought and sold antique furniture and rare books, a brother worked with distinguished automobiles. Two cousins enjoyed a strong business in the sale of rare paintings and old masterpieces. The parents specialized in large manor houses and castles.

Although he appreciated the Eversoll's wide business knowledge, he valued the family's discreetness even more. One couldn't simply employ the Eversoll's for a service. The Eversoll's selected their clients only upon qualification and Gerhard was one of those who qualified. Besides, he and Nicole liked each other. Perhaps it was the respect that educated and successful people often have in common. Neither felt the need to prove anything to the other. It was simply that Nicole was special to Gerhard.

Unfortunately, he didn't see her very often and now was a chance to change that. He picked up his iPad and called her unlisted number. She answered it immediately.

"Good Lord, Gerhard, where have you been? I considered removing your name from my phone directory for fear that you reached the flat end of the earth and dropped off. Now say something sweet and clever so I know it's really you on the other end of this magic pad."

"I did indeed reach the flat end my dear, but luckily, the damn thing kept going."

They both laughed and enjoyed the verbal play between them—something they've done for years, but not often enough.

"I have the feeling that you're not calling from Zurich, because that would mean we could see each other and actually get together for lunch or dinner."

"Oh, I wish. It'd be awesome to watch you eat mussels again—you love them so," answered Gerhard in a teasing tone.

"You know I hate those slimy things. The good Lord did not put us here to eat such foul food. Now fowl, that's another matter—like pheasant. I'd enjoy pheasant."

They laughed together again like old times, and then Nicole felt the need to prime the conversation to another level. "So, my long lost friend, is this a social or a business call?"

"I am afraid it's business for the moment. Do you have a need for some loose ones?"

Now Nicole went into her professional mode. "Not unless they're 'E' and 500 points."

"No, mine are mostly I, J, and K, maybe some L's,

but they're all in the VS1 range—say 100 to 225 points."

"That's not bad," replied Nicole with renewed interest. "I have friends who could use loose ones like that. Let's talk price for a moment. A 100 pointer, G, with a SI2 clarity, and a 'Good' cut would retail from 1.5 to around 2 thousand. Would you take 400 to 500 for it, wholesale?"

Gerhard paused for a moment in thought and responded with, "Okay."

"A 200 pointer with the same marks would retail for 3 to around 4 thousand. Would you take 600 to 700 for it?"

"I'd prefer a 700 to 800 range."

"That's fair. My friends will do business at that level, but not if we were talking only a couple of dozen or so. Could you get a hundred—perhaps more?"

"It'll require a few weeks, but I can deliver those numbers."

"Splendid. Call me with the exact count just before you deliver. You see, I require dinner with you as part of this deal."

"Perfect. You've always been the best deal closer that I know. Now I'm encouraged to really hurry. I'll call soon."

They both rang off and Gerhard put the iPad down just as the train came to a stop on a side track. *Now what. Why did we stop? I don't see anything anywhere.* He opened the door to the rear platform just as a huge "SWISH" sound roared by. The passing "SWISH" literally sucked the door handle out of his hand and slammed the door shut.

It was the bullet train! And it was already out of sight! The freight train that pulled his car had moved to a side track out of the way to allow the bullet train to pass. He marveled at the operational difference between a railroad and a highway, when his iPad began to ring. It was Wolf. Gerhard knew it had to be important, because Wolf would never call him on his private number unless it was a serious matter.

"Yes, go ahead, Wolf."

"Sir. Two thugs tried to steal my car and I killed one of them. I don't think I should call the police and get them involved. What should I do?"

Gerhard was about to respond when he heard a rumble in the distance. It crescendoed down the train ever closer until it included his car. Then the entire car swayed and they were underway again. "When did it happen?"

"Late last night—in the parking lot of the grocery store that I use."

"Where is the body?"

"I took the groceries out of the trunk and put the body inside. It's been there all night. But my groceries are fine."

"Wonderful—glad to hear it," said Gerhard as he shook his head from side to side. "Did you use your gun or your hand?"

"My hand."

"So you electrocuted him. You didn't use the power grip, right?"

"Yes sir."

"That's good because that means there's no hole and

no blood. The body is whole. What does he look like?"

There was a short pause and some stuttering from Wolf.

"Well, he's dead, sir. He looks dead."

"No, Wolf. I mean is he short or tall, fat or thin. Compare him to me."

"Okay. He's about your height and trim. He looks like you except he's younger and he has pointed greasy hair. But what should I do?"

Gerhard sensed that his dependable friend displayed early signs of becoming unraveled.

"Don't worry. I have a plan. Do you still have the key to my garage?"

"Ahhh. Yes sir, I still have it."

"Good. Pack your clothes. You'll be away for a couple of days. Rent a rear car tow. Go to my garage and connect my car to the rear of your car. Drive to Vienna. Drive all night without stopping. Go to the railroad marshaling yard and park near the yard master's office. I'll look for you and you look for me. Wait for me if I'm late and don't be alarmed. I'll explain later. Any questions?"

"No. I understand what to do. Should I leave now?"

"Yes, the minute that we hang up. And don't forget the body. Keep it in your car and bring it with you."

"You want me to bring the dead body with me?" asked Wolf in a confused tone.

"Absolutely, it's part of my plan."

They both hung up. Wolf was pleased that Gerhard seemed so confident about his plan, although he wasn't sure what it was.

Wolf set about implementing all of the details that Gerhard gave him. He left for Vienna and drove all night, with the dead body still in his trunk just as Gerhard had instructed. He felt uncomfortable, like someone was following him.

It was the middle of the night by the time he arrived in Vienna and found the railroad yard. He parked near a shack that had a Yard Master Office sign on it and noticed a man far down the dimly lit tracks who was walking toward him.

Wolf thought he must be a tramp and watched him for any sign of trouble. He didn't need problems with anyone now. It was Gerhard and he was carrying a paper bag and can of gasoline. They exchanged greetings and Gerhard began to issue new instructions.

"Open the trunk and let's get busy while it's still dark."

Wolf popped the trunk lock; the lid opened and revealed the body. Gerhard studied it, even rolled it over a little. He poked. It was getting really stiff.

"Just like you said, no wound and no blood. He'll do fine."

That made Wolf feel better about the whole thing, but he still wasn't sure what they were doing. He was committed to Gerhard and determined to follow every order to the letter. Then Gerhard said something that Wolf didn't expect.

"Take the clothes off of the body, down to the underwear. Shoes and socks, too."

Wolf looked at Gerhard for verification and found Gerhard nodding at him. He swallowed hard and began to unbutton the dead man's shirt. Next he slid the pants off the corpse, finally the shoes and socks. Gerhard pulled clothes from the paper bag and handed them to Wolf.

"Here, put these clothes on the body."

"These are your clothes," said Wolf in surprise.

"Yes, I know. And that's my favorite shirt. I'm giving my clothes, my car, and my identity to this guy and he's going to have a serious accident—one that I hope will retard the effort by the police to find me. Any destabilization of their search will mean a brief reduction in effort, and a reduced effort means more distance between us which translates into more time for me. Here, put my wallet in the left back pants pocket and this gold pen in the shirt pocket while I comb his hair to resemble mine."

"It's your alligator wallet."

"I hope the police are equally impressed. Now let's move him into the front seat of my car."

They looked around and found no one in sight, then maneuvered the body out of Wolf's trunk and into Gerhard's car. They tilted him over so he couldn't be seen.

"Remove the tow from both cars and put it in your trunk."

Wolf took some tools from the box in his trunk, got on the ground and squirmed through the gravel under the front end of Gerhard's car. The strain of the long haul had tightened the nuts on the bolts that held the two together.

Gerhard had to get under the car and help Wolf push the wrench, but they got it. Then Wolf moved under the rear of his car. They had the same problem and solved it the same way. Both men were dirty and their hands were a bit greasy, but that part of the job was done and they could get on their way.

"Where are we going and how are we going to have the accident?" asked Wolf.

"We're going to the park, but there's no time to explain it now. We have to do this while it's still dark, so we must leave now. We'll take both cars. Just follow me, but not too close. Stay back a little so you won't attract attention."

They drove out of the railroad yard as Gerhard led the way toward the northeast part of Vienna. He looked for the B9 highway sign, found it, and left Vienna in his rear-view mirror. They drove on for another fifteen minutes. It was still dark and the lack of traffic allowed them to make unusually good time.

I'd better keep a sharp eye for the sign to the park.

Another five minutes—still no sight of the sign. Now it was Gerhard's turn to become unraveled. *We're going to be in trouble if I miss that sign. I don't know any other quick way into the park and we have less than an hour before it gets light.* Another five minutes passed and it didn't seem quite so dark anymore.

There it is, as he spotted the sign. Dkonau-Auen National Park. He indicated a turn to the left with his signal light and both cars drove into the park. *The spot that I'm looking for is just about a mile further from here.*

Both cars drove on, but slower now as Gerhard strained to see the next sign. The trees made the park seem extra dark and full of irregular shapes. The lack of street lights made the narrow road hard to follow. He slowed down even more. The car headlights picked up a distant sign and he quickly put on the high beams. *That's it, Landschaftlich Übersehen Scenic Overlook.*

They stopped alongside the overlook. Gerhard put the car in park and left the engine running. He pulled the body into the driver's seat, then went around to the passenger's seat and very carefully poured the gasoline out of the little metal can onto the floorboard while Wolf did final adjusting to the position of the body. Both front doors were open.

"Put this empty can in your trunk," directed Gerhard. "I don't want it left around here."

He moved to the driver's side, turned the steering wheel slightly toward the overlook, and closed the door. Then he went to the passenger's side, reached in and nudged the gear shift into drive, and quickly shut the door. The car started to move forward toward the edge of the overlook.

"Come on! Let's help my Passat take its last trip," as he motioned to Wolf to help push. It didn't take much of a push. The Passat drove itself over the side of the cliff. It rumbled a couple of times as it hit rock outcroppings on the way down, then exploded and burst into flames when it hit bottom.

"This thing is going to attract attention. Let's get out of here."

They jumped into Wolf's Jetta, drove rapidly out of the park, and took highway B9 back to Vienna. The sun was just coming up, but it was having a hard time doing it. The clouds were long and flaky looking, like the scales on a fish. The weather was changing from good to bad. Wolf had a question.

"Why did you pour gasoline on the floor board, but not on the body?"

"It wouldn't have been a natural process. We used gasoline to feed the fire and the fire burned the body. Gasoline didn't burn the body, fire did. An object covered with fuel will burn hotter and faster than objects around it. It's unnatural and a dead give-away that outside circumstances were involved. I wanted it to look like I drove over the edge and the gasoline in the fuel tank exploded and caused the fire. The police could scientifically tell the difference between a gasoline covered body that was burned and one that was burned naturally by gasoline in the general area."

Wolf thought about the answer and he was satisfied. But he had another question.

"I guess using your own car was a good way to help convince the police that you were the person in the car. But what will you do now? You don't have a car."

"The car was becoming a liability for me. It was big, easy to spot, and had a registered license number. Now I don't have anything big and easy to spot on the public streets. Nothing's registered with the authorities so I can slip around with less notice. That's a big asset for me."

Wolf had a follow up question.

"You still don't have a car. How do you plan to get around?"

"Well, I have you and your car for the immediate short term need." Wolf nodded. "I plan to present a proposal to the Baker to provide transportation for me. I am still developing the idea and will talk with him about it soon."

The weather was worse by the time they arrived back at the railroad yard. The wind was twirling loose paper and trash straight across the tracks. Gerhard took Wolf inside the railcar for his first look at the new acquisition. He proudly showed him everything—all of the rooms, how the gas, electric, commercial, and generator power worked, everything in the galley, and the arsenal inside the drawing room furniture.

Wolf was speechless.

"Let me show you your room."

"My room? You mean I have a room here?" Gerhard led him to the crew quarters in the forward end of the car.

"This is your private place. Look around and decide how you'd like it to be decorated. We'll change the carpet, the drapes, get some pictures that you like, you know, fix it up to be your home away from home. I'll pay for everything."

Wolf's eyes became moist. He couldn't say anything for a while. It was a good thing too, because Gerhard's iPad rang again. He checked the screen and was surprised to see that the Baker was on the line. The Baker never telephoned him before. This call had to be something special.

"How is my friend today? I hope you have some of your tasty jelly donuts handy," said Gerhard.

But the Baker didn't pick up on the jovialness. His voice was uncharacteristically low, slow, and dead serious.

"Herr Gerhard, I apologize for the interruption. I have been asked by a special person to deliver a message to you. It is a message requesting your assistance in an important matter."

"Okay, what's the message?"

"It is written on paper."

"Please read it."

"I cannot." It is in an envelope, sealed with red wax. It is from the church, sir."

Gerhard was puzzled. The Baker was totally reliable, but this unexpected telephone call and strange message were unsettling.

"Do you wish to deliver it?" asked Gerhard with a hint of concern in his voice.

"Yes sir, but I have been instructed to deliver it only to you. Please suggest how I might meet with you."

Gerhard tried not to feel this way, but he felt himself becoming suspicious. His inner barometer was working. *This sounds like a ploy, like a set up to learn my location. But I've always trusted the Baker."* Where are you?"

"I am in Melk, Austria, sir."

My God, he's only 40 miles away. This coincidence is too strange.

Gerhard thought about what was asked of him, and decided to move ahead because the Baker had been a good and dependable friend for years.

Besides, this may not be a problem at all. Just because it's unusual and a coincidence doesn't make it a problem. I am not going to be unnecessarily alarmed—I'll just be extra alert.

"I'll send Wolf to meet you in Vienna at 2 o'clock this afternoon in front of the Vienna Opera House. Follow him and he'll lead you to me. Will you be alone?"

"Yes sir. I'll be there at 2 o'clock." The Baker abruptly disconnected.

Gerhard sat down with Wolf and reviewed the conversation he just concluded with the Baker. He carefully covered his own concerns as well.

"Remember, Wolf, it's just a suspicion. The Baker has been a good and trusted ally, but I think we should be careful until we know what's going on. Go into Vienna and meet him, but show up about 30 minutes early. Look around. Watch his actions when he arrives. See if he stays in his car or if he meets or talks to anyone.

If he does, drive away in a careful manner so he won't notice you. Make sure no one follows you. Drive once around the block to see if you're followed. Of course, if he checks out, lead him here. But on the way back you might pull to the side of the road and notice if anyone else does the same thing. If that happens the meeting is off. Don't come back here until it's dark and you know you're not followed."

Both men were uncomfortable about the pending meeting with the Baker. Gerhard wondered if his hunch was out of line. Wolf worried that he'd do everything right. Neither wanted any trouble.

44

Noon came and went. So did twelve thirty. Wolf left for the opera house and found a perfect place to park across the street. He turned off the motor and watched, just like Gerhard told him too. Everything seemed quiet.

Several minutes passed and Wolf took his father's artillery field glasses from the glove compartment and checked the people milling about the opera house. The performance was scheduled for tomorrow night so there was very little activity around the place now. It was easy to watch people and look for anything unusual. Nothing was. Time passed.

It was just a few minutes before two o'clock when the Baker arrived in his white BMW and stopped in front of the opera house. He was alone. Wolf watched him. The Baker sat quietly behind the steering wheel and talked to no one. Wolf watched until five minutes after the hour. No unusual conditions developed so he stepped out of the car, waved to the Baker, then started his car and moved into the sparse traffic. The Baker followed him.

On the way back, Wolf decided to go around the block once. The Baker did the same, but no one else did. Then just to make sure, he pulled to the side of the road and remained inside his car. So did the Baker.

No one else stopped, so Wolf continued to the railroad yard confident that everything was proper and that there were no problems with the Baker. He picked up his cell phone and called Gerhard.

"Everything checked out fine. We will arrive soon."

Gerhard was relieved.

CHAPTER 5

Interpol
Field Office
Office of the Section Director
Berlin

The morning started off without much activity. Section Director Gunter Geer carefully reviewed a list of statistics from Lyon. Kamza hadn't arrived yet, and detectives Otto Heydrich and Ernst Nebe were checking their email. Police business at the Interpol station was deadly slow and quiet as a bank vault.

"Jesus Christ! This is unbelievable," yelled Heydrich.

"Whatcha got?"

"Gerhard's dead!"

"Dead?" said Nebe in disbelief.

Both men started yelling at each other in short bursts, as if yelling was a matter of course. But it was the shocking word of Gerhard's death that caused the verbal outbursts. Now Gunter Geer hurried into the detective's office.

"You said Gerhard's dead? Let me see that email!"

URGENT
TO: Interpol, Berlin
FROM: D. Huber, Asst. Dir.
           BK-EKO
           VIENNA
           AUSTRIA
SUBJECT: International fugitive killed in auto accident.
Wilhelm Gerhard was killed yesterday morning when his
car went over a cliff in the Dkonau-Auen National Park
outside Vienna. Vehicle being recovered now.

Gunter Geer's desk telephone rang just as Kamza
entered the detective's office.

"Kamza, get the phone," yelled Nebe.

All of the yelling surprised Kamza, who sprinted into
Geer's office and grabbed the ringing phone.

"Interpol. Section Director's Office. Yes, sir. Just a
moment."

"It's Vienna. Someone named Huber," yelled
Kamza, who quickly got caught up in the noise and
excitement.

Geer ran back into his office to answer the phone and
passed Kamza in the small connecting conference room.

"What's going on?" he asked as Geer zipped past.

"Gerhard's dead!" yelled Geer.

"Woooohhh! How?"

"It's in the e-mail. Let him read it!" shouted Geer as
he flipped his office door closed and picked up the phone."

"Gunter Geer speaking"

"Good Morning, sir. This is Dirk Huber, Assistant Director of EKO under BK, Vienna Police. Our office sent an email to you regarding the death of one Wilhelm Gerhard, who I'm told you've been looking for."

"We've been looking for this guy a long time. How did it happen?"

"Well, he drove off the cliff, you know. Hit bottom and burst into an inferno. Quite a mess, you know."

Geer didn't know, but he felt immediately annoyed by Dirk Huber.

"You needn't congratulate us. Just doing our job. It's our duty to solve all crimes that we come in contact with, even the extra difficult international ones, you know." Geer's feeling of annoyance intensified. "The world was looking for this dangerous criminal, but the Vienna Police captured him."

Geer's blood fast approached the boiling point. It was hard for him to hold back without being rude, but he had to make the effort.

"Sir, you first said Gerhard drove off a cliff, but just now you said that you captured him. Which one is correct?"

"That's right. We have him. And I have more good news for you. I've made arrangements with the German National Police to helicopter you to the crash site in Vienna, so you could watch our recovery team operation first hand. And don't worry; we'll pay for the helicopter because we want you to see our award-winning Vienna Police at work. Hey, I'll tell my officers to wait up until you arrive. Don't want you to miss a thing."

"You must be very influential, sir, because I hear the helicopter on the roof of our building now and the noise from the rotor blades is drowning out your voice. What a pity. We'll board now. I'll see you very soon."

Geer slammed down the phone.

What a screwy nut. He's exactly the type of police officer that we don't need in this world.

Kamza opened the office door cautiously.

"Everything okay?"

"Yeah. Hey, how would you like to come to Vienna with me?"

"Any time sir. When should I put it on my calendar?"

"Don't need to schedule it. Just follow me."

Geer ran through the conference room, then the detective's office and out the side door into the hall with Kamza right behind. He yelled to Heydrich and Nebe.

"You guys watch the office. We'll be back as soon as we can."

"Where ya going?" yelled Heydrich.

"To Vienna," yelled back Geer.

"What for?"

"Coffee break."

They took the service stairs to the roof just as the helicopter touched down—its engine running and rotor blades turning. One of the pilots stepped out of the cabin and yelled out over the chopper noise at the two approaching men.

"You must be the officers that the Vienna EKO Police ordered us to pick up."

"We're the ones," as they displayed the Interpol ID cards that hung around their neck, climbed into the twin back seat, and began the process of engaging the seat belts and head sets. The co-pilot slammed the rear door closed, climbed into his seat, and pulled his door closed. Then he turned around and looked at Geer and Kamza.

"Are you secure?" he yelled.

Geer gave him the thumbs up sign. The engine instantly gained a new deafening noise level; the helicopter lifted above the German Federal Police Headquarters Building, paused momentarily in mid-air as it spun quickly around to the south, then leaned forward on a rush to Vienna. Geer switched his headset to local and motioned to Kamza to do the same.

"What a morning," said Geer, over the noise of the engine. "Nothing was going on, then suddenly all of that yelling and news about Gerhard's death. Now we're helicoptering to Vienna, and I'm still yelling. I feel like I've been jumped by a tiger."

"Beautiful analogy," answered Kamza. "If I didn't know you better I'd say that you've spent time in Africa. That's exactly how a tiger operates. It lays motionless watching and waiting, just like a quiet morning, its prey unaware of the impending attack. Then 'bam' it's got you by the throat and it's all over."

Kamza had a broad smile on his face. Geer shook his head and said nothing. Several minutes passed before he spoke again.

"What do you know about Assistant Director Dirk Huber and the Vienna Police Department?"

"Not much. Never had an assignment there. Don't know anything about Huber. It was pretty well known that they were having problems within the department. They had a major reorganization in 2005, but I never heard that it made much difference."

"What's this EKO and BK thing that he's the assistant director of?"

"It's a result of the reorganization. The EKO is the Cobra Special Unit. It's the Austrian anti-terror force. It's under the Federal Investigation Bureau that they call the BK. There's not much of a requirement for an anti-terror force in Austria, and it appears the EKO leadership is mostly comprised of political appointments."

"I thought you didn't know much about the Vienna Police Department."

"I don't. You should hear me when I know stuff."

Gunter Geer sat quietly for the remainder trip. He felt lucky to have someone like Kamza on his side—even if he didn't know much about the Vienna Police.

A couple of hours passed when a sudden voice in the headset startled them.

"Gentleman, were approaching Vienna. You can see it up ahead. We're going to fly over the city and across the Handelskai River, then I'll adjust my course several degrees and head directly to the crash site. Should be there in ten minutes."

The helicopter was in the Dkonau-Auen National Park in nine minutes and approached the crash site one minute later.

"I'm going to hover over the site and just to the north of it so you could look down and see it. I'd like to take directions from you at that point. Tell me what you want to see and I'll put you in a position to see it, if at all possible."

The helicopter moved carefully into position and the two Interpol officers looked down. The car was easy to see. It seemed totally burned, but the outline of a car was clear. It was in one piece, but badly bent. Scraps of car parts littered the place. The fire that destroyed the car also burned bushes and a small tree in the nearby area.

"The car is right at the foot of the cliff," said Kamza.

"Seems so. I didn't expect it to be somewhere else, did you?" responded Geer in somewhat of a challenging tone.

"Yes, sir, I did."

"Damn it Kamza, you're on to something again, aren't you? You have another idea, right?"

"Oh, I always have ideas. That's not the problem. Confirming the ideas is the problem."

"Okay, the ball's in your court. Take it away."

Kamza spoke to the pilot.

"How difficult would it be to move slowly down and back up the face of the cliff?"

"I could do it easily from this distance. Maybe I could get a little closer."

"Splendid. I'm ready when you are."

The pilot made a number of adjustments and the helicopter engine changed tone—more than once. Slowly, ever so slowly the copper inched a bit closer to the cliff. Geer was uncomfortable as he watched the approaching cliff side appear increasingly larger.

Then the flying machine seemed to actually drift down in a flight action similar to the way a feather flutters. A slight drift to the right, then a slight drift to the left. It felt strange, but it was very effective. They could see everything. Kamza leaned forward as he attempted to study the cliff.

"Here, use my binoculars," said the co-pilot. Kamza took the glasses and continued to study the cliff, but with a close-up view now. He suddenly pointed to a section of rocks that were even with the helicopter.

"See that somewhat shiny outcropping? The rock broke off there." Geer wasn't sure if he saw what Kamza saw. The downward flutter movement continued.

"There's another one," he said as he pointed to a different spot. Geer wasn't sure about that spot either. The helicopter neared the bottom.

"Can't go any lower, sir," said the pilot.

"You're doing great. Please go back up to the top in the same slow way. It would be good if you could find a place to land on the top so we could examine the edge of the cliff."

"There's a clear spot in the road about 100 feet away. I'll land there."

More instrument adjustments and more strenuous engine tone changes and a slow assent began. It seemed faster to Geer this time. Kamza studied every foot of the near vertical cliff wall on the way up. The helicopter suddenly appeared at the top of the cliff and loomed menacingly into the face of several dozen police officers, all of whom stood like sentinels as they watched the wingless flying beast in awe. It landed in a cloud of dust in the designated spot in the road, they climbed out and walked toward the group of officers who were working on the top of the cliff.

"What do you make of it thus far?" asked Geer as they walked along.

"It's not Gerhard in the car."

A man in a business suit left the group of officers and came toward them. Geer thought it was Huber.

"You folks must be the Interpol people that Assistant Director Huber told me about. I am A.B. Cox. I work with Director Huber. He's not here. He's meeting with the press back in Vienna."

The men introduced themselves and the questions began.

"Have you identified the body?" asked Geer.

"Well, we haven't taken any samples to the lab, if that's what you mean. Haven't gotten close enough yet. It's a long way down there, you know."

Geer thought that Cox sounded a lot like Huber. "Mr. Huber sent me an email about the death of Gerhard. I also talked with him on the phone and he said he captured Gerhard. Is that Gerhard in the car below?"

"Well sure. It's his car, you know. We traced it from the license number."

Geer and Kamza exchanged glances.

"Will you please show us the spot where the car went over the edge?"

"It went over that edge," as Cox gestured to the full cliff edge.

"But what exact spot?" begged Geer.

"It doesn't really matter. There's only one edge, you know."

Geer and Kamza immediately lost interest in Mr. Cox. They brushed past him to the area near the edge where the group of officers was working with heavy equipment, including a large cable retrieving crane.

"I had hoped to identify the point of descent, but too many people and too much heavy equipment here to ID anything," said Geer.

"It would have been helpful to learn the angle of approach, straight on or was the steering wheel used to turn the front wheels," said Kamza. "Can't even tell where the approach began—just a foot or so from the shoulder or straight off the main road. This is hopeless."

They turned and headed back to the helicopter. Geer took Kamza's arm and led him aside to a nearby tree.

"You said that it wasn't Gerhard in the car. Talk to me about that."

Kamza took out a handkerchief and rubbed his eyes. Geer wasn't sure if he was tired, hot, or just fed up with the whole thing.

"All of the standard clues that we normally use are gone, obliterated by incompetence. But the tell-tail clues are everywhere. To begin with, why would Gerhard come here in the first place, and just before dawn? He had no history of being a night person. The park isn't a typical destination point at that time of the night. One doesn't just pass by here; one must come here on purpose. The cliff is on a side road that only runs around the park. It's not a main road to anyplace. The incident occurred at a scenic overlook—a place that screams drop off—in fact the scenic overlook sign back there identifies the presence of a cliff. No, a person would only come here at night to commit something or stage something."

"So someone else was in that car, not Gerhard."

"Right. Gerhard put someone in his car to make it look like he was the one who died in an accident. It was all staged in the hope that he would be presumed dead."

"That would change the intensity of the hunt, wouldn't it?"

"Well, it would to some—like Huber, but only for a while. Others would notice that the accident was staged and the hunt would start again, but the delay would provide some temporary relief for Gerhard."

"What did you mean about the location of the car at the foot of the cliff?"

"A car that moved at a normal driving speed would soar somewhat beyond a near vertical cliff and land at the bottom at a distance from the wall proportional to the speed of the vehicle as it went over the edge. It would likely not hit any side of the cliff wall on the way down.

"The car we saw landed next to the cliff wall, which indicated that it moved over the edge very slowly—as if it were pushed by someone. It would likely strike parts of the cliff wall as it fell. I noticed two sections of rock wall from the helicopter that were freshly broken off by a severe force—like that caused by the weight of a falling car. It's my opinion that Gerhard pushed his car over the edge and was then driven away from the park by another person."

The men walked side by side still talking as they headed slowly back to the helicopter.

"Want to hear a riddle?" asked Kamza in somewhat of a lighter tone.

"No. I'm not in any mood for a riddle today."

Kamza didn't pay any attention.

"Well I've got one coming right at you. This park is closest to and primarily used by people who live in what large Austrian city that begins with the letter 'V'."

Geer stopped in his tracks. "Vienna! You think he's here in Vienna, don't you?"

"We probably flew right over him getting here. Come on, let's get aboard and fly over him again."

"You're strange, you know that Kamza?"

But Kamza wasn't finished talking yet.

"I'll tell you what's really sad about all of this. If Gerhard is actually here in Vienna, he's under the police jurisdiction of Dirk Huber."

Geer mulled the comment over in his mind for a second or two. "Then Gerhard's completely safe."

"He's never been safer, and he doesn't even know it," responded Kamza.

They reached the helicopter, quietly climbed into the twin back seat, and engaged the seat belts and head sets for the flight back to Berlin.

CHAPTER 6

Gerhard was seated in the drawing room of his private railroad car and watched the arrival of Wolf and the Baker. They both parked near the yard master's office, got out of their cars and greeted each other just as Gerhard expected friends to do who haven't seen each other for a while, and then Wolf led the way across several tracks to the railroad car.

But a couple of things were different. The Baker appeared solemn and he stared downward, *probably just to watch his step as he walked across the tracks,* thought Gerhard. He carried a black briefcase instead of his trademark white paper bag of pastries. *That's very unlike him. I never saw him with a briefcase before.* Gerhard moved out onto the rear platform and greeted both men as they climbed aboard, but Baker remained unusually serious looking—just the courteous hint of a partial smile. Gerhard invited him to have a seat in the drawing room.

"Wolf, please bring our friend a glass of wine."

"I appreciate your kindness, but no thank you."

He seemed nervous, unsure how to begin, so Gerhard started talking. "I must say that I was surprised to receive your telephone call and even more surprised to hear that you have an urgent message to deliver to me. I am anxious to learn what this is all about."

The Baker reached into his briefcase and retrieved a white envelope. "It's about this," he said as he handed the envelope to Gerhard, folded side up to reveal that the envelope bore a seal of red wax. Gerhard looked at the seal, opened the envelope, and pulled out a note. It read:

Praise Be To God.

My Dear Herr Gerhard,
We have discovered evidence that a great crime was committed within the walls of the Abbey at Melk, specifically within the monastery itself. This was not a crime against the body, but against learning and the history of knowledge. It is an affront to God and to the Holy Church.
We are men of the cloth and lack the experience to seek the truth behind this crime. You have been recommended as one with the skill and experience that we lack. The monastery is prepared to retain your services to investigate this matter.
A Council of Review will be held for you at your convenience in the chamber of the abbey. All matters of evidence will be presented. Details for the Review will be explained by the bearer of this paper.
Obediently Yours,

A

Abbot of the Monastery
Melk Abbey

May The Lord Be With You.

Even though the note was short, he read it again, very slowly. Then he reread key words to himself: *...a great crime...not against the body...against learning and the history of knowledge...explained by the bearer.*

Gerhard looked at the signature. It was the capitol letter 'A' made of hot red wax that was embossed onto the paper—the official mark of the Abbot. There was no doubt in his mind about who this note came from—and no doubt at all that it was genuine. Now it was Gerhard's turn to be nervous.

His blood pressure peaked, his mind stuttered, then soared at mock speed as he spastically retrieved and reviewed bits of information about Melk Abbey. Wondrous. Beautiful. One of the most famous monastic sites in the world. Founded in the 12th Century. Once a castle. Huge Benedictine monastery. Magnificent library. Frescos by Rottmayr.

The Baker sat quietly and said nothing. Then Gerhard began with questions.

"No one hand delivers a private message from the Abbot of Melk Abbey unless that person has proven by deed to be special and trusted. As the bearer of this letter you have achieved that status. I've known you for many years, both as my friend and as a baker, but now I suddenly learn that you have another life, one that includes an association with the leader of one of the largest and most important monasteries in the world. I don't understand how you developed such a relationship."

"At one time, years before we met, I was a member of the Benedictine Order," he said in quiet reverence.

"You were a monk? Oh my God, I had no idea."

"Yes, for one year, that's all."

"But what happened?"

"I loved the time that I spent in the monastery—the peace, the brotherhood, the time to study and learn. It was a year of unbelievable happiness for me. But I discovered that I wanted more. It was strange, but I was unfulfilled, and thus I felt unworthy to remain in the Order."

"How could you be so happy and yet unfulfilled. What more did you want?"

"The year that I spent at Melk Abbey allowed me to examine myself and my commitment to the church with a depth of clarity I never experienced before. It was a time of purity for me. I was experiencing the priestly and holy life that I always wanted only to discover that such attainment lacked the satisfaction that I expected. Further introspection raised doubts about the direction of my life in the Order. Another pathway became brighter and clearer. It beckoned me and I felt compelled to follow it. I wanted marriage, not just to the church, but to a woman. I wanted a family and children. Those human desires were not allowed to be fulfilled within the brotherhood. I had no choice but to resign. I married someone whom I have loved forever it seems, and we have two wonderful boys. We opened the bakery and you helped us resolve those difficult problems with the bank for which I am forever grateful, and you know the rest."

"Oh my dear friend, all of these years and I had no idea about your past and what you had been through. So tell me, are you happy now?"

"I am happier than ever. I have both my God and my family. How could one ask for more?"

"Indeed. But I have more to ask and I hope that you won't mind if I push ahead with a few more questions."

"I expected them and I'm ready."

"If you are no longer a monk, how do you explain such a close relationship with the abbot that he trusted you with his message?"

"I am no longer a priest in residence, but I've been given a priestly appointment as Council to the Abbot. It's not a legal counsel, but one to advise the abbot on matters relating to the community and the priesthood. I retreat to the monastery several times a year to study and learn and to confer with the abbot. It was during my visit last week that he confided in me about the crime that he described in his letter to you. At first I wasn't aware of the depth of his despair. Indeed, the crime had been haunting the abbot for over a year and he revealed his inner anxiety to no one except the prior."

"Who or what is the prior?"

"The prior is a monk who is appointed by the abbot to serve as the Dean of the Monastery. He is usually one of the elders. You could think of the prior as the Chief Operating Officer of the monastery," explained the Baker.

"Very good. Now, just what exactly is this great crime that the abbot referred to?"

"I am sorry sir, but I am not at liberty to discuss it with you. Discussion of such a grave matter is at the discretion of the abbot of the monastery, not a former monk. I listened to him describe the crime to me and I understood the desperation and the deep pain he felt for the abbey and for the world. I knew that you could help us, so I told the abbot about you. He was so excited! Finally, after such a long time, someone emerged who could actually help him resolve the problem and unravel the mystery—a crime that has weighed so heavily on this good man. Please, will you help us?"

"No," answered Gerhard with resolve. "This is not a crime that I am used to. Not murder or robbery. In fact, I don't understand what the crime is and it can't be explained. How can I accept an assignment to solve a crime when the crime itself is a mystery to me?"

The Baker was taken aback. His eyes widened as he looked at Gerhard in disbelief.

"You refuse to help us?"

"Let's just say that I can't agree to something that I don't understand. Allow me to ask it another way. What is it that you want solved?"

"All of this will be addressed during the Council of Review. Questions that I am not allowed to answer will be openly explained by those who have the authority to review and discuss the details with you. You may challenge them, refute them, you may agree or disagree with them, but they will listen and they will respond. You must give them that chance. You must come to the Council of Review and then decide."

Gerhard was surprised by the intensity of the Bakers insistence and by his reasoned plea as well.

"I've always thought of you as an especially quiet person. You listened and seldom talked and I liked that. It was good for business, but I never knew much about you. Today was different, you spoke volumes. I've never heard you speak like that before. My view of you has broadened considerably. No, that's too mundane—my view of you has exploded. You've persuaded me to do as you suggested. I will attend the Review, look at the facts, and then decide."

"Thank you, sir. You'll be happy with your decision. I fear no reprisal when I say that the crime that the abbot spoke of is neither shallow or without merit. It will surround you and pull you inside itself in a manner unlike anything you've previously imagined. Be careful. But the implications of what it could be....ah, that could be the biggest mystery of all."

Gerhard wasn't sure if the Baker's remarks were a warning or not. He moved on.

"How will the Review be conducted?"

"The Council of Review will be conducted on the date of your choosing. I won't be there, but two monks will come for you—one as your driver, and one as your companion. They will take you to the abbey, where you will rest the night and be escorted to the Review after breakfast the next morning. The Review will last until you have decided to accept or reject the request for assistance."

"Very well. I would like to be picked up at three thirty in the afternoon, the day after tomorrow."

"Splendid! Please look for a black sedan with a small gold seal of Melk Abbey on the back door. It should arrive here at two thirty."

"I'll be ready. But I have a final question. It has

nothing to do with the abbey. I no longer have my car and I would like to engage your services for permanent transportation on a contractual basis."

"Your timing is perfect. I am sure that you remember my cousin who owned the restaurant in Amsterdam where you and Wolf stayed before you engaged the Bank of China. He and I have decided to go into the private transportation business together. His eldest son, the one in Italy, will join us. The three of us will run a service route from northern Italy, through France, Germany, and the Netherlands. We also have plans to expand into the UK and other places, just as soon as we can line up the right people and additional cars. We'd like to have you as a permanent client. What did you have in mind?"

"I'd need both local and long distant transportation—often without much notice. But I have an unusual idea that might interest you. Could you use a silent partner? I would provide the funds for you to lease or buy automobiles and grow your business faster than if you did it alone. Use the cars as the business demands; just charge a transportation fee back to me when I need to use one."

"That sounds workable. I'll talk with my cousin and get back with you."

Gerhard's first business meeting in his new private railroad car was concluded. He walked the Baker to his car and returned across the tracks hopeful that he made the right decision about Melk Abbey. And he felt good about the possible business relationship with the Baker.

It could solve a number of problems.

CHAPTER 7

Wolf worked diligently as he poked around, up, over, and under every corner, every cabinet, drawer, and ledge in the galley for places to store all of the food Gerhard sent him to buy. The galley was new to him and it was full of cleverly hidden storage places.

Gerhard, on the other hand, only remembered the obvious places—like the top of the counter.

"Seeded rye," said Gerhard, suddenly.

Wolf took a loaf from the bread box, cut two slices, put them on a plate. Gerhard seemed to stare into space, oblivious to the things that were going on around him. *He must be thinking about something important,* thought Wolf.

"Rare prime beef."

Wolf removed a pound from the refrigerator and put multiple slices on the rye.

"Horseradish,"

Wolf took a jar from the pantry.

"Onions."

"You want onions with prime beef?" asked Wolf in surprise.

"And Cabernet Sauvignon, too. But I'll get that."

Gerhard demonstrated a spurt of awareness, opened the door to the wine cellar and removed a bottle.

"Wine glass. The one that the Pope used."

Wolf handed it to him.

Gerhard took his sandwich and wine to a leather chair in the drawing room. Wolf finished storing the last few grocery items, poured himself a half glass of wine, and quietly joined him, but in a distant chair.

Gerhard continued to stare into space.

...a great crime...not against the body...against learning and the history of knowledge. How intriguing. I'm eager to look into this situation.

"What time is it?

"A quarter after three, sir."

The monks will be here any minute.

"Wolf, I'll go with the monks and spend the night in the monastery at Melk Abbey. The Council of Review will be held early in the morning. At this point I don't know what the crime is or if I'll get involved with it or not, but there are things that I want to move forward with regardless of what I decide. I have a job for you."

Wolf listened intently.

"Lock up the railcar immediately after I leave and drive back to Frankfurt. Check on your parents, then park your car and take the tube to the railway station. Board the first train to Amsterdam that will allow you to arrive at the Bank of China just after they open at nine in the morning.

Call the Baker when you buy the train ticket and tell him that I want him to pick you up at ten o'clock in the morning at the same park bench that he did before, the one on the Hobbemakade side of the canal, just down from the Bank of China. Keep your hand covered so that no one will see the metal parts when you're in the bank. Go to the safe deposit vault and withdraw all five sacks of diamonds. Take that briefcase with you, the one on the floor leaning next to your chair."

Gerhard pointed to the briefcase.

Wolf picked it up and put it on his lap.

"Open it and you'll find a money belt inside."

He pulled the zipper and removed an unusual looking money belt.

"This belt is a little wider than most and it has several well-spaced pouches rather than a single pocket for paper money. I designed it to carry things other than money and had it made of Kevlar, which is a synthetic fiber that's difficult to cut. Wear the belt under a top coat or long jacket, whatever is appropriate for the weather that day. Put the sacks into different pouches in the belt, leave the bank in a casual manner, walk to the park bench and wait for the Baker. Have him drive you back here to Vienna. I'll be waiting for you. Any questions?"

"A couple. Why am I carrying this briefcase if I'm not going to put anything in it?"

"It's a decoy. Remember what happened to you the last time that you went to the Bank of China? You were roughed up and someone sliced the handle of your briefcase. A briefcase is a dead give-away that something of value is inside. So let the thugs think so. Let them take it. You just stay safe with the diamonds strapped around you under your coat. You'll only be vulnerable for a short time—as you walk from the bank and as you wait on the park bench for the Baker."

"And that reminds me—timing is critical. You have to arrive at the bank just minutes after they open, complete your transaction, and be out on the bench waiting for the Baker. And he must arrive promptly, not later than ten o'clock."

"Why is it so important for me to arrive at the bank right after they open?"

"Because the employees will still be getting ready for the day's business and they'll be least prepared for anything different that early in the morning. Statistically, it's the most productive time for a robbery and the safest time for us to make our withdrawal as well."

"If I take the train from Frankfurt to Amsterdam, why can't I take it back?"

"You won't be carrying anything of value to Amsterdam, but you'll have a money belt full of diamonds on the way back. I don't want you using public transportation on the return. Too risky. You and the diamonds will be safer in the Baker's car."

"Just one more question. You said you'd be waiting for me when the Baker and I return from Amsterdam. What if you decide to take the job for the monastery—will you still come back here?"

"I have to. There's so much to do and one thing depends on another. I need to make arrangements to move the railcar. It's been here too long. We'll both ride with it to Zurich if I don't take the monastery job because I've sold some diamonds and the buyer wants them delivered to Zurich. But I want you to come with me if I go to Melk. If that happens I'll ship the car to Zurich, and we'll catch up with it after Melk. We could be at Melk for several days or longer and we have to prepare for it. Everything depends on what I learn at the monastery."

Three short polite knocks sounded abruptly on the rear door of the railcar.

"They're here," said Wolf. "I see a black sedan parked at the yard master's office."

Gerhard picked up his overnight bag and joined a young man on the rear platform who stood straight and tall, had neatly combed black hair, wore a conservative black suit, and sported an interesting black beard that framed a pleasant smile.

Gerhard wasn't sure if he expected the monk to be wearing a robe or not. This one looked well-dressed. Gerhard's companion, at least that's what the Baker said he would be, was Brother Robert. He walked Gerhard to the black sedan with the small gold seal on the door—and actually opened the car door for him. *I can't ever recall anyone ever doing that for me before.*

It took a little over an hour to drive the forty miles to Melk. Gerhard first wondered what it would be like riding that far with two monks, but it was a pleasant experience, made so by their thoughtfulness. The driver was considerate of his passenger, which was a refreshing experience in itself. He never exceeded the speed limit, always slowed in turns without allowing a sway, and accelerated/decelerated smoothly.

"May I ask, sir, if you have been to Melk Abbey before?" said Brother Robert.

"Only through pictures."

"I believe that you will find it to be an intriguing place. Often when I stroll through the garden or walk the hall of the Royal Chambers, I reflect upon the centuries of time these walls have seen and of the thousands of monks and believers that have passed this way before me. I am a young man merely two and a half decades old. I feel privileged to live and worship in a place that is ten centuries old."

Gerhard was impressed with his young companion. He hoped the monk would tell him more.

"It has become a daily practice for me to place my hand on the wall of the abbey and to feel the presence of the past—to know that this holy place—once a fort, a castle, and then a fortified monastery—has lost so many souls to wars and destruction. But now it is a place of peace and learning. I pray you will find a way to feel the history of the abbey as well."

They arrived in Melk and drove slowly through the little town that seemed stuffed into the base of a long rocky ridge. Then it was upon them! Gerhard couldn't believe his eyes. Never had he seen such a sight. The gleaming golden color stone of Melk Abbey occupied the entire ridge above the town. It appeared to be five stories high and a quarter of a mile long. Its presence was startling, defining, dominating, and absolutely beautiful.

They drove to the end of town, made a few turns, went up a slight hill, and arrived at the entrance to Melk Abbey.

The abbey had an east-west axis and the main entrance was at the east end, several marble stair sections above the abbey proper. The view was encompassing. Gerhard paused a few seconds at the top of the stairs to take it all in while Brother Robert stood at his side. Then they walked down the stair sections, passed between the double bastions, through the huge entrance gate and into the forecourt. The grand Prelates Court lay just ahead. They continued walking as Brother Robert led the way between the gallery statues of Peter and Paul, under the coat of arms and the Melk Cross high above the inner entrance arch, and into the Prelates Court.

Gerhard stopped again at the sight of the expansive courtyard of simple gravel with walks of stone, and a fabulous multi-tiered white marble fountain in the center. The surrounding buildings of Melk Abbey provided an impressive protected frame for this striking place. The twin baroque towers and the great dome of the church beyond added extra dimension to an uncommon view.

"The dining hall is this way, sir," but Gerhard didn't hear him. The visual experience of the abbey was overwhelming. The monk allowed some extra time to pass. After a minute, he spoke again.

"It's our practice to have the last meal of the day while it's still light outside."

"Oh, I'm so sorry. I got carried away with the beauty of your abbey. I hope we won't be late."

"It's impossible for you to be late, sir. You're dining with the abbot as his special guest. His table is preferred. He won't start until you arrive and none of the monks will eat before the abbot does."

Gerhard felt embarrassed that he might have delayed the beginning of dinner for everyone and quickly followed his escort into the abbey. Brother Robert pushed open a pair of tall wooden double doors and they entered a large dining hall. The sight of about 100 monks all covered in black habits was unexpected—even startling. It reminded him of a scene from a sinister movie, but no title came to mind. He quickly put the idea out of his head. Brother Robert introduced him to the abbot of the monastery, who introduced him to the prior, the dean of the monastery.

The abbot was tall and slender with curly silver hair that hung around his head at ear length. Overhead lights seemed to seek him out with an aura that reflected from his hair. His presence dominated the hall and he reminded Gerhard of someone famous, but he couldn't put his finger on it. He wore the black gown of a priest with a simple white cross that hung around his neck from a thick purple cord. His round gold-rimmed wire glasses lent an intellectual appearance.

Gerhard thought he looked exactly like an abbot should look. The prior was of average size, a bit pudgy, with straight black hair. He also wore a priest's black gown. Nothing about him seemed outstanding. Gerhard though he looked exactly like a prior should look.

Two staff members arrived at the abbot's table and began filling each glass with red wine. They stood by until the abbot drank first from his glass and nodded to the servers. That was followed by the presentation of food— many plates of it. Additional staff began doing the same for the monks at the other tables, except no one waited to sample the wine. The drinking was instantaneous. The abbot leaned over and spoke to Gerhard. His voice was a bit raspy.

"We're having braised lamb and potatoes with carrots. I hope that you like it."

Gerhard replied that lamb and potatoes were among his favorites and he looked forward to enjoying such a splendid meal.

Gerhard found something interesting in the arrangement of the tables and chairs. The abbot's table was at the back of the hall opposite the entrance. It was wider and more ornate than the tables used by the monks. The abbot sat on the long side facing the other tables. Gerhard was next to him with Brother Robert and the prior on each end. The monk's tables were long and narrow and arranged in the middle of the hall opposite the abbot.

Several monks sat together on the long side, but no one sat on the end. The result was that the monks and the abbot all had a clear view of the other. No one looked at the back of another.

"This wine is delicious," proclaimed Gerhard to his host. "The flavor is hardy and the color is pure. I think it's excellent."

"Thank you. We still grow grapes in our own vineyards, make our own wine, and bake our own bread. At one time the land surrounding Melk Abbey provided food for the entire monastery, even some of the town people, but things have changed over the years. Now we purchase most of our food stuffs from supply companies, just like the hotels and schools in Vienna."

The abbot's voice grew increasingly raspy and then changed to a whisper. He paused, took a sip of wine, and continued.

"Of course, we are here to teach the word of God. Nearly one hundred monks live and study in the monastery and serve the church of Melk Abbey. They also teach religious studies in our school, which has grown beyond our expectations and now boasts an enrollment of nine hundred boys and girls. The Melk Library has become world famous and continues to prepare scholarly manuscripts for religious organizations worldwide. But the tourist industry provides the majority of our income as half a million tourists from around the world visit the abbey every year, many of whom dine in our commercial restaurant just off the Prelates Courtyard. Religion is big business, my friend. Half of me understands and appreciates the value of the business of religion—the other half of me does not. It's a tortuous position. I am afraid that I'm already in purgatory."

The two men continued with polite dinner table conversation, both genuinely enjoyed the company of the other. The lamb was quite good; the pumpkin cream sponge cake dessert was exceptional.

Gerhard felt it strange that the abbot didn't discuss the reason for his visit—the great crime and the important Council of Review, which hopefully was still scheduled for tomorrow morning. But that concern was about to end. Suddenly the abbot rose from his chair and stood quietly in place. The dining hall became immediately silent.

The soft sound of clanking silverware stopped; wine glasses were left on the table. Each monk clasped one hand to the other and both hands disappeared into their habit. All eyes rested on their revered abbot. Then he began.

"Praise Be To God."

The monks responded in kind.

"My dear brothers. It is difficult for me to realize that nearly a year has passed since we first discussed the crime that has been perpetrated against the monastery—a crime that was brought to my attention by you, my own brothers of the church. And although much time has passed, we have been unable to move beyond the incident. It exists today in the library of the abbey, partially hidden, yet to be completely discovered among the volumes, its meaning still unknown. I feel it in my very bones as I move among the stacks of ancient books. I know it is there but I cannot find it. I know the damage it has caused ...."

The abbot began to cough, his breathing quickened. Brother Robert brought him a moist cloth napkin which the abbot dabbed around his mouth. The monks remained silent. They seemed to understand what was happening, but Gerhard was confused. Then the abbot continued, but more slowly.

"Finally, after all of this time, we have a chance to solve the crime."

A murmur arose from the monks. They watched their abbot with rapt attention.

"My guest tonight has the experience and knowledge to solve the crime that we have been unable to solve. He has agreed to attend the Council of Review tomorrow to learn what we already know. I ask each of you to pray for him tonight, pray that God will give him the strength to make the right decision."

Several monks made the sign of the cross. The abbot continued. This time his voice was soft, but clear and easy to hear.

"It is not always necessary to know the identity of someone. Sometimes identity could mean unnecessary endangerment. Therefore, I will not identify the name of my guest."

Gerhard was surprised at the abbot's remarks. Perhaps the Baker had suggested such a course. However it came about, Gerhard felt relieved that he could walk the abbey freely without the need to look over his shoulder.

"But we must call him something," said the abbot, his voice stronger now. "I went to my bible and found the perfect name for him. I decided to call him Matthias, after Saint Matthias, one of the twelve disciples of Jesus. For Jesus described Matthias as the 'brightening of the darkness, the bridging of an abyss, the beginning of a new epoch.' These things that Jesus said represent what our Matthias is to us tonight."

The abbot put his hand on Gerhard's shoulder and motioned for him to stand. He was surprised, but he stood.

"I present Matthias, the guest of the abbot. When you pass him in the hall, greet him. Should he ask for help, give it. If he is busy, do not disturb him. And, whatever his decision tomorrow, know that he is our friend."

The abbot paused and looked directly at Gerhard.

"The Lord Be With You."

The monks responded in kind.

The abbot made the sign of the cross, which was followed immediately by the tolling of a distant bell. Gerhard wondered how the two incidents enjoyed such near perfect coordination. Was it coincidental or did the bell always follow the abbots remarks?

The monks rose, their hands under their scapulars, and formed a line two abreast with the prior in the lead. The procession walked slowly out of the hall toward the other end of the abbey. Gerhard wondered what would happen next. The abbot whispered to him.

"It's time for Vespers. Come Matthias, walk with me. I want you to experience something."

The two men left the dining area and strolled together down a long arched hall that seemed to go on forever. They turned first to the right, then to the left and finally through a huge arch into an open space of a magnificent church made of gleaming white marble. All of the candles were lit. Light sparkled. Frescos were everywhere.

A spectacular dome above gleamed with light even though it was night. Gerhard had seen larger churches, but none more beautiful.

"This is the most important room in the abbey," said the abbot.

They walked down the aisle to the first pew and the abbot motioned for Gerhard to be seated. What escaped his attention for the moment was the whereabouts of the monks. They were all seated in the choir stalls, almost hidden by the baroque design of the stalls.

The abbot remained standing in the aisle next to Gerhard and began to intone the ninety-fourth psalm. The monks responded, the blended mellow sound of their voices rose from the choir stalls and drifted everywhere in the church. The prayers continued for nearly ten minutes. Gerhard was spellbound.

The prayers ended and the abbot moved into the pew and sat next to Gerhard. Then the hymns began. Beautiful music, quietly sung from the monks in half of the choir stalls, then the other half, and finally from all of them. Gerhard felt that he was experiencing a private concert or the celebration of some revered event. Perhaps he was. It was very moving and it was over too soon. He felt the presence of someone standing next to him in the aisle. It was Brother Robert, his companion.

"May I show you to your room, sir?"

He rose and began to leave, but the abbot remained seated.

"What about the abbot?"

"He always remains after the hymns to think and to pray. It's his quiet time."

Gerhard nodded and followed Brother Robert out of the church and down an array of new passageways that he had yet to see. The two walked in silence. Several minutes passed. The monk spoke first.

"Your room is down this hall."

A few more seconds of silence before Gerhard decided to raise the issue.

"The abbot has a bad cough, doesn't he?"

The monk didn't reply. They walked on. Gerhard felt that he needed to press the matter. He just blurted it out.

"Is he sick?"

"He is dying, responded the young monk, his voice high pitched. The abbot has cancer. We pray for him every day. Perhaps you will include him in your prayers tonight."

Gerhard struggled with emotion over the sad news as they stopped outside his room. It wasn't common for him to feel this way. His eyes became moist and he couldn't look at the monk. He just stared at the room door while he fought to regain control of his emotions and then found the strength for a few words.

"I'll do it now."

CHAPTER 8

The first night at Melk Abbey seemed to take forever to move along. The hours were endless and Gerhard lost track of the time. It was somewhere around three in the morning before he fell asleep only to awaken suddenly at six thirty. His first thought was not to keep anyone waiting on him for breakfast. He washed, dressed, and hurried out of his room only to find Brother Robert seated on a wooden bench in the hall outside his door.

Gerhard sat down next to him.

"Have you been here all night?"

"No, I just arrived. The night is my quiet time. I've been strolling in the cloister thinking about the past, wondering about the future, and asking God for guidance. I always talk to Him and He always listens. Come. Breakfast is served and we have to get you ready for the review."

The young monk darted off with such energy that he left Gerhard running to catch up. For some reason it was harder to keep up with him today than it was yesterday. They headed toward the dining hall.

"What did you do before you joined the Order?" he asked as they walked along briskly. "Did you come here right out of school?"

"No. I was in the German Air Force after college."

That answer surprised Gerhard.

"What did you do in the air force and what made you decide to come here?"

"I was a jet pilot. I grew distraught training to kill people. I wanted to save people. That's why I became a priest and joined the Order."

Gerhard was amazed with his companion and decided not to ask any more questions. He already had plenty of answers. The regular breakfast was simple and hardy, but he wasn't hungry.

"Just a small orange juice and coffee, please."

Brother Robert had a pastry and water.

"The Council of Review will be held in the Marble Hall. It is located on the other side of the church, just opposite the Great Library. I am sorry to say that the abbot does not feel well enough to conduct the meeting and he has asked the prior to fill in for him. I hope this change will be satisfactory?"

"Very sorry to hear that about the abbot. Any arrangement will be fine with me. What time is the review scheduled?"

"Any time that you arrive, sir. The prior and the other brothers are prepared and waiting." Gerhard shook his head.

"Why do I always seem to be behind and late for things?"

"It's not you. The abbey is usually ahead of itself on everything that it does. You're the special guest of the abbot and things are done for you, so you're not late for anything. It's our custom."

"Then I'd like to leave now."

Melk Abbey was a plethora of beautiful gardens and striking Baroque architecture. Each courtyard that he walked, each room that he entered, each endless arched hall and soaring doomed ceiling was another example of striking beauty. And so it was when he entered the Marble Hall. Multiple impressions crowded any attempt to experience a single feeling.

The room was made of marble. It was full of light, two stories high, with round windows above thin tall windows that were perhaps twenty feet high. The hall was too long to know how long—except the monks at the far end appeared smaller than those in the middle. A long narrow table was positioned in the center of the hall. It ran from one end of the room nearly to the other—a single chair on each side of the table, exactly in the middle.

The prior stood behind his chair. The vacant chair opposite the prior waited for Gerhard.

He walked slowly into the hall, turned and gazed about. The prior and the half dozen monks at the far end remained at their position. He looked at two inscriptions over the doors, but was unable to read the ornate Latin script. Brother Robert stepped close and said:

"They are quotations from the Holy Rule of St. Benedict. The one over the far door reads, 'Guests should be received as Christ would be.' The other one reads,
'And to each the honor given which is his due.'"

Gerhard studied the ornate words above him and thought about their meaning, then Robert escorted him to the empty chair where he was greeted by the prior. They exchanged greetings of the morning and the Council of Review began. The prior spoke with a steady voice.

"We have placed seven volumes of manuscripts and important religious works on the table to your left."

As he spoke, the monks seated at the far end of the table rose and each one took a position behind a particular book.

"Each volume bears an example of the crime that the abbot spoke of and each is represented by the monk who found it. They are here to describe what they found and to answer your questions. Let us begin with the book on the end."

The prior moved to the monk standing behind his book at the far end of the row. Gerhard walked to the end of the table and stood in front of the monk and his book. The monk spoke first.

"Good morning Matthias. I am Brother Ludwig. I was working in the scriptorium nearly a year ago when I withdrew this book from the library, part of which I was to copy for another monastery. It was written by Athanasius Kircher in 1701. I found that the cover page had been removed and the second page was torn out, but left inside the book. You will notice that most of the words on the third page have been underlined in blue."

Gerhard listened to the monk, looked at the book, and nodded. Then he stepped to the next monk.

"Matthias, I am Brother Axel. It was only a week after Brother Ludwig checked out his book that I found markings on the book that I was assigned to transcribe. I was shocked to find it so desecrated with large number markings on the cover. The numbers 150S and 150N were marked several times over the cover and many times on the cover page in red, blue, and black ink. I don't understand any of it. Then I found additional marks on the clear margins of other pages—many horizontal and vertical lines about three to four centimeters long in different colors."

To everyone's surprise, Gerhard removed a jeweler's eye piece from his pocket and closely examined the numbers and marks. Then he moved to the next position.

"Herr Matthias, my name is Brother Andrew. I worked on my book all day before I noticed the marks. They were big and obvious, but I was so involved with my work that I didn't see them until I closed the book at the end of the day." He pointed with his finger and began to trace the mark. "This heavy four centimeter vertical line runs down along the spine of the cover, then turns to the right and runs another four centimeters along the bottom. A separate thick mark, almost like a scar, runs down the other side of the cover. I studied the marks with my enlarging glass and found that they were not part of the original book. They were added."

Gerhard bent over the book and studied it for some

time.

"Thank you Brother Andrew," he said, as he moved down the line of monks.

"Sir, I am Brother Theodor. I found a strange set of marks on my book. The inside cover page revealed a three centimeter horizontal mark that stopped at the point of a ball or spot, then a space followed by another ball or spot. What do you make of it, sir?"

"Let's take a close look." He put the jeweler's eye piece next to the marks. "Very interesting. Thank you."

"I am Brother Stephan and I found an equally strange set of marks in my book." He pointed to the inside cover page. "My mark is of a chair alongside of a three centimeter vertical line descending from a ball or dot."

Gerhard looked closely. "It certainly looks like a chair all right." He studied it for a moment and then moved to the next monk.

"Matthias, my name is Brother Hans. I have two marks on the inside cover page of the book that I worked with. One is a narrow 'V' followed by the number 450 and a wider 'V' followed by the number 900. I don't have any idea what they mean. But what troubled me most was the complete removal of the entire last chapter of the book. It was written by Johnannes Singrenius in 1519. I was unable to finish my work without that chapter."

Gerhard looked at the numbers then moved to the monk who stood in front of the last book.

"I am Brother Laurenz. I wasn't expecting a problem when the librarian brought my book to me. I opened it and began to work. I got to page 76 and found it wasn't there.

Pages 76 to 126 were gone. They were pulled out. I looked throughout the volume and couldn't find them. I did find something else on the last leaf; it was smeared with different colors of ink. I don't know why."

Gerhard shook his head. He looked closely at the place where the pages were torn out. Then he walked up and down the table and examined each book for a second time. He took his chair across from the prior as the monks waited for him to speak.

"There is no doubt that the damage to the books that you presented to me this morning is despicable. No one has the right to disfigure anything, especially old and valuable books. I don't know who did it or why, but such matters should be reported to the local police so that a case portfolio can be prepared in the hope that the incident can be properly investigated and someday resolved. I am sorry, but as bad as the situation seems, I don't see the evidence of a great crime as was reported to me."

The prior listened with respect, but he wasn't ready to end the discussion.

"I understand your position, sir, but we have not completed our presentation. The Council has additional information that we wish to submit—including a witness. You see, we have only presented Exhibit One, a review of the actual damage that we have found thus far. Exhibit Two will examine the consequences of the damage."

Gerhard liked the prior's persistent attitude and his savvy use of exhibits. The part about a witness was intriguing.

"I am sorry if I conclude prematurely. Please continue."

"You referred to the damaged books that we presented as old and valuable. They are much more than that. They are rare and priceless masterpieces. Suppose you were the curator of one the world's finest museums with exquisite paintings on display by world masters such as Dali, Picasso, Van Gogh, Botticelli, and Da Vinci. Visitors from around the world came to view your magnificent collection every day. But suddenly, tragedy. One morning you discovered that someone broke into your museum during the night and slashed Michelangelo's *The Creation of Adam*. Then you found that Rembrandt's *The Night Watch* had been marred with multiple painted lines and large nonsense numbers. One-of-a-kind treasures, lost to the world forever.

"Our priceless masterpieces in Melk Abbey have been slashed and ripped, too. They have been marred with lines and marks. Entire chapters have been ruthlessly torn out, discarded, never to be read again. These damaged books on the table next to you are one-of-a-kind treasures, parts of which have been lost to the world forever."

Gerhard's sat still, his head tilted to the side. Then he focused on the prior. "I see your point, prior. The analogy was sound and you have given me a fresh perspective. Please continue."

"Brother Laurenz told you that pages 76 to 126 were torn out of the book that he was using. What he didn't tell you was that the book was more than old, more than ancient. It was one of many medieval manuscripts in the

Melk Library that are over two thousand years old."

Gerhard shifted in his chair, disturbed by the new information. But the prior had more disturbing news. Shocking news. He let Gerhard settle in his chair—then he said it.

"These medieval manuscripts were the only known recorded history of the time before Christ. To destroy such a rare manuscript would forever destroy a part of the history of the world."

Gerhard lunged from his chair and walked about in short tight circles. The monks didn't expect such a physical reaction from their guest.

Damn, the prior was absolutely correct. The damage to the books in their library was a major historical loss. It's so clear to me now, why wasn't it before?

He felt himself becoming angry.

"You said that you had a witness. I want to hear from him."

The prior motioned with his hand and an old monk with a cane rose from his chair at the far end of the hall and began to approach them.

Brother Ludwig went to his aid. The distance was long and the walker slow, but by the time he arrived another monk had positioned a chair next to Gerhard and the old monk settled stiffly into it.

The sight of the old monk unsettled him. He was ready to move ahead with dispatch, but the unexpected appearance of an old man changed that. He looked at Gerhard through partially cloudy eyes, both hands clasped over his cane.

What could he possibly add to the situation thought Gerhard? But the monk had something no one else had—first-hand knowledge. What came next was completely beyond anything Gerhard could have imagined.

"May I introduce Brother Felix?" began the prior. "He is 94 years old, the oldest member of the Order. He is also the only living member of the monastery who resided at Melk Abbey during the Second World War. He has something to tell you."

The prior nodded to Brother Felix to begin, just as another monk brought him a coffee cup. He took a couple of short sips and smiled at Gerhard.

"It was early in the winter of 1944. I remember because we were still putting away the decorations from Christmas. I was the youngest and often asked to bring in extra firewood and that's what I was doing that evening when I heard the sound of trucks behind me. I don't know how many there were, but it was a bunch of them, and some cars, too."

He stopped and took another sip or two from his coffee cup. Gerhard began to relax. Somehow the old man's presence was comforting and the slow intonations of his speech were reassuring.

"They were German soldiers, a company of them all dressed in gray uniforms, except the ones in the cars—they wore black uniforms with red armbands. I thought they were officers, but now I think they were Nazis. Maybe they were both. The ones in the black uniforms told the others what to do.

"The soldiers drove those big trucks across our flower

garden and into the courtyard and began unloading ladders, wire, survey instruments, and stone and mortar. I was scared and hurried inside with my firewood.

"The soldiers moved half of the brothers out of their rooms and took the rooms over as their own place. We had to move in with the other monks. The abbot organized meetings that night with groups of us and he decided what valuables to hide and where to put them. There are many places to hide things in this old abbey and we set about doing that all night long.

"I remember how surprised we were in the morning when we discovered that the soldiers didn't seem interested in our treasures. They didn't try to take anything."

Gerhard broke in with a question.

"Did you have a chance to see what they were doing?"

Brother Felix took another sip from his cup.

"Yes sir. The winter nights were long and cold and no one could use lights because of the war, so the soldiers slept at night and worked during the day. The abbot told us all to stay out of their way, but I was young and didn't listen. I felt someone needed to keep an eye on them. I wore my black robe with the hood and crept around the abbey in the shadows of the walls and corners, like the spirit of the night. I was lucky.

"I often wondered what they would have done if they caught me. Half of the gray soldiers were busy sitting up ladders and looking at our books. They took down rows of books and put them on tables in the same order that they were on the shelf. I was surprised that they were so careful. They opened all of the books, checked each one, and then put them back. This went on for days. The soldiers were looking for something—in fact they looked for a whole week, because that's how long they searched through our library. I don't think they ever found it.

"The other half of the gray soldiers were surveying and measuring things—like walls and ceilings and the angles in between. They had lots of problems with the height of the ceilings because they surveyed this room and the Great Library many times. The Nazis probably didn't know about Paul Troger and his *Trompe L'Oeil* ceilings."

The old monk began to laugh, then took another couple of sips.

Gerhard chuckled at the comment too. "Saved by an illusion, perhaps?"

"Perhaps so," responded Brother Felix. "But, there was something that disappeared during that week that I haven't mentioned. I saw it every day and then it was gone. It wasn't anything of ours. It belonged to them. One of the Nazis soldiers with the red arm band constantly carried a locked cloth bag that was banded with leather. I always hoped for a chance to look inside. He didn't have the bag one day and they all drove away the next day along with all of their ladders and survey equipment."

"You said they brought stone and mortar. Did you see where they used it?"

"I am not sure if they ever used it. It was a long time ago and I just can't remember. Besides, it was impossible for me to watch them every minute. I'd watch one group for a while, sneak away and do my chores, then sneak back and watch the other group. I remember how strange it was when I went back to the rooms that the soldiers were in after they left the abbey. Everything looked as it did before they arrived. It was as if they were never here."

"Thank you, Brother Felix," said Gerhard. "Your comments were very helpful. You said you were scared watching the soldiers, but I think you were very brave. I appreciate the time that you took to tell me about your experience."

The old monk smiled and returned to his chair at the far end of the room. Gerhard turned to the prior who put his elbows on the table and leaned toward Gerhard. His voice was quiet and measured.

"You have seen the crimes that we have seen. I wonder how many more crimes reside in the stacks of our library yet to be found."

Just then the door of the Marble Hall opened and the abbot entered. The surprised monks stood. Those seated at the far end of the room walked to the center of the long table, and held the empty chair used by the old one. The abbot settled into it and bid everyone a hardy greeting. They were glad to see him walking about with such ease.

"We didn't expect to see you today, but we are happy that you're here. How do you feel?" asked the prior.

"Splendid. I couldn't stay away—I had to see how the review was going."

"Why don't you ask your guest? He has heard from all of us. We have nothing more to tell. The decision is his."

"Not quite, yet," responded the abbot. He has not heard from me." The monks murmured in agreement. Then the abbot began— his voice steady and firm.

"You have been presented with the evidence, seen the damage, and heard the consequence. You have even listened to a witness. Now hear my view. I believe that there is a direct correlation between the damage to the valuables in our library and the arrival of the German troops, but I do not know for sure—I have no proof. I believe there is additional damage that still exists in our library, but I am unsure—I have no proof. I believe that the German troops either put something in our library or did something to it, but I don't know for sure—I have no proof. I ask you to investigate the matter and provide the proof—so that we know for sure."

All of the monks looked at Gerhard. It was a gathering of the concerned and they longed for a good answer.

Gerhard smiled—his jaw firm. He answered with only a few short words, "I am with you!"

The monks applauded, including the prior and the abbot. Even Gerhard joined in. The Marble Hall was alive with cheers.

"This calls for a celebration! Let's bring out Brother Felix's coffee," proclaimed the abbot.

"Oh, I don't think we should celebrate with coffee," said Gerhard.

"We don't either.   When you're 94 years and the senior member of the Order, you drink whatever you want. Brother Felix wasn't sipping coffee.   His cup was full of the best Irish whiskey we could buy!"

CHAPTER 9

The rail trip from Vienna to Zurich was uneventful—so was the arrival in Zurich's central railroad yard. The Zurich yard was so quiet it was boring. Gerhard loved it. He thought it was a perfect place to spend time unbothered by locals and inquisitive police.

There was an interesting railroad paradox between Vienna and Zurich. Zurich was many times smaller than Vienna, but the little Swiss city was the central European railroad hub and it handled a huge volume of rail traffic, much higher than its larger neighbor in Austria. The difference was technology and management. Just like the traditional Swiss watch, everything worked in Switzerland, and everything ran on time as well. Gerhard's private car was efficiently dispatched to its reserved position on a select track near a clean and sturdy yardmasters office. Then it was immediately connected to the land electrical distribution system and the crew silently disappeared to other parts of the yard without a trace.

Normally, Gerhard would be instantly busy upon arrival at a new station, but this time he remained in his leather chair, seemingly pre-occupied with something else on his mind. Wolf noticed it, sat quietly and avoided any discussion. They exchanged glances, but neither spoke.

Gerhard seemed riveted in his position as he stared out of the window with his chin resting in his hand. Wolf felt uncomfortable with this unusual behavior, but soon learned what it was all about. Gerhard was experiencing stage fright.

I guess this is a good idea. I'd really like to do it and the opportunity is here; it just seemed to arrive so quickly.

"Is everything ready for tonight?" he asked, hesitantly.

"Yes sir. I've attended to all of the events that we discussed and they are all in order."

He remained in his gazed posture without responding immediately to Wolf, as if to fit a little extra time into the conversation. Then he spoke in a voice that sounded somewhat pleading.

"But are you sure? Did you double check everything?"

"Absolutely! We're ready to go," replied Wolf with strength and sureness in the hope that it would do the same for Gerhard.

It worked. Gerhard turned to Wolf and spoke firmly with the confidence of a field grade officer about to charge the enemy.

"Let's do this now!"

But first, he poured white burgundy into the glass with the Papal Crest and took several long sips. Then he called Nicole's unlisted number. She answered before the second ring with one word.

"Gerhard."

It was that soft feminine voice that he loved so and the slow drawn-out way she said his name. She sounded as if she was in bed.

"Nicole. It's wonderful to hear your voice. I'm in town and can't wait to have dinner with you. Are you at home?"

"No. I'm having a staff meeting in the office conference room at the moment, but I told them to go on without me. I've moved to my own office now. I'm so happy that you're here. I always feel better when I know that you're near. When did you get into town? When can I see you? When can we have dinner?"

"I only got in a few moments ago. I thought that Wolf could pick you up around six or six thirty—perhaps seven if that's better."

"You mean tonight, don't you? I don't think I could wait another day knowing that you're here."

"Yes! Tonight! Indeed tonight! Oh! I forgot to ask—are you free for dinner tonight?" *For God's sake man, get yourself together,* thought Gerhard. *You sound so foolish.*

Nicole laughed at the question and said that she was free and would be ready and waiting at home at six thirty.

"And are you ready to deliver the loose ones?" she asked.

"Right. I have them with me now. I have 80 @ thirty two thousand, 20 @ nine thousand, and 100 @ seventy thousand. That totals one hundred eleven thousand euros."

"That's fair. I'll have the money with me, but where are you taking me for dinner and what should I wear?"

"We're going to an extra nice place. It's brand new—very intimate. You've never dined there before."

"That's impossible, dear one. I live here, remember? I know all of the places to eat in Zurich and I've been to all of them. What's it called?"

The name. I didn't expect she'd ask the name of the place.

"Rather not tell you just yet. It's a surprise."

"Okay, but what do I wear? Is it a formal place?"

Clothes! I didn't think about clothes either.

"That's part of the surprise. Just wear something smart. You'll look elegant in whatever you wear—you always do." He hoped he sounded convincing.

"Well, all right, but you'll have to take me the way I come."

Gerhard swallowed hard. "It'll be my pleasure. See you in a few hours."

The conversation was over and he turned his attention to the things that he had to pull together immediately to make the dinner and the night work out just right. Not everything flowed flawlessly as he expected.

Rather than stop at the parking lot near the yardmaster's office, the market truck with the food order bounced over the tracks with great difficultly as it drove directly to the railcar. The food shifted, the bottles tipped over and every box burst open, but miraculously nothing was damaged except a couple of broken eggs. Gerhard checked the order piece by piece and found everything was there and in good shape.

Then Wolf arrived from the airport with Chef Peppie from Le Grand Vefour restaurant in Paris. The surprise was that he wasn't alone—he brought his sous chef with him, who was very short.

Both chefs were enamored to find themselves inside a private car in the middle of a busy railroad yard. They listened very politely as Gerhard explained the peculiarities of the galley and reviewed the food supplies that just arrived. They nodded in agreement to whatever he said and gestured with full sweeping arm movements in support of his comments, after which the two of them immediately rearranged the galley to their satisfaction.

Gerhard felt he should review the menu with the chefs. He gave Chef Peppie a copy of the printed menu that he sent to him earlier and meticulously pointed to various items as part of a general review. They offered 'Oh's' and 'Ah's' and many 'Oui's,' but surreptitiously transitioned to the process of busily chopping and mixing and cooking and baking. They seemed to know what they were doing so he let them alone, hoped for the best, and took two aspirins.

Gerhard felt that there was something odd about Peppie, but he couldn't put his finger on it. What he didn't know was that Chef Peppie was from Barcelona. He only spoke Spanish, knew just a few words of French, and didn't understand German at all. But he was damn good at pretending. He slipped into his standard masquerade whenever someone spoke to him in a language other than Spanish. He used body language very effectively, with accompanying grunts and nods and a few words of French mixed in with lots of Spanish. He would be a model prisoner of war. The enemy would never know by his actions if their interrogation was working or not.

The clothes that Gerhard ordered earlier from *My Ladies Fine Apparel* in Vienna arrived. Wolf opened the packages and began to hang them in Gerhard's bedroom closet when Gerhard came in to check his purchases. Just then a lumbering locomotive passed on the next track with a deafening rumble and a blast from its air horn.

"Wolf, I can't have this noise. It'll ruin the evening. What can you do about it?"

Wolf thought for a moment. "I have an idea. I'll be back soon."

He left the railcar, crossed the tracks, and headed straight for the yardmaster's office. Two big yard switchmen were standing behind the counter. They both wore overalls and carried thick gloves used to handle heavy track switches. An office worker in a shirt and tie was busy on a computer at one of the two desks. He was thin, wore a vest, had little hair, and was typing like there was no tomorrow.

Wolf approached the switchmen, one of whom looked inquisitively at a computer keyboard on the counter and swiped the keys with a paint brush in a cleaning motion. The other man stood next to him reading a newspaper at arm's length.

"I'd like to see the yardmaster," announced Wolf.

"Yeah, what about?" said the switchman brushing the keyboard. The abrupt answer put Wolf on alert. His response was straight forward.

"That's between the two of us."

"If you don't tell us then you don't see no one."

The thin man in the vest seemed to shake a little as his fingers flew over his keyboard. The other man reading the newspaper lowered it a little and Wolf could see that he was smiling, a cigarette firmly lodged between his lips. He knew they were playing with him.

I don't have time for this. Gerhard needs resolution to the noise problem and I have to get back to the car quickly to get ready for tonight. He decided on a course of action.

"How can you type on a computer with a broken hand?"

"I ain't got no broken hand," announced the switchmen sarcastically, just as Wolf clamped it with his metal hand and energized the power cell. Wolf's stainless steel fingers clamped on the switchman's hand in a way that caught his thumb between the keyboard and the wooden brush handle. The thumb broke instantly and the switchman's knees buckled in pain and he leaned heavily against the counter.

"My God you broke my hand. Ohh it hurts. Stop it! Please stop it!"

But Wolf decided not to release the hand—at least not yet. The thin man typed away faster than ever.

"That's only one finger. You've got nine more.

Should I break them one at a time or all at once? Or do I let you go and see the yardmaster now?"

"You can see the yardmaster now. Go right in, mister."

Wolf looked over at the other man who was dazed by the sudden spectacle and still held the newspaper out in front of him, his eyes wide, and his mouth open with the cigarette now stuck to his lower lip. Wolf de-energized his power cell and the switchman collapsed to the floor. Then Wolf stepped to the other man, touched the newspaper with a re-energized finger, and the paper burst into flames. The man held the blazing paper for a second as he stared at Wolf, and then yelled that he was on fire. Wolf did what any good citizen would do—he sprayed the man with foam from the office fire extinguisher—from head to toe. The thin man behind the desk continued to type feverishly.

"I think you two men should see a doctor right away," said Wolf calmly. Both men ran out of the building, one was holding his hand, the other was trailed by a column of smoke. He heard someone laughing behind him. It was the yardmaster.

"Been trying to teach those two a lesson for a long time. Your lesson was better than any that I could think of. What can I do for you, sir?"

Wolf explained that he worked for his employer who owned the private railcar. He tactfully mentioned the arrival of a special guest who was expected in a few hours, and how very difficult it would be with noisy locomotives moving about in the area. The yardmaster smiled.

"No one has ever asked me to operate my yard more quietly, but I think it would be a good exercise in yard management and worth trying. Besides, I owe you one, maybe two. Let's see what I can do."

He spoke to the thin man in the vest, who actually stopped typing on the computer as he listened to the yardmaster's instructions. They conversed for a minute, and then the thin man began to type again, but not as fast as before. The yardmaster entered data into his own computer for a while before he returned to Wolf.

"I've adjusted the car make up schedule and sent all switch engines to the North yard between the hours of seven tonight and six tomorrow morning. That should provide plenty of quiet time for you."

Wolf did it! He felt good as he literally hopped over the tracks on the way back to the railcar. Never before had he adjusted the speed of commerce, or at least the noisy part of it.

* * *

Wolf arrived at Nicole's penthouse apartment at six-thirty sharp. She was ready, excited, and cheerfully hugged Wolf, much to his surprise.

"Do you realize that it's been two years since we last saw each other," she said. They were both in a good mood and chatted back and forth during the ride to meet Gerhard. Then she pressed several questions.

"How is Gerhard? Is he doing well? Does he look the same? Where is he taking me for dinner? Will this outfit be okay?"

"I think Mr. Gerhard is doing very well. He's quite

busy with many projects on his schedule. I think he looks just like he always did—no change, really. But please don't ask about the dinner location. Mr. Gerhard would surely detach me limb from limb if I spoiled his surprise. And your clothes are perfect, absolutely perfect."

Nicole wasn't totally happy about the secret dinner location, but she knew Gerhard's bent for perfection and she accepted Wolf's answer.

They drove on.

The neighborhood began to change from smart Zurich urban to commercial, to industrial. Then the railroad yard appeared.

"Wolf, are we lost?"

"No ma'am. We're just about there. Less than a minute away."

"But this is a railroad place!" There was a faint hint of alarm in her voice. Wolf parked near the yardmaster's office as Nicole stared out over a vast railroad switching yard.

"Oh my," she said.

"Please don't be alarmed Ms. Nicole. I promise that Mr. Gerhard has everything well under control and you will have an exceptionally splendid evening."

"Well, I know it'll be a memorable one."

Wolf took her hand and led Nicole over several rows of tracks.

"I can't believe this. Where are we going?" Wolf stopped at the bottom of the metal steps to the railcar.

"We're here," he said.

Gerhard stepped silently out of the car and onto the

platform above as Wolf helped her climb the stairs..... into Gerhard's arms. They embraced. Then they embraced again and he ushered her into the railcar. She completely forgot about being in a railroad yard. They stood, held each other, and talked insatiably. Finally, she found a moment to ask the burning question that she had to know the answer to before their relationship could continue.

"Where in the hell am I?"

Chef Peppie entered the lounge before Gerhard could answer. He casually balanced two glasses of white wine on a round silver tray, which he held unusually high above his head in a chef type of way. He chatted rapidly in bits of French and Spanish in a happy friendly manner as if he were excited to see the couple, while skillfully presenting a glass of wine to each of them.

Nicole noticed the 'Le Grand Vefour' logo sewn above the left pocket of his chef's coat and was hugely impressed. The chef maintained his constant chatter as he disappeared into the galley.

"Nice touch," said Nicole.

"Yes. Chef Peppie heard that you would be here and insisted on preparing your dinner tonight."

"Oh Gerhard, I like your chef Peppie. Now back to my question. Where are we and what is this place?"

He led her on a tour of his private car while he explained what it was and why he bought it. She listened carefully as they walked slowly together from room to room holding their glass and sipping the wine. They returned to the drawing room to find the shades pulled and the drapes drawn and the coffee table raised and set with two place servings complete with candles. Soft guitar music came from somewhere. Gerhard wasn't aware that he had a music system. They settled close together into the corner of the sofa.

"So, you own part of a train," said Nicole in a teasing way.

"Yes, the back part," responded Gerhard with an equally teasing smile.

"Are we going anywhere in the train tonight?"

"No, we're staying here for the evening. If I wanted to go someplace I'd tell the railroad to connect my car to the train that was going to the place that I wanted to go and the train would pull me to that place."

"Well, it seems like a lot of trouble to me." She was going to say something like—*why not drive or fly*, but she thought it best to dramatically shift the subject.

"I've never known anyone who had a private railcar, but if I did, I am quite sure that it wouldn't look as eloquent as yours."

He gave her a little kiss and then another one.

"You know what you need, dear? You need a chandelier right about there," as she pointed to the center part of the car's ceiling.

"That's very interesting, because a good friend of mine said the same thing. You know all about interior design and fine antiques, why don't you find a really good chandelier for that space?"

Chef Peppie and his sous chef entered the drawing room abruptly. They exhibited a sense of high excitement as they brushed crumbs and vegetables parts onto the floor from the front of their white coats with short sweeping hand motions. They were all smiles.

The short sous chef announced that dinner would be served momentarily upon presentation of the menu. Chef Peppie rocked back and forth, from heel to toe, beaming with pride as the short sous began.

"Lady and gentleman!" he said in an extra loud announcer type voice. "We shall start the feast tonight with escargot stuffed mushrooms in garlic herb butter. Next, we are honored to serve the magnificent main course of brined roast pheasant with heather and whisky raspberry sauce. This scrumptious fowl will be dressed with asparagus and wild rice surrounded by a ring of crispy root vegetables and leeks."

Chef Peppie rocked on; his fore and aft foot movements now allowed his top body arc to reach dangerous proportions.

"And for dessert, the famous Chef Peppie presents his renowned chocolate-strawberry trifle!"

Both chefs burst into rapid applause. Gerhard and Nicole were so impressed with the unique menu presentation that they applauded as well. It was a splendid introduction to a fabulous meal. They dined, talked, and enjoyed. The hours passed and so did the magical evening. Then Nicole made an observation.

"Where did everyone go?"

"Wolf took the chefs to the airport hotel for the night. He has a room there as well."

Then Nicole made another observation.

"Well, how am I going to get home tonight?"

Gerhard didn't answer her question directly. He got up from the sofa, took her hand and said,

"Come, I have something to show you." He led her into his bedroom, opened the closet, brought out two gorgeous negligees, and held them up for her to see.

"What do you think of these outfits?" he asked sheepishly.

Nicole took them both and studied each one.

"Gerhard, there's nothing to them," she announced, with one eyebrow slightly raised. But she continued to look, then hung one back in the closet.

"I think this one will be best for tonight." She looked directly at Gerhard and began to unbutton her blouse, slowly, one button at a time, and let the blouse fall to the floor. She unzipped her slacks and they slid down her firm legs to the floor. She reached behind her and unhooked her bra, and then slid off her panties and they both dropped to the floor. She stood nude in front of Gerhard and smiled. But Nicole didn't slip into the negligee. Instead she returned it to the closet and said.....

"I believe I'll wear what I came in." She sat gently on his bed, reached up, and pulled him down on her.

"Now, what do you think of this outfit?"

CHAPTER 10

The Baker and his cousin agreed that Gerhard's suggestion to become a silent partner in their new private limousine company was a good idea. He provided the money for three additional cars, which allowed them to start the business faster than expected without hindering their cash flow. The arrangement also provided Gerhard with undercover transportation anywhere in Europe, which was priceless to him.

They were being driven to Melk, Austria, in one of the Baker's newly acquired cars, pleased that his custom of providing a box of pastries remained part of the guidelines of the new company. Before Gerhard left Zurich he contacted Alfonso Cavello, the attorney who closed the sale of his private railcar, and left move order instructions for the car to be relocated to Salzburg.

They pulled up to the front entrance steps of the monastery just as Brother Robert and another monk arrived to greet them. The monks carried their luggage and led them to their rooms to freshen up before dinner. Wolf was impressed with the beauty and grandeur of the abbey. Gerhard noticed how his head turned from one striking view to another, just like someone looking at skyscrapers on a first visit to New York City. He whispered into Wolf's ear...

"Don't be late for dinner or anything else around here. They stop everything and wait for you to show up. It can be embarrassing, but it's their custom because guests come first. Nothing starts before the guest arrives."

Wolf was thankful for the tip. Brother Robert escorted them to the main dining room. This time the big wooden doors were open and they entered along with about eighty other monks, all of whom wore black habits—a sight that stunned Wolf at first, but he soon found it intriguing.

The abbot arrived escorted by the prior, and they each put both hands on Gerhard's shoulder as a greeting. Gerhard introduced Wolf to each of them. Unlike other times, Gerhard gave no prior instructions to Wolf that he should hide his metal hand. It was plainly visible, but no one noticed—a refreshing and comfortable feeling for him.

Gerhard and the abbot spent the entire dinner huddled over their food, talking. Gerhard was unusually animated and the abbot highly attentive. The prior listened carefully too, and asked several questions. They nodded often to each other. All of the monks noticed the intensity of the conversation and the general agreement among the participants. The dinner was over and the abbot rose from his chair and stood quietly in place.

The dining hall became silent immediately. The tall silver haired priest dressed in black with a simple white cross that hung from a thick purple cord, looked every inch the leader of Melk Abbey. The abbot's voice was clear and strong without any sign of his troubling cancer.

"Praise Be To God," he began.

The monks responded in kind.

"My dear brothers. Look!" The abbot pointed to Gerhard. "Matthias is among us again."

The monks offered a generous round of spontaneous applause. They were glad to see him.

"And he brought his assistant, who, in keeping with the practice that was decided last time to avoid actual names, shall be called 'Simon' after the apostle St. Simon. Simon was the least known of the 12 apostles, but his quiet ways served Jesus well. I know he will do the same for Matthias. The good natured monks gave Wolf a hardy round of applause. Wolf smiled. The abbot continued.

"You all know by now that our friend Matthias has agreed to investigate the crime that has been perpetrated against the monastery and to discover the cause and the meaning of it. My heart pounds with excitement because we begin in the morning!"

A strong murmur moved in wave fashion over the room of monks. The excitement was building. The abbot continued.

"I used the word 'we' because it will require the efforts of us all to solve this crime. Each of us will have a task to perform."

More murmuring among the monks. The abbot's

comment caught them by surprise. How could they possibly help solve a mystery that's been unsolvable up to now? Then the abbot moved from his chair and stood behind Gerhard, his hands again on Gerhard's shoulders.

"I can tell you one thing for certain—we indeed have the right captain for the job. Seldom have I been more spellbound then when I listened during dinner to his explanation of how he intended to advance the investigation—what needed to be done first, second, and third. Not only the order of the process but the reasons for it as well. They all made sense. I believe in him. I feel that the secrets that remain hidden among the volumes of our ancient books will be known to us soon."

The abbot moved back to his place at the table and looked out over the monks in the dining room. He had everyone's attention.

"This is what we shall do."

Several monks made the sign of the cross, perhaps in resolute, perhaps to insure the success of what they were about to hear. They all leaned forward in their seats as not to miss a word. But they were not completely prepared for the magnitude of what was about to come next.

"By Order of the Abbot, all regular day to day activities at Melk Abbey, except those regarding food preparation, the care of our livestock, and the Vespers will be discontinued at six tomorrow morning until further notice. This closure will include all twelve rooms of the library as well."

A gasp filled the dining hall. The great abbey never closed before and no one could remember a time when the library was closed, except during short periods of danger during the Second World War. The abbot continued in a calm and deliberate manner.

"Matthias will direct the investigation. The prior will coordinate all related activities within the abbey. Tour agencies and schools will be notified of the closure. I ask that the furniture in the main library be removed tomorrow morning and replaced with a single row of eight tables in the center. Four of our tallest maintenance ladders and the garden transit instrument that we use for landscape design will also be required and they should all be brought to the library in the morning. Brothers Ludwig, Axel, Andrew, Theodor, Stephan, Hans, and Laurenz will have initial leadership roles and I ask them to report to the prior at noon. The rest of you will be organized into teams and your duties will be explained shortly after the prior meets with the brothers that I just named."

The monks sat motionless as they reviewed what the abbot said. No one murmured. They wanted more clarification, and waited for him to speak again.

"Any project of worth has a beginning based on a solid and well-reasoned foundation. This project is no different—except for one unique part. It has properties of such voluminous proportions that they cannot be addressed in the usual mode of investigation."

The monks were riveted to the abbot's words.

"You all know that I refer to—books. Our books! We have one hundred thousand of them in the rooms and stacks of our library. Matthias and his assistant could not possibly examine so many in any reasonable amount of time as to advance the investigation to a timely closure. Such technical detail is best addressed by those who are most familiar with the books, those who work with the books daily, know their order, and how to hold and open them without damage. We could do it! There are almost one hundred of us who could do this important technical examination better and faster than anyone!"

The monks erupted with respectful shouts. Some even pounded on the table in support of the idea advanced by their abbot.

"I am sure that some of our brothers who are good with mathematics have already done the math. Don't be alarmed because I too have done the math and find that it is not as bad as it appeared at first. If one hundred of us could check one hundred thousand books, each one would be tasked with one thousand books to examine. Yes, such an amount seems huge, but we need not read every page, nor copy every word as we are used to doing. We will do a 'flip through' as Matthias calls it. There is a reason and a proper way to do it and this Matthias will explain to you tomorrow afternoon.

"Now listen carefully, as the following is a time example of what could be done. If each of us followed Matthias instructions and performed a technical examination of two books per minute, we would complete sixty books per hour per person. If each of us worked five hours a day we could complete three hundred books per person. From this point it's easy to calculate the number of days necessary to check one thousand books per person."

The murmur in the dining room was subdued.

Each monk was doing his own math and the general opinion seemed to be that the process was doable. The abbot continued.

"There will be changes and variations in the time example. Some of us will do more than others, some less, some none at all. Some will find the task too arduous. Some will help in other ways. That's all right. We will do what we can. I feel confident that the entire process will probably take longer than expected. Now listen to these words of hope! If all goes well, it is quite possible that the entire technical examination could be completed in one week's time."

There was much murmuring and nodding among the monks. Their confidence was up and they seemed to agree with the abbot.

"My heart continues to pound with excitement," his voice stronger now and louder than usual as the overhead lights reflected a special radiance from his silver hair. "My spirit is high. The devil may be hiding in the pages of our holy books, but his fear must be enormous, for the monks of Melk Abbey are about to descend on him."

The abbot's arms were outstretched now, his voice crescendoed.

"Once we have identified all of the books that have been desecrated we will have the tools to find the meaning behind these crimes against learning and the history of knowledge. Then the affront to God and to the Holy Church will be no more."

Every monk in the dining room, including those at the

abbot's preferred table, rose and applauded. It appeared that the doable would be done. The abbot dropped both arms, then held one hand high in the air and said...

"May each of you find special pleasure in the Vespers tonight."

"The Lord Be With You."

The monks responded in kind.

The abbot made the sign of the cross, which was followed immediately by the tolling of a distant bell. The monks folded their hands under their scapulars and lined up to leave the dining hall.

There's that bell again, thought Gerhard. *How can he time the end of his comments so perfectly to the tolling of a bell?*

Wolf leaned over and whispered to Gerhard. "That was one of the most moving experiences I ever had. It was a beautiful thing. Where are all of the monks going?"

"To church. They do it every night after dinner. Come, let me show you the closest thing to heaven on earth."

He led Wolf down the same arched hallway that he used before. "*I hope I remember the way.*"

Just then, Brother Robert called out from behind and they stopped for him.

"The abbot asked me to continue as your companion during the time that you'll be with us. I'll serve as your aide-de-camp and try to make things easier for you."

"That's good news and very appreciated. You came at the right time because I need your advice at this very moment."

Surprised at the sudden request, Brother Robert replied, "I'm ready to serve you, sir."

"Is this the right way to the church?"

Robert enjoyed the humor and asked them to follow him. The arched hallway led directly to large open space inside the front of the church.

The sight of so much gleaming white marble, golden frescos, candles, and the spectacular dome above was suddenly enhanced by the soft notes of an organ, which was soon followed by equally soft chants of eighty monks. Gerhard whispered to Wolf...

"Seldom does one see a sight of such beauty. It seems to penetrate the soul."

"You're right. It is like heaven on earth."

* * *

Breakfast the next morning seemed unlike other ones, which were always orderly and dully routine. This one was irregular and spontaneous. Monks darted about hurriedly. The dining hall had a different attitude. Gerhard felt that they were trying to get breakfast over with and move on to other things.

The doing had begun. Brother Robert called out to them....

"Good morning, Matthias. I just came from the library. The prior asks that you come and approve the arrangement of the tables."

"Already! He's cleared the furniture and already has the tables there?"

"Yes, indeed. We started last night. Some of us never went to bed. We're too excited to sleep. As I mentioned before, the abbey is usually ahead of itself in everything that it does."

They hurried to the library and found eight tables placed perfectly in a row in the center of the huge room. There wasn't any need to approve their position, but Gerhard did it anyhow because that's what Brother Robert said the prior wanted.

All of the monks were there, too—nearly one hundred of them. They weren't milling around but were instead neatly arranged into ten groups. Gerhard felt that they looked like an army of black hooded soldiers.

A hush fell over the great library.

Only the sound of the prior's shoes could be heard as he crossed the marble floor to Gerhard and Wolf.

"We are ready for your instructions, Matthias. The monks have been assembled into teams of various sizes and each team has been assigned to a certain library, depending on the size of the room and the number of books and manuscripts shelved in it. Each team has a leader who will run the search to fit the room, monitor the process, tally the results, return the books to their proper shelf position, and bring damaged books that are discovered to the table in this room for your review. Please explain the manner in which the technical review should be conducted."

The prior stepped to the side.

"I spoke to some of you a short time ago during the Council of Review. I saw the damaged books that you found and listened to your concerns. But it took a wise and patient man to help me understand the implications of that damage. I thank each of you for your willingness to assist in the important task of collecting data, without which my investigation would have little movement."

Gerhard cleared his throat and shifted his weight, then continued with the core of his message.

"A sample of a mass is an accepted procedure to verify a whole. Therefore I will use the seven books that I previously examined during the Council meeting as the sample of the mass of the abbey's one hundred thousand book library."

He heard a few low murmurs among the monks and assumed they were murmurs of doubt over the size of the sample. He was ready with an answer.

"It is not uncommon to question the size of a sample so I have a suggestion for those of you who think a much larger one is necessary. The next time you feel ill and your doctor draws a blood sample to examine, tell him to take all of your blood."

The army of monks remained silent for just a second as they processed Gerhard's comment, and then nearly all of them doubled over with laughter. No one questioned Gerhard further.

"There are always exceptions, but we will rely on the rule. The following are examples that will guide the collection of data. In the books that I examined, the marks appeared only on facing pages, not on the backs of pages. Marks appeared on the top, side, and bottom borders spaces. No marks appeared in spaces along the binding. Missing pages were in groups or whole chapters. Single pages that were removed were in the front near the face page. Marks resembled lines, drawings, shapes, and numbers, so be ready for a mark of any type—mostly in a color, including underlined words. No marks were found on the back cover or on back pages although many were on the front cover and pages near the front."

"Here is the process to be followed for a flip through examination. Look at the binding end of a closed book first. Next, look at the front cover, the cover page, and several of the following front pages. Now I offer a warning. The very process of looking will eventually trick your mind into looking for the process. Don't become mesmerized by looking. Instead, concentrate on what you're looking for—marks, lines, word underlining, and absent pages."

The monks nodded to each other in agreement and appreciated the interesting warning that Gerhard offered. It was clear to them that the captain knew what he was talking about.

"Next, hold the book face up in one hand and flip through the pages with the other. Do this three times. I repeat. Flip through the pages three times. Concentrate on only the top margin space during the first flip. Broaden the examination during the second flip to include the side margin space AND word underlining in the text. Broaden it again during the third flip as you check the bottom margin AND page numbers for missing pages and chapters. Be alert should page numbers appear at the top rather than the bottom. Just reverse the checking process if that is the case."

"You'll find the process cumbersome at first. You'll

make mistakes. Don't worry about it. You may need to do six or more flip-throughs at first. That's fine. Soon the process will become more comfortable and your speed will increase. That's the time to remind yourself that you're not here for the process—the process is here for you. Any questions?"

No one had any. The prior stepped forward, thanked Gerhard, and spoke a few parting words.

"We all know the importance of our work during the next several days, perhaps the next week or beyond. We're ready and anxious to begin. Those are good things. But we're new to this type of work and that is food for mistakes. We are also two hours ahead of schedule. Matthias's warning about the process interfering with the task was insightfully astute. Although we're ready to start, we'll wait briefly and use time and meditation as our ally and prepare ourselves to reduce the possibility for error. I ask that each monk leave the library now to stroll in single fashion in the cloister and meditate, after which we shall meet in the dining hall for lunch and fellowship. Let us return to this great library at one hour past noon to begin."

The monks did as they were instructed. They walked, meditated, prayed, and ate. Lunch was over, but the fellowship continued, encouraged by the wine, as nearly one hundred monks walked back to the great library in an unusually vocal manner.

The prior assigned each team to a library room and they happily moved off to collect the data. Confidence was high.

There were problems from the very start.

Although it seemed wise to divide the monks into teams of differed sizes, it quickly became apparent that the teams functioned at different skill levels. The team members were reviewed and some reassigned to improve team balance. Also, no one thought clearly about how to manage the process of book withdrawal from the shelf and return to the shelf.

Books piled up, there was confusion and real danger that some would not be returned to the shelf in the proper order and become lost. The prior redesigned a workable plan, but by that time two hours had passed with little progress to show for the time. However, the monks were determined to press on.

The flip through process started. Only about twenty five percent of the monks had the dexterity to complete the flip. Books tumbled from their hands with regularity. Gerhard had to do something or the project was in solid danger of failing. He stopped the entire process and called all of the monks to the great library for hands-on training. He organized them into pairs, asked one to flip and the other to critique, then he reversed the process.

It was slow going, but improvements began. He noticed that many monks made mistakes with the flip and then passed their mistakes to their partner. He decided it was time for the captain to teach.

"I want all of you to form a two-row circle around me. Think of it as a third of you here, a third there, and a third there. That's right. A circle of just two rows, all around me. Good! Now move closer to me. Just a little more. Good!"

He felt as though he was in a bulls eye, but the arrangement of monks was perfect for what he was about to do.

"May I ask that the prior hand a book to me from the shelf please? Just any book will do sir, just pick one."

The prior selected a book, handed it to the row of monks, who passed it to Gerhard. He spoke in a loud voice so all could hear.

"I will use this book to demonstrate the proper way to conduct the flip through examination, including how to find those important markings that we must not overlook."

He held the book high in the air, as high over his head as he could reach so everyone could see clearly and follow the instructions step by step.

"The very first thing is to look closely at the end binding between the front and back covers for any…….."

Gerhard stopped. He still held the book high over his head, but he didn't move or speak. The monks wondered what was happening. Perhaps he became ill. A seizure of some sort. Then he began to sink slowly to the floor, his arm still straight up, the book still help high, his gaze still fixed on the ancient book.

"There's something here," he said quietly.

The monks murmured.

He continued to lower his body until he was sitting in a cross–legged position on the marble floor of the library. He held the book in both hands now, rested it in his lap, and spoke in a normal voice.

"See, right here on the end—a long single line with a circle or dot at the end followed a number or letter."

The monks crowded in to see; their bodies cast dark shadows over him.

"Move back. Give him some light," said someone in the crowd. No one moved. Then a loud voice in the back said, "Let there be light!" and the monks instantly stepped back.

"Let's flip through and check the top margin," said Gerhard. He flipped and the monks all stared at the sight. They were completely absorbed. Important things were being discovered before their very eyes.

"See, here's another mark, just like the one on the end." The monks saw it all.

"Let's do a side flip now."

The monks watched the process with the eyes of eagles.

"I saw one," said a monk.

The words were quickly followed by the voice from a second monk.

"There's another mark. They both look like the one on the end of the cover. May we do a bottom flip through please?" asked a monk.

Gerhard flipped.

"Nothing," observed the second monk. "Try the cover page and a couple of pages after it," he urged.

Everyone watched as Gerhard opened the book to the cover page and carefully turned several following pages.

"More of them," announced Gerhard. "Two more, just like the first one."

The monks helped him get up from the floor. All of them were buzzing with excitement at the unexpected discovery.

"What do you make of it, Matthias?" asked one of the monks.

"This is an especially good find. The marks definitely mirror earlier ones found in other books. We just have to find all of the pieces, fit them together, and learn what they mean. But more importantly, this find supports the view that there are indeed more damaged books in the library of Melk Abbey. There may be lots of them and they must not be allowed to remain undiscovered."

The monks murmured in agreement over Gerhard's observation.

"This afternoon started out on a low note. We had problems. We worked on them, we didn't give up, and we improved. I think someone was looking out for us and that someone helped us end the day on a much higher note. Let's keep on the high note tomorrow."

CHAPTER 11

The advancing low pressure weather system stalled over Switzerland, blocked by a stationary high over Eastern Europe. Forecasters predicted storms for Austria. A prolonged deep rumble of distant thunder was enough of a sensory stimulus to awaken Gerhard about an hour earlier than usual. He thought immediately of the trials at the library yesterday and decided to return early to check the books again.

Wolf left his room just then as well, awakened by the same sound of thunder. They walked together hurriedly past the closed wooden doors of the dining hall toward the great library. The huge abbey felt strangely quiet so early in the morning. A lone monk was seated at the library table studying a book.

"Brother Robert! What are you doing here?"

"Good morning, sir. All of the brothers who live in my dormitory wing wanted to get a quick start and practice their flip through movements without anyone else around.

We've been here for a couple of hours and look what we've found on the cover page of this book."

Gerhard looked closely.

"More long thin lines with a circle at the end. We're beginning to find what we've been looking for. The seven books that I reviewed during the Council meeting are here on the table, plus the one we found yesterday, and now this new one. That's nine books. It's time to put some order to our collection. Wolf, I want you to locate the marks in each damaged book then highlight the pages with a strip of paper. Next, take a full sheet of paper and draw the single most dominate mark in the book on it. Make the drawing carefully and large so it's easy to see as I walk past the table. Include a small drawing at the bottom of the page of all non-dominate marks. Place all of the books with identical dominate marks in a stack with the sheet of paper next to it as a sort of key to what's in the stack."

Wolf nodded and began to arrange several books on the table. Gerhard turned to Brother Robert.

"Help me find a couple of books with number marks. One I saw earlier that had the numbers 150N and 150S inside."

"Here it is. I was just looking at it. And here's the second book with number marks."

Gerhard immediately turned to the cover page.

"This is it. Look, the letter V followed by the number 450 and another V, followed by the number 900."

A long deep roll of thunder sounded in the distance.

"These books seem special to you. Are you getting an idea?" asked Brother Robert.

"I certainly hope so." He motioned to Wolf and Robert to come close and look at something. He placed one book alongside of the other and opened each one to the cover page.

"I was struck by the multiple placements of the numbers 150N and 150S on most of the front pages of this book. Look closely at the marks with my jeweler's eye piece and tell me if you notice anything different about them."

Both men looked, but neither found anything unusual. Gerhard pointed to the second book.

"This book has the numbers 450 and 900, and different shaped letter V's on most of the front pages. Use the eye piece again and tell me if you see anything different."

Neither man saw anything.

"I'll give you a clue. Look very closely at each number 0.

They studied the numbers longer this time.

Wolf spoke first.

"Well, I don't think it means anything, but the last zero in each number seems smaller than the others." Brother Robert seemed surprised at Wolf's comment. He took the eye piece and looked again.

"If there's a difference I can hardly tell it."

"There is a difference," responded Gerhard. "It's a small one, but it's there. Even a small difference can be a vital clue in a search. Whether this one is vital or not remains to be seen. Let me explain. The numbers are in groups of three and each number ends in zero. The last zero is measurably smaller in size than the numbers that precede it. Remove the last zero and the higher numbers become lower ones, like 15, 45, and 90. Suppose the zero wasn't a zero at all, but a symbol that stood for 'degree.' Suppose the letters N and S in the first book represented north and south, and the different shaped letter Vs–one wider than the other—in the second book were the symbol for angle. Suddenly we have a fresh meaning to the marks that have been hidden in the books for decades. Suddenly we have something like—15 degrees North and 15 degrees South and an angle of 45 degrees and another angle of 90 degrees. This may only be a simple study in how things are perceived—at least it's a start."

"I think it's very well perceived, sir."

"It was so well hidden right in front of us." said Wolf.

Another rumble of deep thunder off in the distance, this one lasted longer than the others.

"It could also be good perception and bad deduction. We'll have to see. In the meantime Wolf, go ahead with your organizational project while I get out the transit and decide where to take a few sample readings."

He took the transit and looked for a place to start, but couldn't find one. Nothing made sense so he triangulated the room from each corner and located the exact center of the great library floor. He told Wolf to mark the spot with a piece of tape and then he set up the transit over it.

Perhaps this spot could be the beginning, but I doubt it.

He randomly twirled the transit head around 360 degrees as he looked about the room for a place to start.

Still, nothing looked right. The voice of the prior spoke to him from behind.

"You need a point of demarcation. Without that, all other reference points are worthless."

"That's about it," agreed Gerhard. "I have a good middle piece of information that was revealed from the marks in the book, an end that's still lost, plus a beginning that remains undiscovered. Perhaps the monks will discover the beginning in one of the books today and I'll be able to move forward. We'll have to look for something else if nothing more supportive can be found."

Then Wolf came over with a question.

"Why not take a shot with the transit? Try 15 degrees north and 15 degrees south and see what turns up?"

Several monks heard the question and came over to watch. The prior stood with them. *I see a chance for a lesson to be learned here,* thought Gerhard.

"All right, let's take a few shots," he said, as he adjusted the transit to magnetic north.

"I'm at north. How can I move to 15 degrees north when I'm already at north?"

Wolf was surprised at the confusing question, but shook his head that he didn't know.

"For the sake of the question let's adjust the transit 15 degrees to the right. What do you see?

Wolf peered through the instrument.

"I see part of a window in the wall."

"Now adjust the transit on magnetic north, turn the instrument 15 degrees left, or to the south and tell me what you see," prodded Gerhard.

"Just part of another window on the other side and the corner of a wall."

"These shots were irrelevant sightings," said Gerhard. "We learned nothing. The numbers and letters that we found in the books looked promising at first. Clues always look good until bad ones are forced to perform. Without a meaningful point of departure, the reference clues led nowhere. But everything could change at any moment should we find more relevant marks in the books. We have to be alert and keep looking."

The monks drifted back with their teams while they chatted about what they just saw. Not everyone understood the point that Gerhard attempted to make. The prior gave a short pep talk and sent them off to their assigned library rooms and more flip-throughs.

Gerhard walked slowly around the edge of the floor, near the walls. He looked at the narrow Baroque balcony above and shook his head. Brother Robert watched, then came over and stood near-by.

"You seem perplexed about something. May I help?"

"Perhaps so. I thought Brother Felix said during the Council meeting that the Nazis unloaded ladders from their trucks and brought them into the library, but these traditional wheeled library ladders are already stationed here. Do you remember what he said about them?"

"He mentioned ladders, but I don't remember where they were used. Brother Felix is outside on the terrace. Let's go ask him."

The expansive stone terrace was impressive,

imbedded on the top of the high rock outcrop at the far west end of the abbey. It spread like a vast smooth blanket from the church entrance and provided a serene walking area between both the Marble Hall and the great library. Anyone on the terrace felt the majesty of the abbey and the history of the famed Danube River below. It was easy to appreciate the view of the whimsical little town of Melk tucked discreetly along the base of the massive stone cliff.

A lone monk leaned on the top of the terrace wall— his black habit and cowl made him nearly indistinguishable against the dark morning sky. Faint far-off flashes of lightning cast an eerie sight against the monk's silhouette. Brother Robert and Gerhard leaned on the wall next to the 94 year old monk and asked him how often he came to this beautiful spot.

"As often as I can, but not often enough. It gives me a chance to think about the past and plan for the future."

They weren't sure how to respond to the unexpected and interesting comment, so they said nothing. They were hugely impressed at what he said next.

"Napoleon captured Melk Abbey during his campaign against Austria—made the place his headquarters. He actually stayed here many times in the early 1800's. The great Napoleon stood on this very spot and planned his wars with his generals. See these three flagstones that I'm standing on now? They're a little higher than the other stones in the terrace. Napoleon had them put in so he could see over the wall better. I'm sure none of his generals ever stood on them—only Napoleon."

He stopped talking for a moment and looked out over

southern Austria. More flashes of lightning in the sky, all easy to see from the high stone terrace.

"I'm a pretty lucky person. I get to live in the House of the Lord and stand in the footprints of Napoleon. Who else can say that they've done that?" He looked at Gerhard and the young monk at his side. "You gentlemen didn't come out here just before a storm to chat. What can I do for you?"

"I'd like to review what you told me about the ladders," began Gerhard. "Did the soldiers use them only in the great library?"

"They started to, but we had our own library step ladders, so they used ours to reach the books. They set up their own ladders to measure the ceiling, which they did several times, and then they moved to the Marble Hall and did the same thing with the ceiling. We don't have any books in the Marble Hall."

Gerhard thought about the two rooms. Brother Felix was right; the Marble Hall didn't even have book shelves.

"So the soldiers worked only in the Marble Hall, the Great Library, and the other library rooms, right?" asked Gerhard.

"No, a group of them went down into the tunnels, into the catacombs, once or twice. At first I thought they wanted to keep warm because it was warmer in the tunnels than it was up here. Remember, it was a cold winter. I was the newest Brother and hadn't heard any of the stories about the things that went on in the catacombs, so I wasn't scared. I followed them."

"What things went on in the catacombs?" asked

Gerhard. The old monk heard him but didn't respond, he just continued with his story.

"The catacombs were always locked so I don't know where the soldiers got the keys. They used the door behind the alter the first time—the one that led down to the tombs. It was so easy for me to hide behind the graves and in the shadows of the tunnel walls. This was the only time that I saw the soldiers act in a reckless way—they tried to tip over some headstones and lift some tomb covers, as if they were looking for something, but they couldn't move any of them. They walked deeper into the tunnel. I didn't know where they were going and I was worried that they might see me so I stayed behind and listened. Their voices faded out. It was so still down there. I got scared and returned to the doorway behind the alter so I could get away fast. I sat still and listened. Suddenly I heard yelling and gun shots, then sounds of running. The soldiers ran back toward me, so I got out of there and hid behind the alter statues of the saints. They rushed out of the tomb chamber door and slammed it shut."

"You ought to tell the other brothers about this," urged Brother Robert.

"I don't want to tell anyone else about it because the next night was terrible—I actually heard the will-o'-the-wisps, the ancient ghosts."

Gerhard glanced quickly at Brother Robert in the hope of an explanation.

"I know a little about these ghosts," whispered the young monk. The Will-o'-the-Wisp ghosts become visible in the smoke of an oil lamp. They're found mostly around cemeteries and have a hideous moan." The young monk swallowed hard. The old monk continued.

"The only other tunnel entrance to the catacombs is in the basement under the great library, near the dining hall—the place we call the cellar."

"Yes, I know of the spot," said Brother Robert. "I've heard that there's a terrible ancient wooden door down there built into the side of a rock wall. I never want to see it."

"I don't know anyone who ever opened that despicable door." Brother Felix began breathing harder. He paused to take some deeper breaths and that allowed Brother Robert to whisper something to Gerhard.

"This old abbey has had many lives, including a castle, a fort, and a dungeon. Hundreds of soldiers have been killed fighting here and lots of people have been murdered within its walls. Stories abound from many sources of two-headed wandering dead people, giant snakes that slither along the dungeon floor, and all types of ghosts that wander about. And those hideous wailing moans."

Brother Robert seemed to be caught up in his explanation.

"But surely you realize that these are just stories made up over the centuries and passed down through impressionable listeners."

"I know they're just stories, but I also know that I've heard the moans—real moans. All of the monks in the abbey have heard those mournful moans—occasionally during the day, but always during storms at night. We all consider the main rooms of the abbey off limits, at night.

Some of us we may not believe the ghost stories, but all of us believe the moans."

How strange, thought Gerhard. *Here's a man of the cloth with a scientific and engineering background—and a military jet pilot at that— who is completely stressed-out over what he perceives to be ghosts.*

Gerhard wasn't sure how to continue. Two reliable and trusted information sources now seemed far less so. He felt it unwise to continue the discussion with Brother Felix and something had to be done to relax Brother Robert. Gerhard put his arm around the young monk's shoulders in a fatherly way and said, "Let's walk Brother Felix back to his room—besides, it's about to storm out here."

The three of them walked slowly across the terrace and into the entrance of the church, then down the arched hall toward the great library. The prior and Wolf rushed out to greet them with news that the monks found two more damaged books. Gerhard said he was happy to hear it, but Wolf noticed that he didn't smile. In fact he looked intense, almost stern. Wolf knew that something had happened—something important.

"Prior, I'd like to go into the tunnels, into the catacombs. Will you take Wolf and me, please?"

The prior stopped in his tracks, the pleasant look on his face disappeared and he stared back at Gerhard.

"Is it necessary?"

"I don't know for sure, that's why I have to go."

Wolf didn't understand Gerhard's answer, but the prior did.

"Now?" asked the prior.

"Yes,"

The prior began to organize. "Brother Robert, take Brother Felix to his room and make sure he's comfortable. Then, stop at maintenance and get four oil lanterns and some matches and meet us at the door to the cellar. I'll get the keys and check on the other brothers to make sure things continue to move along with their project while were gone. Let's meet at the door to the cellar in ten minutes."

As if on cue, several blinding flashes of intense lightning sizzled outside the abbey windows followed instantly by long multiple bursts of resonate thunder. The reverberation was so loud that it startled the group. The weather system had arrived and it was intense.

The four men gathered at the door that led to the cellar. They moved in single file down steps made from old stones worn smooth over the centuries by the feet of trudging soldiers and shuffling workmen.

The prior led the way followed by Gerhard with Wolf very close behind. Brother Robert was last. Each held an unlit oil lantern in one hand and grasped the iron hand railing with the other. They reached the floor below the dining hall and stopped to light the lanterns. Then they began the next level of decent. The stone stairs were narrower and much steeper now, everyone moved more cautiously. They reached a landing, turned and headed down again. The steps became simple foot places chiseled out from solid rock. The railing disappeared, but the flight of stairs kept going. Finally, a bottom landing with an unbelievable narrow wooden door that the prior unlatched and pushed open.

They squeezed into a small room with a single wretched looking wooden door built into the solid rock wall. Gerhard thought of Brother Felix's description of the despicable door and felt he was right, but decided not to comment on it.

The door was made of triple thickness, from wood that seemed to have been both charred and tarred. But that wasn't the bad part. It appeared as though someone, or perhaps many, tried to claw their way out. Deep gouges where abundant.

Light red stains, surely blood from previous times, left ooze marks between the cracks and claw marks. Patches of dried skin remained impaled on charred splinters. Gerhard tried to keep a damning thought from reentering his mind, but it wouldn't go away.

If this side of the door looks that bad, I wonder what the other side looks like.

"Gentlemen," began the prior in a quiet voice. "We're two floors below the great library and the dining hall, but the floors are far apart because this area was once part of a dungeon. I'd estimate that we're three floors under the surface, deep in solid rock."

Suddenly, Wolf held up his hand for silence. Everyone heard a muffled sound in the distance.

"What was that?"

"There's a storm outside," answered Gerhard. "That was thunder, probably very close to the abbey, but the sound was deadened by the mass of rock and stone of the building." Wolf nodded.

The prior pointed to the dreadful looking door and said, "This door leads to a tunnel that was once part of a series of tunnels under the abbey. Many are now closed because of rock falls and modernization. Some tunnel sections have been left untouched and I'll talk about this later. We'll also see another door, but won't go through it. I'll tell you why when we reach it".

The prior was able to turn the key in the old rusted lock after several tries. He and Gerhard pulled the heavy door open, they all walked nervously through, and the two of them closed it again.

"Why did we close the door? Why can't we leave it open?" asked Wolf who, because his parents were blind, had experienced a long and difficult phobia with darkness. The prior was ready with an answer.

"The tunnel serves as a giant air corridor. Under certain conditions, the movement of air in here could easily blow out our lanterns. In fact, I hear the air now. Listen."

There was indeed a sound—in the distance—it seemed to pulsate. Brother Robert said it sounded like the wailing of a ghost. They walked on with lanterns held high. Water dripped from spots overhead and seeped from cracks in the wall, parts of the tunnel floor became slippery. Each person could hear the others breathe.

"This tunnel was used hundreds of years ago as a passage way for military maneuvers when the abbey was a castle and a fort," explained the prior. "Soldiers secretly outmaneuvered the enemy by sending extra troops through the tunnel to bolster its forces on the other side. They also secretly entered the castle through the same tunnel."

"Look!" said Brother Robert. "A trail made by something. It's slimy." He became obviously uncomfortable at the sight.

Gerhard dropped to his knees and placed his lantern next to the shiny stream of slime. Then, to everyone's surprise, he put his index finger into the slime and touched it to his tongue. "It's not a slimy trail; it's just moss growing in this moist darkness." Gerhard got out his iPad and took a couple of pictures. Brother Robert relaxed. They waked on. Another serious clap of intense thunder, this time it was more intense and easier than ever to hear deep inside the rock tunnel. One could almost feel the sound.

"We're getting closer," said the prior. Everyone stopped in their tracks at a strange sound. It was a pulsating sound, a wobbling sound from high to low and it got louder, much louder. It seemed to float in the air of the tunnel and surround them. This time Wolf joined Brother Robert in feeling uncomfortable.

"I've heard this sound before, at night, the sound of the Will-o'-the Wisp," said the young monk.

"I've heard it too," said Wolf in a frightened voice— "In the house of terror at an amusement park!"

The prior asked them to come over to the wall and pointed to a narrow vertical opening that was cut into the wall. The piercing noise came from the opening. It was an absurd time for a history lesson, but the prior began one anyhow. He had to yell to be heard.

"Leopold II gave his palace in Melk to the Benedictine monks. That was in the eleventh century and they turned it into a fortified abbey complete with a library. That's how our Melk Abbey began. They had lots of problems, not the least of which was how to keep the damp and stale air from mildewing their books. They built a system of corridors in the walls so air could move about and the books would stay fresh. Openings in the outside walls allowed fresh air to enter the abbey. This tunnel was part of the main air corridor and this opening in the wall connected to smaller tunnels or ducts, which opened into the rooms of the abbey. It worked well."

But the prior had to stop talking. The sound of the screaming moaning wind became too loud. The storm outside had increased several fold. Sheets of rain smashed against the abbey and bursts of violent wind pulsated around the walls and towers. It roared through the stone chambers, it wailed and screamed, first at an eerie high pitch, then a vibrating low pitch. It sounded exactly like the dreaded cry of the Will-o'-the-Wisp.

Then, cracks of thunder, one after another.

Brother Robert was terrified and Wolf was nearly so. Gerhard moved quickly to the narrow vertical opening in the wall and pushed his back firmly against the open space. His body blocked the sound; the noise was somewhat muffled. The group was amazed at the difference. He motioned Wolf to come over and do the same. Gerhard got out of the way, the wailing became louder, Wolf took his place against the opening, and the sound diminished once again.

Wolf actually smiled. Gerhard waved him aside and motioned for Brother Robert to take his place. The monk hesitated at first, but made the move, his back now against the opening. The sound became muffled again, just like before. Gerhard cupped his hands around Brother Robert's ear and yelled.

"I know you can feel the wind on your back, but go beyond that—try to sense the sound of the moan as it pulsates through various levels of the spectrum. Some of the air tunnels have been sealed up and the size of some passageways restricted by cave-ins. What remains now is a giant whistle, which changes notes on a musical scale—or moans—as the wind speed and pressure change, depending on the intensity of the storm."

Brother Robert's scientific background kicked in. He knew what Gerhard meant and he was anxious to see if he could actually feel sound. Gerhard yelled in his ear again.

"The high frequency sound will feel like fast moving tiny pinches, the low frequency more like a push. You may have trouble distinguishing the difference at first, but prepare yourself to sense the point of adjustment or transition from one sphere of the spectrum to the other."

The terrifying moaning seemed to fill the tunnel, but Brother Robert no longer seemed afraid. He was busy with an experiment. Gerhard's plan to allow the monk to feel and understand the scientific principle behind the once dreadful sound of the Will-o'-the-Wisp, was working. The group continued to watch, the moaning became softer, as did a distant clap of thunder.

The storm was moving on. The prior motioned

everyone to follow and they moved still deeper down the dark tunnel, lanterns held high. A small wooden door appeared unexpectedly and they gathered around it. A few bones were scattered on the ground at the base of the door.

"For some of those who passed beyond this door, the trip was their last one on earth," said the prior softly, as he crossed himself. "It leads beyond the wall of the abbey and under the monastery's cemetery. The tunnel on the other side of the door is also a 'safe exit' from the abbey— to a cemetery slab that slides from its base via a system of drums and ropes, to allow an escape from this place. It was last used to escape the Nazi occupation of Austria during the Second World War. The Benedictine Order at Melk Abbey is charged with the serious responsibility of maintaining the operating mechanism of this escape route." The prior waited for a comment, but there was none. "I think it's time to go back up to the abbey." The group nodded in agreement.

The tunnel was long and twisted, and required several minutes of slow and careful walking to reach the dreadful door in the cellar. Gerhard and the prior pushed it open, then Gerhard paused at the door before he helped the prior shove it closed. The pieces of dried skin impaled on the splintered wood was a sickening sight,—but not to the prior. His comment and actions shocked everyone as he pulled big pieces of the dried stuff from the splinters.

"This wonderful fungus grows year round on the wood of this door. We serve these delicious mushrooms on the salad in the dining hall."

The startled group had absolutely nothing further to

say.

They reached the top of the staircase and reentered the top floor of the abbey. The unexpected morning journey through the dark and moaning tunnel was stressful indeed. It felt good to be back. Now, the sound of chanting monks filled the abbey.

"They knew where we went," said the prior. "They were worried, so they went to the church to pray for us and to receive the strength of the Holy Father. Come, let's show them that we're safe."

The group of explorers walked into the large open space at the entrance to the church, then single file down the center aisle of the majestic church—their lighted lanterns still held tightly at their side—right through the chanting black robed monks seated on either side of the aisle. It was quite a sight. They reached the first row, turned around and faced the monks. The chanting stopped and the applause began.

The prior explained everything: why they went into the tunnel, about the ventilation shaft, the moss on the wet floor, why the sound of the Will-o'-the-Wisp was so terrible, everything.

The congregation of monks sat motionless, careful not to miss a word. It was a good review. But then the unexpected happened—Brother Robert stepped forward to be recognized. It was unorthodox for a brother to ask to speak while the prior still had the floor, but the prior nodded his approval. The brothers readied themselves to listen to one of their own. The Holy Church leaned forward in expectation.

Brother Robert began.

"My grandfather died before I got to know him well. I miss him. I think about the things we used to talk about and it makes me feel better. Once he told me something that I thought was most unusual. He said, 'Robert, I'm only 82 years old and I have so much to learn.' I am but a third of his age and I wonder if I'll ever learn as much as he did. But I got a good start today. I learned how easy it was to lose sight of what is real and I literally felt the difference between fact and fiction. I also witnessed the partnership between the miracle of God's work and the blend of science that supports it. All of this added fresh meaning to my life. I am ready to move on and look forward to completing our present project regarding the books in the library."

He stepped back into the line as the prior added concluding remarks.

"Our beloved abbey is a place to discover truth and meaning. I see the discoveries every day."

He made the sign of the cross. The monks responded in kind.

"Let us meet in the great library at one hour past noon and rededicate ourselves to the swift completion of the task at hand."

CHAPTER 12

Nearly ten days had past and the project of examining 100,000 books in the twelve rooms of the library remained unfinished. There was high hope that it would be finished today as only a quarter of the great library was left to check. It was a daunting task to manage over eighty monks all working at the same time in the same space, but the prior said he was up to it and the room was large enough to handle everyone.

They were well under way early in the morning.

Gerhard used his time during the preceding day to check the ceiling of the great library while the monks were working in other rooms. He set up the transit on the narrow balcony that ringed the room and painstakingly elevated it on platforms to reach both the real ceiling and Paul Troger's Trompe L'Oeil imaginary one.

He shot azimuths and angles, and looked for protrusions. Everything was in order. Then he took readings from the floor corners, in reverse, back to both ceilings. Nothing.

Why did the Nazis spend so much time and effort to set up ladders and take measurements here? It had to be important, yet I can find no evidence of what they did. Brother Felix said they also took multiple measurements in the Marble Hall. What were they looking for? I'm confident that I'll find nothing there as well, but I've got to look—I've got to check behind them.

Gerhard, Wolf, and Brother Robert drudgingly moved the equipment through the huge open foyer of the church and into the Marble Hall. There was no convenient balcony to use in the Marble Hall so they set up the heavy, long extension ladders and leaned them against the walls. Wolf removed the transit from its case and looked at its complex dials, gauges and delicate telescope lens. Then he said something so penetrating, so accurate, that it shocked Gerhard and reshaped his approach to the entire search process.

"Why would the Nazis use all of this equipment just to hide something? After all, they were just ordinary soldiers."

Gerhard's body stiffened, he stared into space. He muttered the words to himself, and then said them out loud—slowly.

"Just ordinary soldiers! They were just ordinary soldiers! That's all they were. Good Lord, Wolf, you're so right. They were just ordinary soldiers. Why didn't I see this before? They were told to use this equipment to locate a hiding place for something. But the equipment was complicated and awkward to handle. I'd wager that none of them knew how to use it, so the ordinary soldiers just went through the motions, because they were ordered to use the equipment. Brother Felix watched them set up the ladders and take them down. He watched them measure walls and ceilings over and over, but it was just an act. The ordinary soldiers faked it."

"What did they use to find a hiding place and how are we going to find it?" asked Wolf.

"That's still the mystery and the answer is still hidden somewhere in the books. But we can forget about the ladders and equipment and all of the angles and degree numbers. From now on we concentrate on simplicity, because—they were ordinary soldiers. Wolf, if I had some wine, I'd offer you a glass—you deserve a toast for your astute observation."

"I can get some wine," said Brother Robert. "Remember, I'm a monk and this is a monastery."

But that was yesterday.

The examination of the books was still on-going today and it appeared as though the work of the monks had reached a fevered pitch.

"With the Lord's help, we'll finish within two hours," announced the prior excitedly. We're going to skip lunch and keep working until we're done."

"No lunch! What dedication!" said Gerhard.

"Not exactly. We fast on a regular basis and I felt this work project was basis enough."

Gerhard decided to skip lunch, too. The stacks of books with identical dominate marks had grown to the point that they resembled the outline of a city sky scape—tall buildings in the center. He began to thumb through some and quickly noticed a pattern—in fact, more than one.

There was now no doubt that the thin straight line with a dot or circle of some sort at the end and a companion symbol had become the dominate mark. Interestingly, he expected the line mark to appear in just one book, but he was wrong, it appeared repetitively in multiple books, at least that's how it looked at this point.

He watched the number of unexamined books dwindle quickly and motioned for Brother Robert. He told him that the long arduous examination of 100,000 books was almost at an end and reminded his aide-de-camp that this was a milestone of major importance to the abbot.

"It should not pass fulfilled without the abbot in attendance."

"What do you suggest, sir?"

"Find him. If he is well enough, either escort him here in one hour, or make arrangements for him to be brought here. There is something else, but it would require the expertise of an especially innovative and dedicated monk. I was told by one who exhibited such qualities that he could get wine. So I say to you—bring wine and glasses for all—and maybe cookies—in one hour."

"That's a huge task, sir!"

"Not for a jet pilot," responded Gerhard with confidence.

The examination continued until only a few books remained. Then the last one was checked. It was over. The sound of cheering monks was unforgettable.

Brother Robert's given task turned into a real honest-to-goodness house party—the type seldom experienced in a monastery. The red wine flowed freely. No one bothered with the cookies. Gerhard wasn't sure who brought it, but somehow a small phonograph machine showed up complete with a group of 78 rpm records—mostly polkas. He thought the sight of black robed monks in a group dance in the great library was among the most unusual sights he had ever seen.

The brothers relaxed after more than ten days of non-stop work. They deserved the fun and fellowship. The monks could hardly believe that the long and meticulous project was over and they were finished with it. The abbot was joyous about the conclusion too, mostly because he remembered his doubts that it would ever start. He lifted the closure order for the abbey, except for the library.

Then the party suddenly kicked up several notches as three staff members arrived pushing kitchen carts full of beef and pork complete with a small carving station and a basket of rolls.

The monks applauded the unexpected arrival of such succulent food, only to let out a roar upon the arrival of three more carts—of Austrian beer and mugs. Gerhard saw Brother Robert chatting with other monks as he waited in the carving line and went over to him.

"This performance was above and beyond the call of duty."

"It's just standard get-the-job-done pilot training, sir."

The unique house party continued without a hint from either the abbot or the prior that it should wind down. In fact, the abbot made the unusual suggestion that it should continue and become dinner—right there in the great library. Of course it was only a suggestion, but it came from the abbot and that's all it took to resemble a proclamation. However, the Vespers would be held at the regular hour.

Gerhard and Wolf enjoyed the festivities and stayed for a while, then Wolf retired early and Gerhard strolled about the abbey thinking—first in the ornate scriptorium, then slowly down the long Royal Way, and finally the pathway outside in the beautiful cloister.

The morning would arrive soon, and then all of the damaged books carefully stacked on the tables in the great library would be his. The more he walked, the more he thought. Ideas began to flow. He strolled on.

Every theory has both hard and soft spots, he reasoned. *The best hard spots always stand tall and resist repeated challenge—the soft spots fade and finally fall because they can't withstand the scrutiny. A solution would be swifter and clearer by first identifying the soft spots. The ladders and the transient were the first to fall and I no longer include them in the equation. What other soft spots can I eliminate? The pages—those that have been torn out of the books—regardless if they're a single page or an entire chapter. Pages that have been removed can tell me nothing and offer no clue or direction because I don't know what was written on them in the first place. They were probably taken by the soldiers as souvenirs or to be sold for money. What's next? Underlining. Ordinary soldiers would be unable to read Latin, Greek, or Hebrew, thus they wouldn't know the meaning of the words in the books that they underlined. The underlining was random and meaningless and best eliminated from consideration.*

So, where does this take us? To the end of the soft spots. Only the thin lines with a type of circle at the end followed by a symbol of some sort remain. I believe these lines are the hard spots of the theory, the core of the equation. I have to learn what they mean, and then I'll have the answer to the secret of why so many valuable books were defaced.

I wonder if that'll be the only secret we'll find.

Gerhard had a tough night. Lots of tossing, not much sleep. It went on for hours as he thought about the books, the clues, the hard and soft spots. Sleep finally came when there was only an hour left to do it. The knock on his door startled him. It was Wolf.

"I'll wait for you out in the hall. They have your favorite thing for breakfast—blueberry pancakes."

The words sparkled like a huge stimulus. Blueberry pancakes were indeed one of his premiere breakfast items. It seemed as though he was ready in less than a couple of seconds, quickly threw open the door and burst into the hall. Wolf was standing at the ready, but way off to the side, because the serving of blueberry pancakes had put him in a precarious position before.

Breakfast was terrific. The blueberry pancakes were cooked on an extra hot griddle that caused the edges of the pancakes and the berries inside to singe ever so slightly, which resulted in an unbelievable aroma and an exquisite flavor. Breakfast was over too quickly and they hurried to the great library. Gerhard reviewed his thoughts with Wolf on the way—about the soft clues and those hard ones that he felt were so important. Wolf listened and expressed complete agreement.

Wolf went to work immediately and moved all of the disqualified books to the far end of the table while Gerhard gathered books with identical thin line marks. He was surprised at how many he found. He ended with eight stacks of books with identical marks, the same round circle, and eight different symbols. The number of books varied in each stack, but totaled thirty. Thirty-two books were discarded, so the number of defaced books that were located by the monks totaled sixty two.

"We're at a critical point," said Gerhard. "We need one last step. Each stack should represent one identical dominate thin mark with the same circle at the end and the same symbol or mark, regardless of the number of books actually in the stack. The final step is to eliminate redundancy. But remember, there are eight different symbols. Don't mix them up. Make sure we have the same symbol in each stack."

Wolf nodded.

"Let's each examine one stack at a time—slowly and carefully—and compare each book with the next one. If the first book displays all three parts of the mark and the marks are identical to those in the next book, discard one book. Continue with this process until only one book remains. It then becomes our core book. Put the other books that you discarded behind the core book. They will become our back up books. Any questions?"

Wolf shook his head. They both began.

Gerhard was meticulous. He felt they were advancing toward a critical key to a secret that had been hidden in the library for six decades. He turned each page with that thought in mind. One page at a time—swiftly, but carefully. Wolf felt Gerhard had entrusted him with an important job that was critical to the project. He would do it perfectly. Nothing would distract him.

Just then Brother Robert entered the great library.

"Good morning. Did you gentlemen have the blueberry pancakes for breakfast?"

Wolf kept his eye on the book, put his metal hand high in the air, and yelled, "Not now!—Not now!"

The young monk stopped in his tracks, stood motionless for a second as he watched Gerhard and Wolf in the midst of serious concentration, and quietly backed out of the library.

They worked on. The library was so quiet that one could hear the stillness. One page turned at a time. It was the only sound. An hour passed, the size of the pile of ancient books began to dwindle. Another hour passed. Now only one short three book stack remained unchecked. Gerhard pulled it to him and began. Wolf watched. The first book was finished in twenty minutes; the second in about the same time. Wolf could tell that Gerhard was tired. The last book was nearly eight hundred pages. Gerhard's shoulders slumped, but he continued with diligence. He closed the book forty minutes later then rested his eyes for a moment.

Brother Robert entered the room. "Sorry I interrupted your concentration earlier, but I kept everyone else out while you worked. Any progress?"

"We've made some decisions. Those books at the end of the table are no longer part of the project. They can be returned to the shelves. Each single book on the table in front of us is a core book. They're central to solving the puzzle. Those behind it are back up books. We're going to break for lunch and a brief rest, and then we'll return to the library and begin to unravel the mystery of the defaced books of Melk Abbey.

They returned at two in the afternoon. The unnecessary books that Wolf moved to the end of the table were gone. The eight core books were carefully centered on the table, each with a group of back up books stacked neatly behind it.

Two tablets of lined paper were in a row, along with several tablets of plain paper, several pencils, erasers, and pens. But there was more—a large bottle of water packed in ice, two bottles of wine, and most surprisingly—the traditional white box of the Bakers pastries. Gerhard looked at what had transpired while they were gone and said, "Brother Robert should be a Broadway producer. He can arrange anything."

Gerhard sat at the table and began to look at each book, from left to right. Wolf sat next to him and passed things back and forth, but he always returned items to their proper position. Order was critical. Gerhard studied one book, then another. Then he sat and thought.

"Let's make another round of drawings. Make a full

page drawing of the complete mark in each of our core books and place it in front of the core book. I'll watch but I won't help, because I want the drawings to be made in a similar manner by the same person."

Wolf began. The drawings were simple to make and he completed them in about fifteen minutes. Gerhard gathered them up and moved to a free table. He spread them out, looked at each one, and then rearranged them. Then he did it again and again. Wolf watched and wondered where this was going. Gerhard just stared at the drawings.

Brother Robert entered and looked at the drawings.

"These are the drawings of the core marks, the ones that I believe hold the secret," explained Gerhard. "I've arranged them into many different positions to see if there is an obvious relationship somewhere and I found nothing. This is what they look like in groups of vertical and horizontal marks, along with their symbols. What do you see?"

"I don't see anything in the symbols, except a strange jumble of lines and random numbers. But I see something surprising in the thin marks that I haven't even thought of since I was a kid."

The monk had Gerhard's attention.

"Did you ever play with a game of sticks the length of pencils and wooden circles with holes all around the edges?"

Gerhard's mind raced to his youth.

The monk continued.

"The idea was to build something. I remember that I pushed a stick into a hole, and then pushed the edge of a circle into the other end. Then I added another stick, maybe two, and more circles, until I had a design. I made a bridge once, and a building. But it was so simple that I lost interest in it quickly."

Gerhard looked down at his arrangement of marks.

"I remember that game. My father gave it to me. I can't remember the name, it was too long ago, but it doesn't matter. They were popular with little kids in Frankfurt, where I grew up. I can see why this arrangement of marks reminded you of it."

He pointed to the thin lines. "These were the sticks." Then he pointed to the circles. "These were the wooden circles with holes around the edge. These marks are on paper so we don't have holes around the edge, but we could lay one paper circle over another and achieve the same result as if they were objects of wood. Let's see if we can build something."

Gerhard and Brother Robert began adjusting the papers while Wolf watched. "There's too much paper. It gets in the way of the placement. Wolf, get some scissors and cut along the mark—careful not to cut off the symbol."

Wolf made the cutouts and returned them to Gerhard, who continued with the arranging. Nothing developed.

"We're getting nowhere, probably because we've ignored the symbols so far. I think the symbols will dictate the arrangement of the lines and how they should be connected. Let's start over and put the thin lines back into vertical and horizontal groups and see what they look like with the symbols."

They only looked for a second before Gerhard said, "That's interesting! Look, all of the horizontal lines have symbols on top of the line; the vertical ones have symbols on the side. The lines all have a little circle on one end, the other end has nothing. Finally, a pattern has developed—wonder if it's a good one."

They re-examined the marks in a new light. Then Brother Robert made an interesting observation.

"I was very young and couldn't read instructions when I played with my game of sticks and circles, so I just stuck pieces together. I remember that I wouldn't make anything interesting if I connected pieces end to end and made a straight line. But I had fun when I made angles."

"I had the same experience. Let's try right angles with different horizontal and vertical marks." They stopped after ten minutes without any progress.

"I'm stressed about these symbols," said Gerhard. "I know they're important, but I can't understand how to use them. There's no statistical or functional relationship between the symbol and the line."

He and the monk sank back in their chairs and stared at the elusive paper marks. Wolf came over and began his own arrangement.

"I've always liked this chair symbol, and the number 2 looks like a rocking chair, so I'm going to put them together like this."

Gerhard and Brother Robert sat up and watched Wolf engage in steps of logic that had not yet been applied.

"This dot is simple so I'm going to stick it into number 3, like this, because 3 has always been my favorite number." Gerhard and the monk stood at their chairs and looked down at what Wolf had just arranged.

"Very Good. You just made two reversing right angles," announced Brother Robert with a smile.

Gerhard turned white and left the table. He walked slowly toward a wall, then turned and walked back to the table. Brother Robert watched with confusion. Wolf watched with alarm at his unusual movement and sudden change of color.

Wolf offered him a chair, but Gerhard remained standing—hunched over Wolf's arrangement in deep concentration. Finally, he looked at Wolf.

"You've done much more that make a couple of reverse right angles. My dear friend, I think you just solved the damn puzzle."

CHAPTER 13

Interpol
Field Office
Office of the Section Director
Berlin

Dawn was just breaking as detectives Otto Heydrick and Ernst Nebe reached their office on the top floor of the Landerpolizel Headquarters Building. The three small Interpol offices were squeezed into an impressive facility shared by the German State Police and the Berlin Municipal Police, neither of whom paid much attention to Interpol—except when they needed something.

Heydrick spoke first.

"Someday I'll find a job that doesn't start with a staff meeting at six in the morning."

"Mr. Geer called me around four o'clock and said to be here at six for something important," replied Nebes as he hung up his coat. Man that was just a couple of hours ago. I didn't even have breakfast. That reminds me, Otto, where's Melk?"

"The closest spot is the market down the street next to the new tobacco and cigar store."

Kamza opened the door just then. He heard the question and offered the answer.

"He didn't mean milk—he meant Melk, as in Melk, Austria." Kamza sat heavily in the only guest chair in the office, still wearing his hat and coat. "I trust you gentlemen are ready for the meeting, because Mr. Geer is right behind me, and he's moving in a serious manner."

The door to the little conference room opened abruptly before anyone could answer. It was Gunter Geer, the section director. He almost sounded rude.

"In here! Let's go!"

His tone and the brevity of his remarks left little doubt in everyone's mind that something was either especially important or terribly wrong.

Each officer quickly took the nearest seat at the table while Geer stood next to his chair and fingered some papers at the bottom of his briefcase. Then he snapped the case closed with a loud cracking sound of the clasp. Geer was nervous.

"I don't like to be awakened from a sound sleep at 3:30 in the morning, especially when the caller is the Investigations Director in Lyon."

Wow, this has to be about something especially important, thought Heydrick.

"The Director was very uncomfortable because he just received a pressing call from the head of security for the Vatican."

My God, something is terribly wrong, thought Nebe.

"Now hold onto your seats. Listen carefully and do Not—I repeat, do not—get ahead of me. I don't need anyone here to jump to a conclusion. This is a perfect example of how something so very important can get totally screwed up."

Geer took out his handkerchief and wiped his mouth.

"I don't know who it was or how they did it, but someone reached the Pope's secretary—a Bishop somebody, and told him that a band of Germans had taken over Melk Abbey. It's reported that one of the Germans has a metal hand."

Heydrick and Nebe interrupted Geer and both began to talk simultaneously. "That's got to be Wolf! It's Gerhard and Wolf all right. They're going to make the abbey their fort. We have to do something."

Both Geer and Kamza called for quiet. Geer even rapped the table, a move that brought the two investigators to their senses.

"Damn it," said Geer. "I told you guys to listen and not spin off into a conclusion. There's more, and most of its bad."

Now it was Heydrick and Nebes' turn to be nervous. "Kamza, why don't you tell them about Vienna."

"You recall that several weeks ago this office received an email from the Vienna Police that Gerhard was dead. That was followed by a call from Dirk Huber, Assistant Director of EKO under BK, Vienna Police. He was about to retrieve the body and he made arrangements with the German police to fly Mr. Geer and me to the site to watch him operate in all of his glory. Huber turned out to be a bumbling idiot, who I'm sad to say, has since been promoted to Director. It wasn't Gerhard in the wreck, but Huber couldn't accept it. That was then. Now we fast forward to today."

"Again, we don't know how Huber came to this conclusion, but he believes there are dozens of German terrorists involved in the takeover of the abbey and he has requested that the German State Police join with his department and storm the facility."

The two investigators sat spellbound. Kamza looked over at Mr. Geer and suggested that he tell the last saga.

"Immediately after I talked with our investigations director at 3:30 this morning, I telephoned the chief of the Melk Police Department. I wanted current information about activities at the abbey. He was in bed, too. It was hard not to be specific after awakening the chief, but I couldn't afford to tip my hand or unnecessarily alarm him. The conversation was pleasant and smooth. It turned out that he had a great lunch in the public restaurant at the abbey that afternoon. He chatted with the prior about raising money for school supplies, and met with a couple of tourists who talked endlessly about the beauty of the place. He did tell me that the great library was closed for a few days for repairs, but he said nothing about German terrorists. My view of his remarks was that activities at the abbey were normal."

"Unfortunately, I can't afford any more third party information. It has to be first hand and it has to be now. Otto, I want you on a plane ASAP, or sooner. Fly to

Vienna, rent a car and drive quickly to Melk. Use your Interpol ID if you're stopped. Keep a low profile once you arrive at Melk. Dress like a tourist and take the standard tour. Be alert, do some snooping, look through the library windows, chat with a monk or two, ask non-threatening questions—you know, do a little investigating. And call me several times with your observations as I'll need information quickly and often. We're going to be busy here at the office trying to put out a few fires. Need to calm the Vatican, keep Dirk Huber in check, and insure that the German State Police won't be sucked into a stupid inferno. "

CHAPTER 14

Gerhard slid down into his chair slowly, right in front of Wolf's impressive arrangement of marks. Wolf and Brother Robert moved to the side of his chair to get a better view of what might happen next.

Gerhard seemed to only stare at the arrangement, but he was pulling it to him with his eyes and examining it with his mind. Then he put his hands on the paper cut-outs and physically gathered them in. His concentration was intense and several minutes of silence passed before he said anything. He seemed to talk out loud to someone, perhaps himself.

"Wolf's choice of symbols was indeed unique. Their placement, however, was immensely revealing as it provided a direction for those pieces that remain. I was intrigued that it seemed natural for him to use one horizontal and one vertical mark for each right angle. He could have used two vertical ones to make an angle, but he didn't. He also maintained the vertical and horizontal lines in their original position with the symbols on the outside of the vertical lines and on top of the horizontal ones. It was all very natural. And he used exactly half of the eight marks. The unused marks match the used ones— two vertical and two horizontal, so it stands to reason that the remaining marks can be similarly arranged to make a new design that will match the previous one. Wolf's design is a perfect reflection of what has yet to be arranged. But what is it?"

Gerhard took Wolf's marks and arranged them in a row, first the chair, the 2, the dot, the 3.

"Now watch what they become when I slide the two reverse angles together."

Brother Robert was the first to notice that the shape became.....

"Half of a swastika!"

The tone of his voice was one of astonishment.

"Exactly. Now let's make the other half. The soldiers made their swastika as a standard stationary design where the horizontal section was dominate and used first. Now we'll make the dominant vertical section, and that requires the reverse of Wolf's design. The horizontal mark will go first."

Gerhard put the remaining marks before him and began to put them in place.

"First a horizontal number 5 connected at the circle with the vertical scroll. Then the last vertical mark with the reverse slant connected at the circle with the short angle mark. There—we've made two more reversing right angles, which become the other half of the swastika. Now I'll place the new vertical group over the center of Wolf's horizontal group."

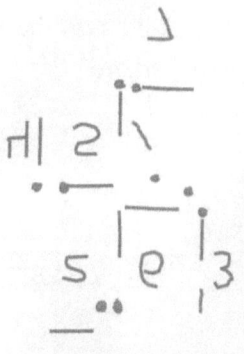

"The full swastika!" said Brother Robert in the same astonished tone as before.

"This swastika is the clue that the Nazis left to guide the finder to whatever it was that they hid in the abbey. The Swastika adds the Nazi authenticity, the confirmation, that this thing, which is before the finder, is indeed the real item. However, the marks are but a structure for the symbols. The symbols are the key. They are the letters in a secret word. They identify the location of what is hidden."

"I hear what you say Matthias, but your words add no clarification for me."   Brother Robert's voice was troubled.   "The symbols, like the puzzle, remain a jumble—they make no sense. I feel that we're still at a dead end."

"The letters are themselves purposely misleading, illusionary, like the ceilings in the Marble Hall and the great library—like an unknown language, until we learn to speak it. Wolf, take paper and pen and record the symbols in a line as if they were the letters in a word."

Wolf wrote the symbols on the paper as he was told and presented them to Gerhard.

"Like this?"

$$\sqcap 2 \cdot 35 \mathsf{P} \backslash \rfloor$$

"Perfect."   The secret to this illusionary language is to speak it upon reflection. Wolf, take the shiny silver tray that holds the ice water bottle and stand it on edge behind the symbols."

Wolf got the tray and set it on the paper close behind the symbols. Brother Robert watched closely. They were unprepared for the results. The line of symbols reflected off the tray in reverse.

"Everything changed," said Wolf, in amazement.

"Yes. The rocking chair changed into a number 4, the 2 became a number 5 and what we thought was a 5 became a number 2. And there's more; the upside down scroll mark changed to a number 6, the slash changed directions, and the short angle became a number 7." Gerhard grabbed his pen and transcribed the new word. "So now we have this.....45.326/7. But what is it?

"Oh my God in Heaven," said Brother Robert in a strained voice as he made the sign of the cross. "I know what it is."

Gerhard let out an unexpected robust laugh that startled the young monk. "Tell us Brother Robert, tell us!"

"It's the standard catalog reference number for one of the books in our library."

"You hit the target precisely, my friend. The Nazis hid their secret in one of your very own books. They may have been just common soldiers, but they were clever ones. Brother Robert, please find the prior. Tell him that we need his help in locating a single book in his 100,000 volume library."

The monk darted off while Gerhard and Wolf reexamined the new number word. The door to the great library reopened sooner than they expected with the return of Brother Robert and the prior, along with the head librarian and a couple of other monks who were most familiar with the workings of the library.

I was just down the hall when Brother Robert came in search of me," announced the prior as he crossed the large room and headed for Gerhard. "He explained about the swastika, the symbols, and the reflection in the silver tray. What does it look like?"

Wolf held the edge of the tray immediately behind the symbols as Gerhard pointed out how the reflection of the symbols changed and they became something else. The prior watched with keen interest, as did the head librarian and the other monks, all of whom leaned over the prior like pigeons looking for crumbs.

"What is the catalog reference number of the book that you wish to retrieve?" asked the librarian. Gerhard handed the number to him and he read it out loud.

"45.362/7. Humm. That's a work by Carl Goedeke, from Hannover. I believe it was printed by Goethe und Schiller in 1859."

"How do you know that by heart? There are thousands of book in here?" asked Wolf who was duly impressed with the head librarian's memory.

"These books are my friends. I know them all. As a matter of fact the volume you seek is there... (he pointed to the center of the north wall)...between the sections of theology and jurisprudence." He nodded to his assistants, who pushed a tracked library ladder along the wall to a position midway between two tall windows. Two monks climbed up about eight feet, just below the baroque balcony. One of the monks traced along the volumes with his index finger until he found the number 45.362/7 on the edge of the binding. Then they carefully slid a huge book from the shelf, cradled it in their hands, and slowly backed down the ladder. They placed it on an empty table and everyone gather around it—wondering.

"That's a large book," said Wolf. "It's as thick as a telephone book, but twice as long."

The head librarian chuckled. "Yes, Goedeke was known not only for his content, but also for the size of his hand. Goethe und Schiller printed it just as Goedeke wrote it—large."

Gerhard motioned to the prior to open the book.

"I need a moment, please" He closed his eyes, bowed his head, put the palms of his hands together close to his habit, and said a silent prayer. He concluded with the sign of the cross, which the other monks made as well.

"I'm nervous, but now I have His strength."

The prior opened the cover, slowly turned the cover page, and each of the following cover pages. The first chapter appeared then the second chapter, and the third. The speed of the page turning became faster. Nothing. The prior looked at Gerhard.

"Perhaps I might try," suggested Gerhard. He began a flip through from the back, but the book was too large and the pages flipped in groups, so he flipped in small sections of pages—first checking the top, then the bottom. Nothing.

"May I try?" asked the head librarian. He turned the book around and started from the middle, one page at a time. Nothing.

The group stood silently. They were dismayed and confused. Each wondered what happened. Wolf finally broke the silence with the question they all wanted answered.

"What went wrong?"

Gerhard slid down into his chair, slowly, just as he did earlier. It was easy to tell that he was thinking. He stared across the vast space of the magnificent great library, directly at the empty place on the shelf that previously held volume number 45.326/7. A warm smile came to his face and he looked up into the frowns of the others.

"Nothing went wrong. We just didn't finish looking." He rose abruptly, crossed the room with quick bold strides, and climbed the ladder to the empty space on the bookshelf. His head disappeared into the space.

"A huh," came a muffled sound. Then the hard sound of his fist as he banged on something. A smiling face popped out of the hole and looked directly at the prior.

"What does this metal plate cover?"

"It's the opening to one of the old air ventilation shafts. It was closed when the air conditioning system was installed."

Gerhard climbed down the library ladder and crossed to the prior.

"There is something else there. I saw part of it, but it's covered with other books. Will you please have someone remove all of the books that surround the shaft cover—out to about half a meter?"

The other monks heard Gerhard's request. They all moved simultaneously to the other side of the room and began to remove the books from around the opening— each book placed in proper order on a library table. They finished quickly.

Gerhard climbed back up the ladder. He looked, thumped, and called the others over. They gathered at the base of the ladder.

"The lower part of the shaft opening appears to be filled-in within recent times. See here?" He pointed to mortar joints. "The mortar is a different color and texture than when this narrow wall slit was built centuries ago. I'd like to have this metal plate removed. If it covers what I think it does, I'd like a hammer and chisel to see what's buried inside this false bottom."

The monks quickly returned with the blacksmith of the abbey, a stout man with a hefty set of tools. He dispatched the bolts with ease and removed the metal plate. Gerhard climbed back up and looked into the shaft. The others remained at the foot of the ladder.

"It's as I thought. This shaft has a false bottom."

He took the hammer and chisel and tapped away carefully at the mortar. He didn't want to damage the original stones or anything hidden inside the mortar. It didn't take much effort or time. The mortar flew in chunks, then clank. He hit metal.

"I hit something. I'm going to remove the rest of the mortar on top. Perhaps then I could look in and see what's buried here." The mortar was brittle and came off cleanly. "I see metal. I think I can remove it." But the metal object wasn't ready to let go of its hiding place. He wedged the chisel between the metal and the mortar and gently tapped all around the sides. It loosened and then came free. "I've got it." He lifted it out of its burial site. What he saw provided instant credibility that he found what he was looking for. It was a narrow stainless steel box, complete with an embossed swastika on top. Gerhard said nothing, he just backed down the ladder and handed the box to the prior, who saw the swastika and quickly put the box on the table. As if on cue, the inner door of the great library opened and in hurried the abbot.

"The prior sent word that you were making wonderful progress and appeared on the threshold of solving the puzzle."

"It's been a series of ups and downs, sir," smiled Gerhard. "First it looked like we had it, then we didn't, things changed and now it appears promising again. We found this stainless steel box buried in a false bottom of an old air shaft in the wall of the library." He pointed to the spot. The abbot looked at the hole in the bookshelf, then bent over the table and looked carefully at the old box.

"It was hidden by the Nazis during the Second World War," continued Gerhard. "I can tell you with complete confidence that the Nazis vandalized the books in your library. They made some of the marks on purpose to chart a path to a hiding place for this box, other marks were made in mischief. Some of the pages and chapters that were torn out were likely sold for profit. The Nazis perpetrated the crimes against the history of knowledge—they caused the affront to God and to the Holy Church. But half a century has past. Those who caused the destruction are surely dead by now. There is no one to punish. It is time to stop the pursuit and the worry. It is time to put the matter aside. But only you can decide if it is time to forgive."

"Your words are wise, my friend. I am grateful for them." He looked back at the dust covered box on the table. "What's in the box?"

"We don't know. We found it only a minute ago and haven't opened it. Inside is the secret that the Nazis worked so desperately to hide. It's the reason they destroyed your books. It seems only appropriate that you open it."

A mummer went through the small group of dedicated monks. They knew how strongly the abbot felt about the damaged books. A year had past and the struggle was over. The answer to the puzzle was in a little box in front of the one who cared so much. The monks felt it was right that he open the box.

The abbot sat in the chair in front of the box and pulled it close to him. He put one hand on the cover over the swastika. With the other hand he slid a little sliding lock open, then lifted the lid. Inside was a single piece of slate marked with a confusing list of numbers. Gerhard knew they were a simple set of geographic coordinates, which he entered into his iPad. The electronic miracle quickly spit out the answer—a particular spot on the southern shore of the Sognefjord—Norway's grandest, longest, and deepest fjord.

Just then the door to the great library thrust open and a worried monk ran to the abbot.

"Police! Soldiers! Trucks full of them! They're at the front gate and they want the Germans that are hiding here!"

The abbot went into action. First he took the simple white cross that hung around his neck from a thick purple cord and held it in front of him while he gave instructions to one of the monks. Next, he put one arm around Gerhard, the other around Wolf and hugged them both. "May the Lord watch over you and keep you safe. Take the box and go quickly with the prior."

They followed the prior down the worn stone steps to the cellar, through the despicable door, into the tunnel to the old door in the far wall—the one that opened to another tunnel that led under the centuries old cemetery outside the monastery's walls. Then, up through a grave plot next to a weathered tombstone, where they were met by another monk and whisked to safety.

The abbot walked rapidly into the church and stood under the spectacular domed rotunda. The overhead lights reflected from his silver hair and cast a shimmering aura over him. Framed with a background of the great alter, white marble statues, shimmering candles, and golden frescos, he was a dominant presence.

"I shall wait for the police here."

The abbot could hear them coming. Their boots clunked on the white marble floor, their police equipment rattled, their voices too loud. They passed through the Royal Way, rounded the front of the church and were confronted by the holy sight of a majestic priest, complete with an aura of light, who seemed to stand at the very entrance to heaven. The police stopped abruptly. They stood, quietly and respectfully in awe of such a Godly person. Finally, their leader took one step forward and bowed.

"Your Grace, I am Dirk Huber, Director of EKO under BK, Vienna Police."

But Dirk Huber wasn't prepared for what happen next and his voice fell off. A long line of slow moving black robed monks, cowls lowered over their faces, their hands under their scapulars, entered the church and formed between the alter and the first row of pews—directly behind their abbot. They were quietly chanting the abbot's favorite psalm.

He began again. "Your Grace..." But it was no use. He couldn't be heard over the chanting. Then to Dirk Huber's surprise, the abbot stepped forward abruptly, to within a foot of Huber's face. He towered over the director. The chanting stopped.

"Why do you enter the House of the Lord with guns?" demanded the abbot. His voice echoed in the vast space of the magnificent church.

"Well, sir, your Grace, aaah, we were told that a group of German terrorists were holed up right here in your church. We asked some of the monks outside to tell us where the terrorists were, but they didn't answer us. We're here to save you."

"The LORD is my SAVIOR!" The abbot's booming voice resonated throughout the entire abbey—his eyes riveted to Huber's eyes.

"Not the Vienna Police!

CHAPTER 15

Gerhard and Wolf emerged from the grave with an eerie appreciation of what it felt like to return from the dead. Being helped out of the hole in the ground by a black robed monk, his cowl lowered tightly over his face, added a chilling dimension to the experience.

"Follow me!" said the monk in a whisper. He led them along a narrow gravel path edged with small pointed rocks, past gnarled branches of small olive trees that hung in wrenched distortion over ancient tombstones that marked the places of the dead—all bordered by a high wall of stone. Ahead were the iron bars and scrolled curves of an ornamental gate, beyond which waited a black sedan with a gold seal centered on the rear door. They entered the car and drove quickly away. Gerhard looked back over his shoulder at the site of the lone monk next to the tall iron gate. The car picked up speed and the wispy figure in a robe and hood faded into just another feature of the cemetery.

"Where may I take you, sir?" It was the same polite and careful driver Gerhard had before.

"To the railroad yard in Salzburg."

"Are you catching a train, sir?"

"Yes, in a manner of speaking."

The get-a-way from Melk Abbey went smoothly. It took just over two hours to drive the 145 kilometers to the Salzburg rail yard, including the quick stop at a small market for provisions. They found the yard without much trouble.

Wolf carried the food into the private car then checked in with the yard master while Gerhard put things away in the galley. The blinking red light on the desk top computer caught his attention. It was an email message from André Beau, his Swiss agent. André didn't like computers. His messages were always short and to the point, a trait that Gerhard appreciated:

> Herr Gerhard:
> I have a client who wishes to make a significant long term investment in something of lasting value. Please contact me if interested.
> Respectfully,
> André

Gerhard called him immediately and André answered after the second ring. They exchanged brief pleasantries, then got down to business.

"I have something exceptional with unique worldwide appeal," said Gerhard. "Purchase of this item would require an equally exceptional buyer who appreciates both rarity and opportunity, one who is capable of operating at the highest financial level. Do we have a matching profile, thus far?"

"Yes. It could be a match."

Gerhard had to be careful. He was worried about entrapment. The police could easily orchestrate a sting operation with a fake millionaire ready to buy anything Gerhard wanted to sell. He could even be André's client. He had to find out.

"Tell me about your client," he said bluntly.

"I've known him for over three years, but I've only meet him once. He is from Qatar, works in investments—more like international finance. I met him at a hotel in Paris when he flew in to inspect a manor house that I found for him in the Loire Valley. He brought his wife with him to look at the house and two business associates who constantly handled his incoming calls. Occasionally he'd take one. He is fluent in several languages. I was there when he took some calls and he appeared to be very business savvy. He was disappointed that the manor house lacked a modern security system and that nearly squashed the purchase. I contacted him later when 500 hectors of land adjacent to his manor house became available. He purchased it immediately. I might add that he didn't pay with check or electronic transfer. He sent an envoy with cash."

This sounds interesting. There's no hint that this guy is part of a set up. It's all natural, all real. His comment about the security system was convincing.

"He sounds like a perfect client for you André, but tell me what type of a long term investment is he looking for?"

"It's difficult to pinpoint. He has houses and land in other parts of the world and doesn't want any more property. I think he wants to get something and put it away to mature. A world masterpiece, a rare work of art—that's what I think he wants now—something no one else has. You know what I mean, the type of art that's only available on the black market. He seems to have a lot of money all of a sudden and he wants to move it fast." Do you have anything that fits this picture?"

Gerhard knew this was the time to move forward with the critical question that would determine if the conversation expanded or stopped completely.

"There are only two original and available Gutenberg Bibles left in the world and I can get both of them. The price is thirty five million euros each."

There was no response from André. The line seemed dead. Gerhard allowed the silence to hang suspended and said nothing further. He waited.

"Interesting," was André's singular comment. More silence. He knew André was thinking.

The more he thinks about it the more he's seriously considering it.

"I'll get back with you."

By then Gerhard and Wolf were exhausted. They each had a bowl of cereal and retired early.

Compared to other places where he kept his car, the Salzburg rail yard was quiet. Sleep was easy, but Gerhard had an important early morning call to make and was thankful for the 4 AM buzz of his alarm. He was dressed and at his desk in the drawing room only minutes later, thumbing through the telephone section of his iPad for Karl Olsson's number. He knew that Karl would be up by now and at the cannery wharf to meet the first group of his returning fleet of fishing trawlers.

"Gerhard, my friend, it must be three years since you were here in Norway and we fished together for salmon. Where are you and what's going on?" asked a surprised Karl Olsson.

"Yes, it has indeed been a long time since our fishing trip, and I remember how upset I was when you caught more fish that I did."

"But your fish were much larger than mine."

"Doesn't matter, the guest should always catch more," as they both laughed. Then the tone of Gerhard's voice changed, so did his words.

"Karl, I need your help."

"Of course. My brothers and I are forever indebted to you and we are ready to assist you with anything. What do you need? How can we help?"

"I'm involved in a project for the church and it has led me to Norway. I'm trying to find a particular item that has ties to the Second World War. The government and the police are not sure what I'm doing and that makes the search a bit awkward. That's the overview. I'd like to meet you in Bergen, bounce some thoughts around, and ask for help in locating the item. I'll need a place for Wolf and me to stay, a guide, and transportation, but I don't want to arrange this myself over the phone or computer. I'd rather have a trusted local person do it."

"I understand. My brothers and I qualify as local and trustworthy. Consider it done."

Gerhard said he'd explain the details of the project when he arrived in Bergen, and that he'd call again very shortly with the date and time of his flight. Karl had a meeting place in mind that would provide good security. It was the end of a short conversation, but the beginning of a long and intriguing adventure.

Gerhard and Karl Olsson had been friends for over two decades. They met each other on a fishing trip shortly after Karl's parents died in the mid-eighties. The five Olsson brothers lived in Sweden then and wanted to move to Norway to start a fishing business, but Norway denied them citizenship and a business license because they were Swedish. It was all part of a long standing anger that Norway held against Sweden because the Swedish government allowed the Nazis to cross through their country and invade Norway during the Second World War.

Gerhard's relationship with the Olsson's began when he was a young electrical/electronic engineer with "Das Auto", a new electronic equipment supplier to several major European manufacturers, especially the auto industry. One day he received a request from a yacht owner who wanted to operate his yacht remotely from any location on the vessel—not only the bridge, but also the bow, the stern, either side of the yacht—even below. It was a unique request because the equipment that the owner wanted had never been made.

Gerhard considered it a challenge and worked on it day and night. He developed a design after only one week, and completed a workable performance unit after the second week. It was a remote, wireless, hand held radio guidance controller that did exactly what the owner wanted.

What Gerhard didn't know at the time was that the yacht owner was also the vice president of Norway's largest ship builder. He had Gerhard's controller installed on all of his ships. The equipment increased the steering capability of the ships, especially in docking maneuvers. Expensive tug boats were no longer needed to nudge the ship into a berth. Docking time decreased and profits increased.

Gerhard's fame as someone who could solve problems using the emerging electronic technology spread quickly. Sweden's largest car manufacturer contacted him with a requirement for ultra-high performance controllers for DC systems.

Within days, he engineered an unusually small controller that handled all of the car's dashboard instrument systems. It worked perfectly and the client ordered thousands. Das Auto took over the processes of manufacturing the controllers.

Business was brisk, but Gerhard was exhausted. He took a brief vacation for a few days and chartered a fishing boat to rest and relax. The captain was Karl Olsson and they became good friends. It was during one of their conversations while fishing that Gerhard learned about Karl's problems with Norway.

Gerhard felt that the Norwegian government's attitude toward Sweden was not only outdated, but it interfered with post war development between the two countries, both of whom needed each other to improve economic conditions. He told the Olsson brothers that he'd make inquiries and try to get Norway to reverse its decision. The Olsson's were appreciative, but they really didn't expect this young German engineer, whom they had just met, to make any difference. They dismissed his effort.

They didn't know how persistent Gerhard was. They also failed to realize that his recent successful work with two huge corporations in both Sweden and Norway provided important contacts in very high places. The car manufacturer gave him names and introduced him to high officials in the Swedish government.

The vice president of the ship building company in Norway did the same thing. He even accompanied Gerhard to meetings with Norwegian officials. One can't underestimate the enormous political influence such important business leaders have on governmental officials, especially in the conduct of their regular day-to-day decision making process.

It took about ten days. The government of Norway granted citizenship to the Olsson brothers and issued business permits to allow them to engage in fishing in Norwegian waters and to conduct other related activities. The Olsson brothers were more than overwhelmed, they were stunned. They expected nothing to happen only to find that everything happened. They remained indebted to

Gerhard to this day.

Karl Olsson set up a business structure that earned high praise from the Norwegian government. He contracted with the big Norway ship builder to construct his fishing trawlers. He hired only Norwegians to work on his vessels. A Norwegian contractor built his docks and his canneries.

Later the brothers formed a land reclamation company, built wharfs, and developed an undersea fabrication company that supported the state gas exploration efforts. Thousands of Norwegians worked for them with a payroll in the multi-millions. The five Olsson brothers had become an economic and political force of their own.

Gerhard put down the iPad and wondered about the feeling that came over him when he talked with Karl. *Suddenly I felt uncomfortable about identifying an arrival date and time. I think I said I'd call later with the flight information, but I know better than to reveal that over the phone. It felt as though my inner self was warning me about this trip—and my inner self has never been wrong.*

Gerhard decided to change his plans. He climbed down the steps of his private car and crossed the tracks to the yardmaster's office to discuss his thoughts about a move order to Oslo.

"You can get to the North Sea by rail without much trouble, but it would take forever to cross into Sweden, Norway, or Finland. No, there's a better way to do it."

Gerhard stood and watched the yardmaster flip through log pages and check schedules on his computer.

"How does this sound? I can get you out of Salzburg at 9:02 in the morning and arrive in Berlin at 5:23 PM, just in time to go out and enjoy a good dinner at one of Berlin's fine restaurants. Out of Berlin at 8:38 the next morning and arrive in Amsterdam at 2:59 mid-afternoon."

"Excellent connections, but I need to get to Oslo, so I can take a train to Bergen."

"Well, you can always fly from Amsterdam—it's fast and cheap, but my wife and I like to take the overnight ferry. Nice and peaceful. The ship docks in the middle of Bergen. You can buy ferry tickets right at the central train station when you arrive in Amsterdam."

"Nice and peaceful. That's what I needed to hear. Book it. Oh! Put in a storage order, with power, for my car in Amsterdam. I might need to keep it there for a week or so."

CHAPTER 16

Eeeeeeeeeeeeeeeee. It was that damn high-pitched electronic sound again, but this time Gerhard knew what caused it—the train crew, as they disconnected the commercial power from his car to get ready for the trip to Berlin.

The muffled sound of the back-up generator started almost immediately and it allowed the electricity and life to return to normal. He waited for the expected gentle nudge of the switch engine to couple onto his private car, but instead the engine hit it with such force that it literally threw him off the bed.

The sound of profanity came from Wolf's stateroom so he assumed that Wolf was on the floor, too. He heard Wolf shuffle to the rear platform door, presumably to complain, but the engine was already in the process of abruptly pulling away and there was no one in sight to complain to.

This whole experience of being coupled onto a train in Salzburg was different than any other place and it caught him off guard. In the past they were connected to the end of a train that was being made up for a run.

This time there was no train in the yard. It was already on the road and hadn't arrived yet from Vienna. And it wasn't a slow freight train like before, one burdened by fifty cars of oil, grain, boxes, steel, autos, etc. They were about to experience a thrill ride.

A sleek passenger train of less than a dozen cars was streaming toward the Salzburg station without any intention of slowing down. It was late. Gerhard's car sat waiting on a side track still coupled to the idling switch engine. He wondered why they hadn't yet been connected and what was going on. Wolf had time to make breakfast while they waited, which he served in the drawing room. The blueberry pancakes were among his best.

They heard the swooshing sound too late to determine what it was or where it came from. The passenger train swooshed past at what seemed like just inches from their breakfast table and came to an unbelievably quick and smooth stop.

Gerhard's car jerked from the yank of the switch engine as it backed onto the main line, then forward with a thankful ever so gentle connection to the sleek passenger train. The air hoses were attached, the power feed switched, two sharp blasts from the big passenger diesel's air horn, and they were on their way to Berlin.

Unsure what to expect from a passenger train, they literally held on to the furniture in the drawing room as the train accelerated rapidly to 60 kilometers, then inched toward 70. The car began to sway. Gerhard hadn't felt this type of speed before and he wasn't sure if the car had either. Each looked at the other and smiled like a couple of kids on a carnival ride. All went well. The car actually held together without difficulty—all the way to Berlin, with a twelve minute ahead of time arrival.

It was surely the grand train ride that put them both in an up tempo relaxed mood. He took Wolf to the two starred Michelin restaurant, Fischers Fritz, where the chef de cuisine Christian Lohse prepared an exquisite meal of wild sea bass. Wolf insisted on a desert of walnut ice cream topped with white chocolate. He got it.

The next day was nearly a repeat of the previous one, except the performance of the Berlin yard crew was a cut above the one in Salzburg. They were connected to another passenger train, but this one originated in Berlin so they didn't have to wait for it to arrive.

Departure was prompt and as posted—8:38AM. Arrival in Amsterdam was precisely at 2:59PM. A yard person came along after they pulled into the station and taped a Storage Notice on the car door so Gerhard knew that his storage order was being activated and not overlooked. He quickly checked his briefcase … the small stainless steel box was still inside. They packed their bags for an extended stay in Norway and bought tickets in the Amsterdam central railroad station for two cabins on the overnight ferry to Bergen. Gerhard paused for a moment and sent a text message to Karl Olsson.

"Arrive at 9 AM. Where do I meet u?"

The cab ride to the ferry yard was short. They went onboard, put their luggage in their cabin, had a sandwich and a beer in the bar, and walked the deck. It felt good to be in the open air after two days in the rail car—so good that they grabbed a couple of chairs and decided to remain on deck during the departure and enjoy the scenery. They ordered two glasses of wine from the deck waitress just as Gerhard received a text back from Karl.

"Walk fish market. We'll find u."

He noted that Karl didn't ask for anything specific, like a flight number. Karl understood his reason for the ambiguity and supported it. The night was quiet, the sea was calm, the passage uneventful. Everything was perfect, thus far.

Gerhard was on deck around six in the morning when the ferry made a starboard turn away from the Atlantic Ocean, and headed into the wide ship channel toward Bergen. He watched the turning movements and was intrigued with the unique engineering feats of the ferry.

It was a big ship with a bow that was hinged at the top and swung open like a huge mouth that swallowed vehicles as they moved into the ship and regurgitated them again as they left. The ferry moved closer to Bergen. He could see the seven small mountain peaks that surrounded the city.

Several minutes passed as the ship steamed steadily toward the entrance to city harbor. He had been here several times before and liked it. The sparkling small city wasn't trendy—just naturally elegant. The only thing that he didn't like was the abundant rain.

Bergen has had a love affair with its harbor for centuries. Everything began and ended at it—from buildings to lives. Each time Gerhard saw the picturesque harbor, he was reminded of the accident.

Norwegians regarded it as tragic; the Nazis considered it an embarrassment. It happened during the war on April 20, 1944. Germany confiscated a Dutch fishing trawler and converted it to a supply ship, but never maintained it. The ship sought repairs in Bergin, but the city denied it permission to enter the harbor because the vessel was loaded with 124,000 kg of explosives.

The Nazis overruled the city and the ship entered only to explode in the middle of the harbor. The blast created a tidal wave that flattened the city. Whole neighborhoods disappeared. The waterfront was gone. Later, the ship's anchor was found near the top of one of the seven mountains. Nearly 160 people died, 5,000 were wounded. Norway never forgot. Gerhard couldn't help but think of the paradox that surrounded the event … the intense suspicion that the explosion was sabotage. April 20th was Adolf Hitler's birthday.

The ferry slid into its berth alongside the Skoltegrunnskaien pier. They disembarked and ordered their luggage delivered to the Radisson, which was harbor side and very close to the fish market. Gerhard didn't check his briefcase … he tucked it under his arm. Then the two of them walked slowly along the water toward the city center. It would have been easier to take a taxi, but not as pleasant. It was only a ten minute walk to the hotel with the fish market just five minutes further.

He remembered that the hotel had one of the best buffet breakfasts in town. They were ready for it and had the time. Gerhard talked with the bell captain after breakfast and tipped him handsomely to keep the luggage safe for the rest of the day.

By then it was nearly nine o'clock so they strolled past the historic wooden warehouses transformed into chic shops toward the fish market, which was spread out on a cobble stone plaza along the top of the harbor.

Old fisherman and young ones, and women of all ages and dress proudly displayed a wide variety of fish, snails, eel, and a few other things that Gerhard wasn't sure of. Some were boiling water, building a charcoal fire, and getting ready for the lunch crowd.

Colorful vendors hustled about their stalls arranging T-shirts, leather purses, jewelry, and homemade wooden items. It was only mid-morning and the market wasn't crowded yet with shoppers, but he couldn't help feeling uncomfortable with all of the people milling about.

Old ladies with shopping bags were probably all right, but the small groups of men that just stood around for no apparent reason put him on edge.

They glanced about as they walked through the market stalls. There was Karl Olsson. He didn't speak, but slowly shook his head from side to side and faced the palm of his hand toward them—all signs that things were not right. They stopped in their tracks. Wolf touched his pistol. Then Karl motioned for them to follow as he walked through the stalls in a casual manner. They followed in the same manner, around the edge of the old market to a new section, which had a roof and walls with sliding doors. More fish stalls were inside, but these were big ones with counters, display cases, and glass freezers. Wide aisles separated the counter sections with tables and chairs along the edge near the sliding doors.

The old wooden support beams overhead added a contemporary look to what had previously been just an old fish market. Karl moved to an unoccupied table and Gerhard and Wolf joined him.

Karl made no move to shake hands. He kept his distance, Gerhard followed suite. He knew something was wrong. Karl's face was expressionless so Gerhard decided to speak first.

"This doesn't seem like a safe place to meet—too crowded."

Karl's expression changed to a warm smile. "It's wonderful to see you again. Actually this old fish market is an exceptionally safe place for our meeting ..." Gerhard cut into his words.

"Your actions speak otherwise. You seem concerned about something and all of these people won't make it easy to talk."

But Karl didn't seem to hear what he said. His eyes were in another part of the room and his index finger was on his ear, so Gerhard began again.

"I said that you're acting in a very cautious manner......"

Now it was Karl's turn to interrupt.

"I am sorry for appearing rude. Allow me to explain. I'm wearing a new LAN (Local Area Network) radio receiver in my ear and someone sent me a message while you were talking. A whole lot of people seem interested in you. We've noticed their appearance in the area ever since you telephoned and said you were involved in a project for the church and looking for something in Norway regarding the Second World War."

Gerhard was shocked. Multiple groups of serious thoughts cascaded through his mind. *They're on to me again! Is it the government? Which one? And whoever it is they can monitor my calls. They know where I am, where I'm going, and what I'm doing. This is damn bad!*

"What people are interested in us?" asked Wolf. "Who's showing up around here looking for us?"

"It doesn't make much sense," responded Karl. "They don't seem to understand how to stay under cover— like they never heard of the word, incognito."

"You're confusing me. What do you mean?" asked Gerhard.

Karl thought for a moment, as if searching for the right words. "Norwegians all drive small cars. The roads are narrow and parking is hard to find. Car ownership per capita is high. We're frugal and keep our vehicles in good repair. These guys show up in big Mercedes that are dented and dirty. They ride around town and look, then park and watch, with four or five men in a car."

Gerhard and Wolf shared a long stare.

"I'm beginning to get the picture," said Wolf.

"Scandinavians are generally fair skinned. We're not big

on beards either. These are stocky guys, dark hair and beards—big bushy ones."

"I have the picture," said Gerhard.

"There are lots of ways to blend in and not stand out so blatantly," added Karl.

"I have some terrible news for you—and it's also terrible for us as well. The people you described are from Pakistan. Most are part of the al-Qaida group, and all of them are terrorists. They're after us for work we did in Washington."

He thought it best to stop and not go into more detail.

"Christ!" was Karl's quick response. "I better call the police!"

"No! Don't do that!" They're not here to hurt anyone or damage anything in Norway. They only want to get us. We don't want the police to know we're in the country because that could interfere with the church project and the item we're looking for."

"Okay, I won't call the police." Karl scooted his chair up closer to the table and leaned toward Gerhard. "You asked for my help and I'm anxious to do anything I can for you. So let's talk. Tell me what you need."

Gerhard looked around at all of the people in the market and quietly said, "How can I talk to you about something so serious in this public place—a fish market?"

"I should have explained it to you earlier." Karl took a moment to decide how to start. "About a dozen of the fisherman, vendors, and shoppers in the market outside work for us. We put them in the stalls today for extra security because you were coming."

Gerhard and Wolf were startled at Karl's blunt words. They wondered if he'd have more—and he did.

"We own this new market that we're sitting in now—actually, we built it for the government and they leased it back to us. You may not have noticed, but half of the tables in here are full and the people sitting at them haven't moved away since you arrived. They all work for us. Two of my brothers are seated among them and my other brother is outside in the fish market. He's the one who sent a message to me while you were trying to talk to me a minute ago. All of my brothers are armed, including me. We have other security measures in place, but there's no need to go into them now. My point in telling you all of this is to assure you that you're safer here with us in our harbor side fish market than you would be in your hotel room."

Gerhard was so taken aback by all of the preparations Karl made for their safety that he didn't respond immediately. So Karl continued.

"I knew something was wrong when you called, wanted to talk, and asked for help. You didn't offer any specifics about your arrival—just when you'd arrive not where or how. You didn't text where I could find you, rather you asked how you could find us. Your ambiguity spoke clearly, and I figured you needed some protection. And now you tell me that Pakistani terrorists are after you, so I believed I guessed right—you need protection immediately. I will also tell you that one of those dented

Mercedes with four big guys in it has been parked alongside the market since early this morning. They watched you walk through the fish market and into this building. We've been watching them, too."

Suddenly Karl sat straight up in his chair and put a finger to his ear. Someone was talking to him on his LAN.

"That was my brother in the market outside. Two of the men left their car and are headed our way, but they're coming in through different doors on separate sides of the building. Our table is in the middle—so we're going to do something about them."

He turned his head to his coat collar and said, "Do it now."

Then he smiled, looked back at his two guests, and in a calm and quiet voice said, "Let's sit here and see how it goes."

Both men smiled back in an automatic way, completely unsure what would happen next and with a bit of doubt about how effective it might be.

A door on the far side opened and a chunky man with thick hair entered. The bulge under his jacket was telling. The second door opened. But suddenly there was a commotion of some sort outside. The men stopped and looked back. Gerhard saw yellow smoke, lots of it coming from the market parking area. People outside yelled, " Fire! Fire!" Then sirens. A long hook and ladder truck from the Bergen Fire Department arrived and stopped crossways behind the dented Mercedes.

A second fire truck pulled up along the other side. Yellow smoke billowed from underneath the Mercedes as high pressure water hit the car from several hoses. Four men, who looked like foreigners, ran around and around the car shouting, "Fire!" only to be blasted by a fire hose with each yell.

A tall blonde waitress hurried to Karl's table. "Go with her, quickly!" then he, too, darted off. The girl led them to a side street just as a big white American diesel pickup truck screeched to a stop in front of them. She opened the door. Karl was behind the wheel. "Get in." The truck disappeared down the street.

It all happened so fast that Gerhard wasn't sure what happened.

"Looked like someone had a car fire back there," chuckled Karl in a mocking manner.

"But the fire made yellow smoke," said Wolf. "I never saw that before."

"Aw, my little brother tossed a marine smoke flare under their car, that's all." The pickup darted through the narrow streets and neared the edge of Bergen. "I think it best that you stay with some special friends of ours while you're in Norway. Much safer that way."

"Wait!" shouted Wolf. "Our luggage! It's still back at the Radisson."

'What's it look like?" asked Karl as he continued to drive on without a hint of turning back.

"Two black duffel bags with a blue stripe," came the nervous reply.

Karl calmly removed a microphone from the truck dashboard and said, "Number seven this is number one. Pick up two black duffel bags with a blue stripe from the

Radisson and bring them along."

A contented smile appeared on their faces. Things seemed to be under control now.

"Wait!" yelled Wolf again. "How's the bell captain going to give our luggage to a perfect stranger?"

"Danny's the bell captain. His father is a foreman in one of our canneries."

Karl turned the big pickup to the left and headed northeast toward Balestrand.

CHAPTER 17

Balestrand, Norway. Population, 1,400. On the north side of the Sognefjord. That's where Karl was taking them.

"It's a small pleasant village. You'll like it, especially the Knudsvig Hotel. I think she's the most classic grand dame hotel in all of Norway. Owned by the same family for well over a century. The village and the hotel are both on land that's bumped out into the fjord, so penetration by anyone without being noticed would be difficult. Security will be a snap."

Gerhard heard Karl's words, but they were just fringe sounds. He wasn't interested in where he was staying. His thoughts were on the little box in his briefcase. He didn't want to waste time by reviewing the historical or geographic reference of the place, but he owed Karl an explanation about what had happened and where he was going next. The truck ride seemed like the perfect time and place to do it.

Gerhard was good at summarization. He covered everything in five minutes...Melk Abbey, the call from the abbot, the markings in the books, the tale from the old monk about the Nazis during WW II, searching the great library, uncovering the old air chamber, locating the stainless steel box, everything. Karl listened passionately.

"Fascinating! I can't wait to start. What's our first step?"

"This Balestrand place that you're taking us to...it's not up in the mountains is it? It's on the water, right?"

"Right on the water. The village sits at fjord side in a small valley surrounded by nearby mountains."

"I need a boat and a marine chart. Can I get these things in this little village?"

"You get them from me." Karl looked at his watch. "One of my crew boats should be at the Balestrand marina now. It'll serve as administrative headquarters and the housing base for our security group that's been assigned to watch over you in Balestrand. The charts you need are onboard."

"The steel box that I found in the abbey wall behind the bookcase held a piece of slate inscribed with numbers. They're coordinates for a location somewhere on the Sognefjord. Thus far, I've only checked it using the Web. I need a local marine chart for absolute verification. I want to go to the spot on the fjord after we identify it on the chart."

Karl thought for a moment. "We need something different than a crew boat ... a fast launch. I'll have one sent over now."

He used the dashboard microphone again. "Number 10 this is number one. Send *Mollie* along with the crew boat and tie her alongside."

The big American pickup covered the miles comfortably, but the ride was long and increasingly arduous. They left the main road and drove north on one that was noticeably narrower and increasingly twisted all the way to Vangsnes, where they drove onto a ferry and crossed the Sognefjord.

Gerhard was annoyed and dismayed to learn that it was necessary to cross it again, because the Sognefjord formed a "T" at that point. They only crossed the stem of the fjord on the first ferry, now it was necessary to board another one and cross the arm. The trip continued. They made the second crossing, drove around the beautiful little Eselfjord, and finally arrived at Balestrand.

Karl parked directly in front of the crew boat in the marina. The old wooden Knudsvig Hotel was next door. Gerhard couldn't help but notice the grandeur of the stately hotel. Karl introduced them to the crew, but only a few were onboard. The rest were somewhere on the grounds.

"Your luggage has been picked up, gentlemen," said one of the men, who Gerhard felt must be the crew master. "It should arrive here in about an hour and it will be brought to your room."

"Let's see your charts," said Karl. The crew master led the group into the pilot house and pulled several rolls of charts from an overhead rack and placed them on the chart table. He stepped aside as Karl unrolled the large main chart. Gerhard placed his briefcase on the pilots chair, removed a small stainless box with the embossed swastika on it, and handed it to Karl. He took it carefully, like one might a delicate antique.

"Slide the lock back," instructed Gerhard. He slid it, raised the top, and looked down at the valuable jewel of slate.

"It's just as you described," he said quietly.

Gerhard reached over, removed the slate, and put it on the chart. He pointed to the numbers. "These are the coordinates. Let's find them on the chart."

Karl looked at the clear marks on the gray sheet of stone and traced them gently with his fingers. Everyone watched and wondered what thoughts passed through his mind at that moment. The pilot house was silent, except for the sound of water washing against the lap boards of the hull, as if the small waves were anxious to move on. Karl reached for the protractor and parallel ruler and leaned over the chart.

"61 degrees," he said

He slid the parallel ruler to the mark.

"4 minutes." He adjusted.

"47.9 seconds-North."

He adjusted, ever so finely—against the flat edge of the protractor.

Everyone in the pilot house leaned over the chart to see the marked line. It ran from land, to water, to land again.

"That's the latitude. Let's plot the longitude."

"5 degrees," said Karl. He slid the parallel ruler to the mark.

"30 minutes." He adjusted.

"30.9 seconds-East." He adjusted, ever so finely.

The two lines crossed. Everyone leaned over the chart to see where.

"Oppedal, Norway," said Karl with a sigh of bewilderment.

'What's there?" asked Gerhard anxiously. "What type of place is it?"

Karl sat down on the side of the pilot house berth. "Nothing much has ever been there, but actually it could be one of the most important locations on the whole fjord, because it's the only place I remember that people talked about."

"That's very confusing," said Gerhard with a bit of annoyance in his voice. "Clarify please."

"Oppedal is now and has always been an important crossing point. That's all. It's the shortest and most direct route from Bergen to the Sognefjord and places north. People don't go there for anything except to cross the fjord. The road is important enough that it has been designated European Road—E 39, but in earlier times it was just a short straight road without a designation."

Karl took his index finger and traced the road. It was indeed a straight shot north from Bergen, but far west of where they were in Balestrad.

"People would boat across the fjord from Oppedal to Lavlk on the North shore even before there was a ferry. It was an important crossing point during the war, too. The parents of my Norwegian workers often talked about Oppedal because they said it was full of German soldiers. They seemed to concentrate there … not anyplace else on the Sognefjord, just around Oppedal. Unfortunately, we're losing our older citizens, and I never hear those war time stories anymore."

Karl unfolded another chart on top to the first one. The scale was different and allowed an enlarged view of Oppedal and the surrounding area.

"There's something else about this place that's unusual." He pointed to the location where Oppedal touched the water.

"I've always been fascinated by the way this sharp pointed bay extended several kilometers from the side of the fjord directly south into the land. It's a safe harbor, a significantly narrow one, and an exceptionally good one—but always an empty one—no buildings of any type."

Gerhard looked at the enlarged view on the chart. Karl was right. The chart clearly verified a sharp "V" shaped wedge of water that unexpectedly detoured from the main fjord. It looked exactly like a hanging icicle.

He also noted that Route E-39 followed the side of the hanging icicle bay to the Sognefjord, then east across land for a short distance to a wide open space of water. It looked like a bay, but a very marginal one without much protection.

"That spot you're looking at is now the terminal landing site for the ferry," said Karl.

Just then a launch pulled up alongside and tied to the crew boat. Karl motioned to the crew to stand by. He pulled the main chart out of the stack and pointed to a position on the north shore.

"We're here in Balestrand. Oppedal is here, farther west and on the other side of the fjord. We can make it in about an hour in the launch."

They boarded the launch, the crew shoved off, and they were on their way. The steep mountain sides of the fjord served as a wind shield and kept the waves low. The launch picked up speed and flew over the tops of the ruffled waves like it was walking on water, with hardly any wake behind the boat. About forty five minutes passed and Karl pointed to the outline of a large vessel off their bow.

"That's the Oppedal ferry. She's crossing to the north shore. We'll be there soon."

Once they arrived at Oppedal, Karl had the captain stand several hundred meters off-shore so Gerhard and Wolf could get their bearings. He pointed to various positions and explained what they were. Gerhard found the sighting from the sea more challenging than he expected. The shore line looked dimensionless from the boat, much different than it did when he looked down on it from a paper chart.

"There's the ferry landing. It's in that marginal bay that you saw on the chart."

It all looked flat to Gerhard.

"There's the entrance to that long narrow icicle bay. You'll note the interesting hook at the mouth of the bay—there's plenty of shelter back in there."

Gerhard could see the bay opening, but not the hook.

"Several cars on E-39. They'll line up for the ferry soon."

Gerhard could see the cars.

Karl motioned to the captain and the launch took off for icicle bay—past the hook of land at the entrance, and into the safe water behind it. The boat slowed to a stop, and then just floated within the circular ripples of its water space.

"What's the depth?"

"Four hundred meters," answered the captain.

Gerhard looked around. Karl gave him binoculars and he traced the shoreline along the E-39 side.

"Lots of trash—old steel beams, timbers."

He switched his gaze to the opposite side.

"Just big rocks. Let's go in further."

The captain heard him and put the launch in gear. They moved forward at six knots—a good speed to look carefully. They moved well into the bay before Gerhard said: "That's enough. I've seen all that I need to from the water. Let's go back and return tomorrow with a truck. I want to walk about and climb down the side to the water. Maybe collect a few items from the shore."

The sleek launch made a comfortable 360 degree turn and headed back toward the bay opening, then out into the open waters of the fjord, a ten degree turn to starboard, and full throttle to Balestrand.

The Norwegian sun wouldn't set for many hours, but the air had turned cool and it felt like evening. They went below where a crew member served everyone a gigantic mug of coffee with several shots of Irish whiskey.

Suddenly, there was an era of cheeriness aboard. Wolf nudged Karl and gestured for him to look at Gerhard who sat motionless with a gazed look on his face, his hands clasped loosely around the hot mug.

"He's thinking about something," said Wolf.

Then Gerhard came alive. He looked up at Karl and said, "I'd like to have a party."

The comment surprised everyone and brought an immediate hush to the chatter.

"Well, join in. We've got one going now."

"No. I used the wrong words. I'd like to have a luncheon—a luncheon for the senior members of the surrounding villages who lived here during the Second World War and remember seeing the German soldiers around Oppedal. I'd like to meet them, talk with them, and listen to their stories."

"Now that's a great idea," responded Karl with gusto. "Having a luncheon for our senior citizens is something that we should have been doing all along. When do you want to do it?"

"Tomorrow."

"Tomorrow?" repeated Karl, with some doubt in his voice and wrinkles on his forehead. "I'll put my people on it and I'm sure we can get it arranged in time."

Karl began to get caught up in the luncheon idea. Ideas formed and spilled out as approved plans. "I know that some of the people can't drive anymore so I'll send a car ... or even a boat to pick up each one. We'll begin with light hors d'oeuvres ... say shrimp ... maybe berries and cream ... then the main course could be salmon or something. I'll talk with the chef ... we'll figure it out. We'll have the luncheon at the Knudsvig."

"I'll pay for it," said Gerhard quickly, as he tried to get a word in between Karl's rapid fire thoughts.

"No thank you, sir. This will be my pleasure. I hope this luncheon for seniors will become a regular part of the Olsson Brothers civic duties. More Irish anyone?"

The launch kept a solid plane on top of the waves and was making good time. Karl went forward into the pilot house and talked with the captain, then made a few calls on the radio. They arrived in Balestrand with plenty of daylight left and tied up next to the crew boat.

"I'd like to get an early start in the morning so we can get back in time for the luncheon," suggested Karl. "How about 7 o'clock?"

"We'll be ready. Are you still okay with the luncheon plans and how many guests do you think you can contact?"

"I talked with my office about that during the run back. We hope for six guests, all of whom should have been called by now. I'm going to check with the office soon and I'll let you know the latest news in the morning. I'll be parked right here."

Gerhard and Wolf found their luggage in the room and got ready for dinner. It was a smorgasbord, literally, and a grand one at that. Sleep was easy, but the Norwegian night was short.

The sunlight beamed through the wide room windows and made an extra morning doze tough to get. So they got up and dressed for the drive to icicle bay. Neither Gerhard nor Wolf had any interest in breakfast—more food now was out of the question after last night. They were at least thirty minutes ahead of schedule so they ambled out of the hotel to the marina—only to find Karl sitting in his truck waiting for them.

Actually, he had his cell phone in one hand and the dashboard microphone in the other. He was at the office doing business. They both walked to the shore to wait. Wolf skipped a couple of stones across the water to pass the time.

"Okay, I'm ready," yelled Karl.

They climbed into the cab of the big pickup and were on their way.

"We're going to take the north shore road along the Sognefjord this morning to Lavik, then we'll drive onto the ferry and cross to Oppedal. Should take about thirty minutes in the truck and fifteen more on the ferry. What do you plan to do when we get there?"

"Look for signs of German troops. I know it's going to be difficult to find anything because the war happened seventy years ago. I'm willing to take a shot in the dark. You never know what might turn up."

They drove on. Wolf commented several times about the severity of the mountain sides. "They're so sheer ... the sides just disappear straight down into the water. It must be tremendously deep around here."

"One thousand three hundred meters deep," replied Karl in a low and resonant voice.

The answer jostled Wolf's mind and he had no further questions.

"Tell me about the arrangements for the luncheon?" asked Gerhard.

"Six people confirmed that they'll attend. Seemed happy to have been invited. I think they'll be a good group for you."

"What can you tell me about them? Any insight up front would be helpful."

"We have four women and two men, all were in their late teens or early twenties during the war. One of the men had a position in a shipyard, the other was a headmaster of a small school system outside Bergen. We have a newspaper editor, a nurse, and two housewives among the women. They're all around ninety years old now and we may not have many more chances to learn first-hand what it was like around here during the war. I'm so glad that you thought of this luncheon idea. We're going to learn something about our own history from the folks who lived it."

The ferry was boarding cars when they arrived at the north landing, so they drove through the gaping mouth of the boat and crossed the Sognefjord without delay. The first thing Gerhard wanted to do when they exited the ferry was drive along the top of the ridge above the ferry landing. Good thing Karl had a four wheel drive truck because they formed their own road among the rocks the moment they left the smooth concrete of E-39. No one seemed to mind the bumpy ride.

"We're pretty much above the ferry terminal now," Karl said as he stopped the truck. Gerhard jumped out and scraped the ground aside with his foot in various spots until Karl gave him an axe handle from the truck bed. All they found were modest amounts of modern day trash. Nothing special.

"What's this?" asked Wolf as he held up part of an old boot.

"Bring it over to the truck bed," said Karl as he lowered the tail gate to serve as a table.

Gerhard looked at it closely. Only part of a side remained, but it was a leather side—a scuffed section of a heel clung to it. The old boot had been in that spot for a long time, but was it long enough to be there 70 years? He put it in the truck bed and closed the gate.

"I'd like to get down to the water on the other side of the road—the place where I saw the timbers."

There wasn't an easy place to pull off of the road on the icicle bay side, so they stopped on the other side and walked across the road to the bay. Karl chose well—the timbers and steel girders were almost directly below their position—far below. All three of them looked down at the water. Gerhard started slowly down the steep side.

"Can you swim?" asked Karl in a commanding voice

Gerhard paused and said, "No." He felt Karl's hand on his shoulder.

"Come back up, please."

Gerhard followed the instructions.

Karl looked him straight in the face and in a quiet calm voice said: "I can't keep you from going down there, but I can keep you from drowning."

He got a boat line from his truck and tied it around Gerhard's waist.

"Explore away," he said.

Gerhard inched his way down the steep side as both Karl and Wolf played out the line. He reached a group of timbers and checked all of the visible sides. He pointed to a place on one narrow timber and waved to Karl and Wolf. Then he moved to the nearest steel beam, dropped to his knees and actually laid on the ground upside down to read something, waved his hand, and began to climb back up the slope. Karl and Wolf retrieved the line as he advanced.

"This could be important," said Gerhard as he reached to top. The others gave him time to catch his breath. "You can't see it from here, but that narrow timber is banded in steel. The word 'Germany' is etched on each band—it's worn, but still readable. It's also etched on the beams. The words mean that either the Norwegians ordered it and built with it … or the Germans did."

CHAPTER 18

Karl's office staff found their boss's positive attitude about the senior luncheon highly addictive. There wasn't a complicated list of things to do, just a shortage of time—they only had a few hours to contact the guests and arrange the luncheon at the Knudsvig Hotel.

Karl usually initiated a project and followed it through to completion, but he never did any of the hands on work to get it done. The staff did it. That was okay with them because he was a good CEO with many companies to oversee. But this project wasn't about business as much as it was about local people. That made it personal.

The invited guests were special local villagers who had a unique perspective into an historical era that ultimately affected them all. They were pleased to have been invited to lunch by the Olsson Brothers.

Frankly, they liked to reminisce about their experiences during the war. The fact that a guest would be present who actually wanted to listen to their stories was like an extra dessert. The staff found the seniors alert and feisty, which in retrospect, may have triggered the events that were to come.

Mrs. Knudsvig reserved the finest private dining room in her hotel for the event. She put extra leaves in the table to make it longer.

"More space, more comfort," she said.

Even the chef and the serving staff were excited. Karl arrived at 11:45, just to check for unexpected problems, but his administrative assistant was already on the premises and made sure that there were none. Of course, no one ever had to check behind Mrs. Knudsvig—everything was perfect whenever she was in charge of anything.

The luncheon guests arrived in groups all about the same time and each took a chair that Mrs. Knudsvig had tactfully placed in a large circle just inside the entrance of the dining room. Gerhard arrived at the same time. Wolf decided not to come because he didn't want his steel hand to intimidate the conversation.

The staff served a glass of white wine to everyone while Karl walked around from chair to chair, introduced himself, and made sure that the seniors knew each other. Most did. They were having a good time. The conversation was peppy. Karl tapped on an empty wine glass for attention, but most of the seniors were hard of hearing and didn't hear the cling.

Mrs. Knudsvig noticed the lack of response and feared a broken crystal if Karl tapped harder. She reverted to a procedure in common practice in her hotel—she walked into the middle of the circle of chairs, removed a small dinner bell from her apron, and rang it. She got everyone's attention.

"Thank you Mrs. Knudsvig," said Karl as he began some short introductory remarks, which included a warm welcome to the seniors. "We have a special guest with us today who has traveled all of the way from the famous Melk Abbey in Austria to meet you and listen to your experiences along the Sognefjord during the Second World War. He's currently gathering information for a project about activities around Oppedal. Please welcome Herr Wilhelm Gerhard from Germany."

There was very light and only scattered applause, then complete silence. Mrs. Knudsvig noticed the lack of response and rang the bell again.

"Luncheon is served."

The table was a rectangular one. Name cards were in place, three seniors along one side, three along the other side, with Karl and Gerhard on the ends. A small cup of soup was served first followed by the main course of baked salmon. The seniors talked with each other and with Karl, but not with Gerhard. The dessert of snowberry ice cream was a big hit.

Karl cleared his throat and began to speak. He thanked the seniors for attending the luncheon and expressed an interest in having it again on a regular basis. They agreed. He asked the woman on his immediate left the retired newspaper editor and author of two books regarding the history of economic development in Norway, if she would describe some of the economic hardships that confronted Norwegians who lived in the

Sognefjord area during the war.

She said there were many problems, most of which were caused by the Germans, and that she had nothing further to say. Her sharp abruptness was a shock to Karl and Gerhard, but apparently not to the other seniors.

Karl moved on to the next person, the man who worked in a shipyard for many years, and asked him what it was like during the war and if the Norwegian shipbuilding industry was viable then. He answered that the business was a disaster and only improved after the war was over. He had nothing further to say.

Karl asked the housewife who sat next to Gerhard to tell about her experiences.

"They killed my husband," she said. She looked at Gerhard.

The anger that was on display was obvious to everyone. Never-the-less, Karl asked if anyone else had anything positive to add to the conversation. No one did. Gerhard recognized the harsh attitude of the group, got up, excused himself, and slowly walked from the room.

Karl exploded.

"Your actions today were an embarrassment, not only to me personally, but to every Norwegian. Gerhard wasn't even alive during the war. He had nothing to do with it. In fact, if it was not for Gerhard, my brothers and I would still live in Sweden."

He explained how Gerhard convinced the government to allow his family to move to Norway and start their many businesses, which now employ thousands of Norwegians. The seniors sat motionless, their expressions unchanged. Karl continued.

"You showed the same prejudicial disrespect to my friend because he is German, that Norway showed to my family because we were Swedish. Will this hatred ever stop?" pleaded Karl. The retired headmaster offered a sour response.

"He's German and Germany started the war."

Karl shot back with his own stinging response.

"The German people didn't want the war. The Nazis did."

He stormed out of the dining room.

What transpired immediately after Karl left the dining room was unclear. Some said the seniors sat at the table and talked. Some said they left in little groups, just like they arrived, and moved to the veranda to talk.

Others said the whole bunch went home. Regardless of which version was correct, no one could have foreseen what happened next. It was a spontaneous life changing event that left the harsh comments around the luncheon table in the distant past.

Gerhard was unnerved by his treatment in the dining room and retreaded to his room. Wolf found out what happened and decided to let him alone for a while. He felt Gerhard would recover best with some quiet time.

Thirty minutes passed. Wolf ordered one of Gerhard's favorite cocktails and brought it to his room. He was sitting on the patio staring at the gleaming Sognefjord. Wolf sat with him. Gerhard wondered what to do next and they talked about various alternatives.

There was some type of a sound. It was off to the side of the hotel—around the corner. Neither of them paid any attention to it and continued to talk. There it was again, but now the sound was clear and definite. It was the sound of a screaming young woman.

Gerhard leaned forward on the low wall of his patio for a better view. She came around from the side of the hotel in clear view now. She was running ... chasing something down the parking lot. It was a little kid in a red wagon rolling straight for the water and picking up speed. It all happened so fast. The wagon went right over the edge into the deep fjord.

Gerhard put one hand on the short patio wall and flung himself over it. He raced at top speed with all of his might across the lawn to the parking lot and jumped in the fjord feet first. He went under. He opened his eyes and saw the little kid floating next to him in the clear water. Gerhard kicked and pushed the kid up.

They both surfaced, but they faced the wrong way, towards the open fjord. Land was behind them. Gerhard grabbed the kid by his arm and flung him around the other way. It took several tries. Then he kicked and pushed the kid toward shore. Someone else jumped in. It was Karl. Together they got the kid to shore where other people pulled him out of the water. Then they pulled Gerhard out. The little boy sputtered water out of his mouth, but he was okay. Gerhard looked down. Karl was still in the water.

"You son-of-a-bitch," yelled Karl back up at him. "Why the hell did you jump in the water when you couldn't swim? You could have drowned!"

"I forgot," replied Gerhard in a slow solemn voice.

A wobbling sound of an old siren wound down upon the arrival of the Balestrand police car (Police office hours, Monday through Friday, 9-5, closed weekends). They made sure that the youngster was in good condition, and then dispersed the curious crowd of under twenty. Gerhard returned to his room with Wolf's assistance, to shower, clean up, and rest.

Karl was whisked away by his staff for the same purpose.

The hours passed.

It was seven o'clock in the evening. Wolf convinced Gerhard to go to the dining room for something to eat.

"Just a bowl of soup. It would do your body good."

They walked together, slowly, toward the dining room. Gerhard wasn't interested in another huge buffet or being around lots of people. He almost turned back when he spied the waving hand of Mrs. Knudsvig held high in the air. She pointed to a quiet table for two in the far corner and they plopped into it with a sigh of relief.

"Just a bowl of soup for each of us," said Wolf.

Mrs. Knudsvig served the soup almost instantly— along with a rolled up note, tied twice with a dark colored ribbon. Gerhard unrolled the note and read it.

> Dear Herr Gerhard,
> May we have the honor of your company
> for breakfast tomorrow morning at eight?
> Respectfully,
> The Seniors

He handed the note to Wolf, who read it, then shook his head and said, "What a surprise. This is actually a friendly note. You're going, aren't you?"

Gerhard didn't answer at first—he just sipped his soup. Wolf wondered why the delay. Gerhard still didn't answer—he just sipped. Then a response.

"I have a funny feeling, Wolf. For some reason, I just don't give a damn. At least fifty percent of me wants to get on my private rail car and ride away from here. The other fifty percent tells me to stay. What do you say?"

Wolf was surprised that Gerhard asked him such a personal question. He thought about how to answer.

"It's only natural to feel pulled in two directions. They said mean things. I think that was because they saw the war—we didn't. We don't owe them anything … except, possibly, the benefit of the doubt. I think you should go. I'll be with you this time."

Gerhard and Wolf walked into the hotel breakfast room at eight the next morning. Mrs. Knudsvig waved them into the same private dining room where they had the luncheon the previous day. The six seniors were seated at the same table, but they all rose and applauded as Gerhard entered the room. He was stunned at the reception.

The retired headmaster asked everyone to take a seat, but he remained standing. Then he offered some brief and unexpected comments.

"Herr Gerhard. We were mean and hateful to you yesterday and we apologize. We're old and stuck in our ways, but that doesn't make up for how we acted. Your heroic action yesterday demonstrated the worth of a human being without regard of who they were or where they came from. That little boy you saved yesterday was my grandson. You didn't know that, and it didn't matter to you because saving his life was something that needed to be done and you did it. I'm forever grateful that you came our way. Now, we've ordered breakfast and included some items which I understand are among your favorites. We have many interesting stories to share with you about Oppedal after we eat."

The hotel staff served Gerhard first, then Wolf, then the seniors. They put a Norwegian sized plate stacked high with hot blueberry pancakes, slightly burned on the edges, in front of Gerhard. The aroma was sinful. Then a second plate... fried eggs, over light, with sausage and potato slices.

Everyone dipped with a ladle from a big bowl of sliced peaches and cream for dessert. The staff cleared the table, left the coffee, and closed the door behind them.

They talked for about an hour—maybe more. It seemed that something most unusual did indeed occur at Oppedal during the war.

Regular German soldiers weren't part of it, they were mostly Nazis. According to the seniors, the soldiers had a tall fence built along the bay vehicles. This shut down the little ferry that was in service and stopped the local people from crossing the Sognefjord. The Germans discovered the closure was also very inconvenient for them and ordered the ferry to keep operating.

The seniors tried to describe what was under construction, but couldn't agree on the name for it. The retired ship yard worker called it a dry dock because a small part of it was built with timbers to create a type of under water slide, and the rest of it was constructed above the sea. However, it was completely covered and that wasn't normal for a dry dock. It was also narrow and long, perhaps 50 meters long with a huge winch motor at the far end. The construction above the water resembled a lean-to. The roof was made of steel sheets with steel beams driven deep into the side of the ground above the water, but parallel to it— and made to lean over the water.

Apparently the Nazis first tried to pound the beams into the water bottom in the normal way, but couldn't find the bottom, it was too deep, thus the lean-to shape. The soldiers put rocks, branches, and even boulders on top of the lean-to. It blended into the land and looked very natural, like a normal outcropping of land. A couple of the seniors brought old photos of the site, four in all. The pictures were taken secretly, of course, but their visual description of the lean-to idea and the way it was covered with rocks was very accurate.

Gerhard found it interesting that up to this point no one had discussed the purpose of the site. What was the construction for? He was about to ask when the ship yard worker offered the answer. It was a shocker!

"Our neighbors in the village came back from working at the Oppedal site one evening with the damnedest news you ever heard. They said we wouldn't believe what they found in our lean-to when we got to work—a submarine. We all talked about it and decided that the lean-to/dry dock was made not to build or repair submarines, but to store them— not any submarine, just this particular one because it fit on and within the timber supports so perfectly. It wasn't a one man mini sub or a big ocean going war one with torpedo slots and deck guns. It was more of a mid-sized submarine—and a real special one—no guns, just slick and smooth with a real window on each side. We found out later from the Nazis, that the submarine was being readied for Hitler."

Gerhard was thrilled at the information he was being given. It was far more exciting than anything one might expect from a breakfast meeting. But the seniors weren't finished. More thrilling information was just ahead.

The seniors told how the Nazis didn't allow any more local people to work at the Oppedal site after the submarine arrived. Only soldiers were allowed in the area. Some of the villagers started to keep records of how the area was guarded and when.

One guard was stationed on the shore opposite the 'hook' during the day, and two more patrolled the submarine as it rested in the lean-to, but this was only during the day time. They were gone during the night. Only two guards walked about on the road above during the night.

The seniors said they couldn't believe that only two guards represented the entire night time security force for Hitler's submarine, and they were above on the road, not below at the submarine.

For some reason, Gerhard got the idea that the submarine was hidden in the storage building for a short period of time, and then it was to be taken away, but he was dead wrong. The stories and conversation continued.

The seniors explained that the Nazis were busy preparing the sub for a trip, they thought. Trucks arrived daily with boxes of various sizes, which the soldiers put on board—lots of equipment, freeze dried food, expensive clothes—and surprisingly, several cases of Beaujolais Nouveau. A small group of sailors worked all around the sub for long hours—connecting systems, running motors, and turning things on. The Nazis were getting the submarine ready for someone special.

The required lights-out policy at night allowed the villagers to easily sneak about town and hold small meetings with each other. Sometimes the discussion was simply which of them had chickens that were laying or where they could get some milk or bacon, but they always talked about the submarine, and what to do about it. They decided to destroy it, if they could. The retired school teacher lady, who had been relatively quiet up to now, burst dramatically into the discussion.

"I remember the meeting at our house that night. I was so young and timid, but my uncle was just the opposite. He could do anything. He said he could get dynamite because his job was building roads and they used dynamite to clear road paths. He wanted to blow up the submarine. The villagers liked my uncle's idea. After much discussion about the best way to do it, they decided to swim to the submarine during the night, set the dynamite, and swim away. All of the men volunteered to be the swimmers, but my uncle said no, only the best and strongest should go. All of the men said they were the best and the strongest. We had a problem. No one knew how to pick the men, except my uncle. I can see him now as he walked around the room and said, we'll have a contest. Someone asked how they could stage a swimming contest in the water in front of the soldiers. We'll do it without water. We'll hold the contest tomorrow night. All those who want to be in it should be at our house at midnight.'

The people around the breakfast table were riveted in place. Gerhard listened with his mouth open, motionless. The seniors had never heard this story before, especially from one with such first-hand knowledge of it. All elbows were on the table, bodies hunched forward waiting for more. It was a pretty good bet that this teacher never had a more interested audience.

"Word got around about the contest," continued the teacher. "Small groups of people wound through the dark village streets that night, straight to our house. It was packed. Some were there to watch, others to participate, but no one knew what they were going to participate in, except my uncle.

"The men were getting noisy when our big hall clock chimed midnight. My uncle told the men to take off their shirts, get on the floor, and lie on their stomachs. About twenty did. Then he explained the rules. The contest was going to be pushups, but to his count of cadence. Up on the count of one, down on the count of two. Anyone who broke the cadence or couldn't keep up with his count would be disqualified and should leave the floor. The three men who remained would be declared the strongest and best. They would be our swimmers . My uncle didn't waste any time. All quiet! Everyone became so. Then he said: Get ready…get set. One … two … one … two … one….two .. .one……two. He changed the cadence. It was tricky. The men quickly learned that they had to pay close attention to my uncle's cadence. The spectators realized it too and they kept absolutely still. He went faster … one … two ... one … two. Then he held them in the up position. One……..two… one…There was a lot of grunting. The men were having trouble.

"My uncle kept up the cadence and the men followed. Suddenly one man plopped on his face. He dropped out and left his space. My uncle continued and so did the men…one…two…one………..two..one. A man in the middle missed the cadence and dropped out.

The count went on. Another dropped by the side. Soon, only five men were left. It was so very exciting, probably the most exciting contest I ever watched. By that time the number of remaining men dwindled to four. Only one to go. My uncle went faster. One .. two..one … two..one ……… and the fourth one fell. We had our strongest and our best. We had our three swimmers."

Everyone at the breakfast table cheered for the winners. It just seemed like the proper thing to do. The splendid story of the strenuous contest exhausted them all. The seniors called Mrs. Knudsvik to take away the hot coffee and bring ice water. The need for a short break was real. Something else was real, too.

Gerhard and the six retired seniors bonded. It was probably the story telling and the way they interacted with each other that made the difference. Gerhard leaned back in his chair during the rest period, and in a casual voice posed a question to the great story teller.

"Did the villagers actually dynamite the submarine?" The once timid little school child, and now retired school teacher replied: "Hell yes!"

The laughter was spontaneous. The stories continued.

The villagers talked about how to destroy the submarine during several night meetings. They made an important decision to do it during bad weather, because there was a chance that the two guards on the road might be inside and least likely to see anything outside. Rain was predicted for most of the night, the day after tomorrow. It would be done then.

The day arrived and the rain started on schedule. Light amounts began to fall at dusk. The villagers were fisherman with a good understanding of weather. They knew that the rain and wind would pick up later and could interfere with reaching the site.

They decided to jump ahead of the bad weather. Darkness set in as the three swimmers were taken by an outboard motorboat to the side of the Sognefjord just above and north of icicle bay where they waited on the shore line in the shelter of crevasses and boulders for night to arrive. Each man carried a sealed bag with three sticks of dynamite inside. They didn't have to wait long.

Night fell and the rain started as predicted, but harder than it needed to be. The wind was unnecessarily gusty—it drove the rain in sheets, than backed off for a while, only to repeat the process a minute later.

The wind blew from the east, directly out of the Atlantic Ocean, right down the fjord. Swimming into it would have been impossible so they were glad they took the preemptive move by boat ahead of time. One of the swimmers wanted to start, but the other two felt it would be best to allow the clock to move deeper into the night and the rain and wind to worsen.

Each swimmer worked at the submarine site at one time or another so they were familiar with the location of the beams and timbers and how to place the dynamite sticks. Although they previously reviewed the mission and how to accomplish it many times in the past, they discussed it again and again, while they sat hidden and sheltered among the rocks. An hour passed. The weather worsened. Part of another hour ticked away. They decided it was time to do it and slid into the water.

There was no need to swim just yet. They only had to guide themselves past the rocky shore as the wind pushed them along effortlessly. They reached the hook at the entrance to the bay and maneuvered themselves into its quieter water. It was dark. They swam along the shore, sometimes under the water, sometimes on the surface—cursing the wind for constantly driving them into the sharp rocks. Although it was dark and their vision blurred by wind and rain, they could see the dark mass of the lean-to ahead. They swam hard for another two minutes and reached it. They held on to the structure and remained absolutely still for a full minute.

The wind and rain masked their heavy breathing. Their eyes roamed around the submarine, every corner of the building, back to the submarine, then up toward E-39. Nothing moved. No lights. Just wind and rain. The submarine was all theirs.

The three men went to work, just as the wind calmed a bit. Perhaps it was the overhang of the structure that helped. It not only shielded the submarine from view, but also from the wind.

Two men placed charges at six floor supports that cradled the submarine. The other man placed his three sticks on the supports for the over-hang. They taped them in place on the leeward side of the supports—the longest fuses farthest from the entrance—the shorter ones closer to the opening.

Then the three men met in the middle of the building to confer. They double-checked each other's work and agreed that all charges were properly set and ready. They looked around the structure again and up at E-39—still nothing moved and no lights were visible…just rain. They looked at each other, nodded, and began.

The man responsible for the charges farthest away left first, the overhang man left ten seconds later, followed by the last man who set the closest charges. They each had a Weather-Proof Zippo lighter and every 2.5 minute all-weather dynamite fuse lit immediately with the first try, despite the wind. It was done!

The men waited for each other in case of problems, then dove into the water and swam hard for the bay entrance. They didn't look back. They just swam as hard as they did during the competition that got them here. One minute passed. Each swimmer tried to pick-up their pace, but the effort was inconsistent. Two minutes passed. They began to separate.

BAM! The first charge went off, then another, followed by many more. The men kept swimming, but now they felt renewed and the swimming seemed easier. The rainy sky lit up with a fire ball, then a second one. The swimmers reached the Sognefjord, where the blowing wind picked them up and added extra distance to every stroke. They heard a grinding crunching noise far behind them. Two more explosions. They passed the ferry station. A group of villagers were on the shore waving. They pulled the swimmers out, wrapped them in towels, and took them home.

The seniors were weary. The conversation was intense and they would soon be too exhausted to continue. But they still had three more surprises in their quiver and Gerhard had three more questions.

"Did the swimmers ever get caught?'

The Nazis never found out who they were. A high ranking officer was brought in to conduct an inquiry and required all of the men in the nearby villages to attend. Soldiers with guns stood around the room. The officer demanded to know where everyone was that night and required every villager to verify the activity of his neighbor. But the villagers had their story ready for him.

They told of seeing two black patrol boats loaded with men near the harbor entrance.

The boats weren't challenged by the guards so the villagers assumed they were German ones—after all, the Nazis had a superior security force in place all around the area. That revelation unnerved the officer in charge and changed the tone of the inquiry. The villagers were dismissed shortly thereafter.

"What happened to the submarine?"

The villagers didn't try to blow up the submarine, their intent was to destroy the support structure so it would fall into the water and sink. The hatches were open and the blowers were operating to keep the submarine ventilated. It filled with water quickly and sank, just as planned. The Nazis felt the water was too deep to recover it and never tried.

"So Hitler's private submarine sank four hundred meters to the bottom of the bay—intact, but unrecoverable. Is that how it ended?" asked Gerhard.

The seniors weren't sure how to answer. Surely technology had advanced well beyond were it was during the Second World War, but they were not familiar with modern recovery equipment. It was a question better left to younger people.

The seniors shared the strong conviction that the little bay in which the submarine was stored wasn't what it was always assumed to be. It didn't drop almost straight down on all sides as was commonly thought. They explained that the movement of the glacier that created the Sognefjord caused a sub-sea outcrop to occur—a ledge—

that was about 200 meters below the surface along the side where the submarine was stored.

Anything that slid from the shore would surely rest on the ledge and not slide beyond it into the deeper water. Perhaps the submarine was indeed recoverable.

CHAPTER 19

Wolf's eyes shot open at the clicking sound of a key being slipped slowly into the lock of his hotel room door. He was a light sleeper, alert to anything unusual. The sound of a small key sliding through metal tumblers was unmistakable.

Now it was being turned...one way, then the other...then removed. Unsure if it was a mistake or a threat, he bolted from bed and stuffed pillows under the covers to resemble someone still there.

Again, the slow deliberate sound of a key as it was pushed in his lock. No time to attach his metal hand.

Where's my gun! Damn, I must have pushed it under the covers with the pillows.

The sound of tumblers—the key was being turned. He dove behind the overstuffed chair. The lock clicked. A pause, then the room door flew open—someone stepped partially through, but the hall light cast two shadows. He saw a hand and a gun. PUM, PUM....PUM.

God! They have a silencer. They're pros! The door closed.

He remained behind the chair for a few seconds and listened to see if they'd come back, then he twisted around and sat on the floor. He started to sweat. The experience was draining. His thoughts were jumbled. *They killed me…they just killed me.*

He sat hidden behind the chair for a minute or two in a recovery mode, until a fresh thought occurred.

Gerhard! Is Gerhard all right?

He found his gun, opened the door, and peered into the hall. No one was there. He stepped next door and rapped soundly on Gerhard's door.

"Sir! Sir! Are you okay,"

Gerhard opened it.

"I'm fine. What's going on? It's four in the morning. You look upset. Come in."

Wolf explained what happened. Gerhard could clearly see that his trusted friend was rightfully shaken by the incident and did his best to calm him down. He automatically looked out of the room window and searched the patio area for any sign of the Olsson crew member that he often saw guarding the area. He was on a bench several rooms down. He opened the door and waved him over. It was the crew master.

"Someone just tried to kill Wolf," began Gerhard. Then he reviewed everything that he knew. The crew master was a take charge type of man, with a calm demeanor—just what everyone needed. He mashed a button on his belt radio and spoke into the epaulet-mounted microphone.

"All Crew! Red Alert! Red Alert! Someone attempted to shoot Wolf. Surround the hotel. Advise should any male attempt to leave. Mr. Olsson, please report to Herr Gerhard's room." It was just moments later when Karl was spotted running across the lawn from the crew boat, dressing as he ran. They met him at the door and Wolf explained what just happened. Carl rubbed his chin in thought.

"At this point, no one has been spotted leaving the hotel, so the gunman is still in here with us."

Wolf didn't like the sound of that.

Karl looked at Gerhard. "Your rooms are next to each other and easy to get them mixed up. There's a 50/50 chance that the gunman was after you."

Gerhard didn't like the sound of that.

Karl continued with his well-reasoned thoughts.

"I think it best that we don't let the gunman know the truth, that he shot a pillow instead of one of you. Let's go along with the game and make it appear as though his action worked and someone was shot. We can more easily intercept his thoughts and deeds by misleading him. It'll give us the edge. You two need to stay out of sight. I'm going to put into motion those things that would normally be expected when someone is shot, while the rest of us begin checking and asking questions. First, I'm going to call the police and get an ambulance."

"No, I don't want the police involved," said Gerhard sternly.

"Hold on, my friend. Look at this from the gunman's

perspective. He'd expect the police to arrive if a body was found. Otherwise, he'd know something was wrong."

Gerhard nodded his head. Karl was right.

"Don't worry. I fortunately have some wonderful advantages in this game that we're playing. Local people know me and I know them. I can get special things done easier than most. The tourists and visitors don't know me. I can move about them unnoticed."

He turned to the crew master.

"Check with the men, see what they know, and meet me outside the hotel entrance."

Both Gerhard and Wolf stood in silence and watched Karl orchestrate. The game swirled about them and they could only watch.

"I know this rubs your grain the wrong way," said Karl in an understanding manner, "but I know what I'm doing. Now, both of you stay out of sight and in your room. Don't forget, one of you is supposed to be dead."

He hurried to the front desk where Almar the night clerk was completing the books for the day manager, who was Mr. Knudsvig's younger son.

"Almar we have a problem! There has been a murder in the hotel."

Almar stiffened in shock.

"My crew and I are on top to it and we'll take care of everything. We must keep your guests safe and not mention anything to them about the matter now. I want to speak to Mr. Knudsvig as soon as he is awake. But first I need information from you about some guests."

Just then the day manager, Helmut Knudsvig arrived for work, early. Karl was delighted and repeated what he just told the night clerk, then explained what he needed.

"We're looking for two men who are guests of the hotel. Don't know when they checked in, probably yesterday." Helmut began to check the register, then stopped and looked at Karl.

"I know who you're looking for. I was on duty yesterday when two men checked in without a reservation. We're out here in the middle of the Sognefjord. No one just drops by and asks for a room. But they did. And they acted like they didn't know each other, but they came in together. And that's not all. They didn't come over on the ferry either. It gets here during mid-morning and they checked in around three in the afternoon. I think they had their own boat. Said they wanted to check out in the morning."

"What's their room number?"

"Mr. Smith is in room 307 and the other Mr. Smith is in room 309."

"They both used "Smith?" asked Karl in amazement.

"Right. 'J' Smith and 'R' Smith. Paid in cash. We get all kinds here."

"Did they look English, like they came from the UK?"

"Oh no. They looked like they were from India."

Karl noticed the crew master outside of the front door and waved for him to come inside. Then he turned to the hotel manager.

"Now don't get nervous, Helmut, but I'm going to

step behind the front desk and use your phone in the office to call the police. Don't want any of the guests to hear me." He put his hand on the shoulder of the crew master and drew him close.

"Any change outside?"

"No change."

"Wake up the harbor master and tell him that you're calling for me because I'm busy calling the police. Tell him we need his cooperation dealing with a couple of bad guys. Find out if two men arrived yesterday in a private boat and where it's tied up. Let me know."

The crew master hurried away. Karl dialed the police department.

"Chief! This is Karl Olsson. Yes, fine thanks. Listen, we have a situation here that I want to handle myself, but I need some help from you. No, I don't want to go into it, I have it under control. Just help me out a little, okay? Good. Besides, didn't you tell me that the department needed a new police car, but didn't have the money? Well then, work with me on this and I'll help out with a check. Good. It's simple. Just bring your police car over to the Knudsvigs Hotel and park it in front. Do you have an ambulance? That'll do. Bring the pickup with the ambulance card in the front window and park it in front, too. Yes. I'll fill you in when you get here."

He saw the crew master on his way back to the hotel and hurried out to meet him.

"What did you find out?"

"Two stocky guys with dark hair and beards arrived yesterday afternoon and leased slip A-7. Said they chartered the boat in Bergen and wanted to motor back this morning. It's the same run-a-bout that my son liked. Remember, it was cheap and he wanted to fix it up? Told him, no."

A look of surprise flushed over Karl's face. "I remember that beat-up old boat and the guy who had it for sale. They rented it from Hugo at Bergen Harbor Boats."

He picked up his cell phone.

"Hugo, this is Karl Olsson. How's business? It'll get better soon. Tell me about the two guys that rented the old run-a-bout yesterday. Oh, I just find out these things, you know. Did they just walk up or did they drive up? So, you're keeping their car until they return. What make is it? Yah, it's a shame how some people keep a fine car. Tell me Hugo, is the run-a-bout insured against loss? Like if it sank. Good. Let's have lunch next week."

"Walk with me," he said to the crew master. "These two men are al-Qaida terrorists from Pakistan and they want to kill my friends."

The crew master stopped abruptly, in shock at Karl's words.

"Keep walking. Now listen carefully because we don't have much time. I bet if the locking nuts on both stuffing boxes in their boat were loosened just right, that the shafts would spin the nuts off after only a minute underway from the dock and the boat would fill with water. Probably sink in only a couple of minutes. What do you think?"

"Probably would. I hear that if the transmit wire in the radio came loose that the captain could receive and listen, but not talk or transmit. He'd think the radio was working fine, but no one could hear him if he tried to send a message."

Karl smiled at his crew master. "I wonder if that run-a-bout has any life jackets on board."

"I doubt it," winked the crew master.

"Hurry. We'll cover for you on this end."

The police chief didn't know if Karl wanted any sirens, so he told his driver to blow it a couple of times on the way over just in case. "It'll help keep it in operating shape," he said. Karl pointed to the spot near the hotel entrance where he wanted them to park the police car.

"I want it close, but not too close. Need space for the ambulance. Keep the police car door open and have the officer stand outside and lean against it."

Good staging is everything, he thought.

One of the crew members approached Karl with news.

"The two men left their rooms and were on the way down to check out."

Karl nodded and told him to go over to the police car and engage the policeman in some type of serious conversation.

"You've got to look serious—remember, there's been a shooting," instructed Karl. He waved another crew member over and told him to do the same thing. Karl walked inside the hotel entrance. The two men were checking out. He noticed that Helmut was attempting to delay the checkout, just as Karl suggested. The checkout was over now and the men walked outside. They saw the police car and the ambulance and stopped in front of them.

"We heard the police siren a short time ago. What happened?" asked one of them.

Karl approached from behind with a response.

"No one is sure. The police are quiet about it. Someone may have had a heart attack."

The men smiled, nodded at each other, and walked toward the harbor—just as the crew master headed back toward the hotel. They passed each other in the parking lot and exchanged greetings. The crew master reached Karl and stood next to him. They both watched the harbor. The two men climbed into their boat, tossed off the dock lines, and drifted away out into the harbor. The engines turned over several times, but didn't start until the fourth try.

"Neophytes," said the crew master. "You're supposed to start the engines first, and then cast off."

The boat moved straight across the fjord at high speed, without any engine warm up time. Karl and the crew master watched and checked the time.

Thirty seconds.

A crew member came over with binoculars, took a sighting, and gave the glasses to Karl.

One minute.

They passed the glasses around and each took a good look. The boat was getting smaller, but they continued to watch. Almost two minutes. The white water of the wake behind the boat diminished, and then stopped.

Then the boat disappeared.

Karl told the men to call off the Red Alert and contact the Chief to get the police car and ambulance returned. He walked to the front desk and told Helmut that everything was okay and the hotel could return to normal. He continued down the hall to Gerhard's room and knocked on the door.

"It's me."

Gerhard opened the door.

"It's over. Let's get Wolf and have some breakfast."

CHAPTER 20

A good breakfast helped Wolf get over his near death experience. Karl was tired from the stress of dealing with the gunman and just picked at his food. Gerhard couldn't keep his mind off of the submarine and had no interest in eating.

"The seniors said the sub didn't sink to the deep bottom, but slid off of the land support to an undersea ledge just 200 meters down."

Karl listened and Gerhard talked.

"It's hard to believe that a ledge might actually be there and that Hitler's sub could be resting on it." Karl nodded. "I'd be a remarkable thing wouldn't it?"

Karl nodded again.

"Everyone around here has heard these stories before. I don't mean to sound like a downer, but I've heard variations of this theme over and over again to the point that they're more of a folk tale than a reality."

"You mean they're not true and you don't believe them?" asked Gerhard in surprise.

"Let's just say that I had more faith in the stories when I first heard them, but I believe them less after hearing about them repetitively for decades. The great story about Hitler's submarine has become a Norwegian myth. It's an interesting story, fun to tell and intriguing to hear, but hard to believe for most people. But not everyone. It seems to be part of the mindset of the older people. You know, the 'still believe' type of thing."

Gerhard sat dumbfounded. He never considered that the stories weren't true. He felt tricked, but only for an instant as he recalled how the seniors spoke with clarity and accuracy unlike a story teller searching for images to describe. No, they told the truth.

Perhaps fewer people believed them now, but that doesn't make the story less likely. Time may have changed the perception of things and repetition dulled the belief, but not the reality of the event.

My God! Is it possible that no one ever checked the story?

"What makes you feel that the stories are mostly made up?"

Karl thought for a moment. "Oh, I don't know. It's too far out. It just can't be true, I guess."

"Did anyone dive on the location to look for the submarine?"

"No. It was too deep for the equipment we had them, besides folks were busy working and no one had either the time or the money to prepare an exploration of the site."

"But the equipment is available now?" pressed Gerhard.

"Right. New deep dive apparatus has been developed, but it's expensive and no one around here has it."

"There were a couple of educators and teachers in my group of seniors who told me that Norway's geological history books described the glacier that created the Sognefjord as the same glacier that also caused a sub-sea ledge in the bay at Oppedal. If Norway's history books mention the ledge then that part of the story must be true. Do you know if anyone ever checked the charts for an outcropping at that site?"

"Damn it, Gerhard. This is why I have such respect for you. You get an idea in your head and won't let go. I never heard that the ledge was written in our history books. I thought it was just part of the legend. Now I'm intrigued. I've not heard of anyone who tried to verify it either. I think we should do it. Let's finish breakfast and walk over to the crew boat. She carries the latest charts with a good scale. If the charts show the ledge, I'm willing to motor to Oppedal with the launch and hit the spot with sonar."

The crew master retrieved the charts from the overhead rack and unfolded them on the chart table. Karl immediately found the one he wanted and bent over the chart for a close up view of the east side of the bay. The crew master slid the three legged enlarging glass across the chart to Karl who positioned it over the exact spot. He straightened up almost immediately.

"Oh my God. The ledge is there, just where you said it would be." Karl stepped out of the way for Gerhard to see ... then Wolf ... then the crew master.

* * *

The high speed launch flew over the nearly flat Sognefjord and arrived at Oppedal in less than an hour. The crew master knew exactly what was expected of him as he slowed considerably to pass the hook safely and positioned the launch in the middle of the narrow bay perpendicular to the shore. He shifted both engines into neutral and came to a complete stop.

There was no forward momentum. The iron beams and old timbers were dead ahead, still resting on the shore. He switched on the sonar. The screen came alive with a flashing green light, and then stabilized in seconds. Karl explained what would happen next.

"The sonar should now have a position relative to the target. We're going to maintain its present 45 degree angle for just a short time. The crew master will move the launch in a nudging fashion. He'll slip the throttles into forward and then quickly return them to neutral so we slowly coast toward shore and close on the target incrementally. I'll adjust the sonar angle as necessary. The crew master will watch the shore and operate the boat. I'll operate the sonar, you watch for images on the screen. Any questions?"

"What should we look for and what will we see?" asked Wolf.

"I don't have the sonar pointed at the bottom—it's positioned to view the side of a steep slope. Look for a line outline. Look for shapes. The line of the ledge will be horizontal, and perhaps the submarine will be too, maybe not, but the sub is all metal and the sonar has a feature that is engineered to look for metal. I don't know if the sub is on the ledge, but it'll show bright green if the sonar signal hits it. I'll stand next to you so I can adjust the sonar for reception and to allow for the movement of the launch. I'll help you read the screen. Is everyone ready?"

Karl nodded to the crew master.

He nudged the throttles, then brought them back to neutral. The boat coasted slowly forward a little. He repeated the process. The launch moved ahead. Nothing showed on sonar. He nudged the boat again. Again. Something began to show up on the screen—fuzzy at first. The boat nudged forward. Suddenly a full bright green shape of a submarine!

"Holy Christ, that was fast!" exclaimed Karl.

"It's so clear," declared Wolf.

"And it's not a debris field, either. The sub is intact. Only a few beams and timbers scattered about," said Gerhard.

The crew master held the launch in position as everyone pointed to different places on the green screen and raved over the find. Karl wisely took several pictures of the screen with a digital camera. Gerhard looked hard and long at Karl, but he had to say it.

"Well, well. What do you think of your fairy tale myth now?"

"If I had a hat I'd eat it. This is truly exciting. Thanks for pushing on with the idea."

The water of the Sognefjord kept its morning smoothness as the launch literally skimmed across the surface like a polishing cloth. The water gleamed. The spray picked up rays of the sun and formed a rainbow that raced with them all the way back to Balestrand.

Wolf rode up forward in the pilot house with the crew master. Sitting in the second pilot chair gave Wolf an opportunity to thank the crew master again for his help when the gunman tried to kill him.

Gerhard and Karl were seated in the salon, thinking. Gerhard made some sketches while Karl thumbed through technical manuals and made a few telephone calls. The magnificent wooden Kaviknes Hotel dominated the shore line as the launch pulled into the town harbor.

"I know it's a bit early, but the bar is open and I'd like to have a drink and talk," said Karl.

"But you don't drink," responded Gerhard in a teasing way.

"I know. I'll just have my usual."

The carved wooden table and chairs along the paneled bar wall didn't look comfortable, but the deep red seat cushions helped a lot and the location next to the huge slab stone fireplace provided unbeatable ambiance. They were the only ones in the bar, except for a middle aged couple having a light lunch of a beer and sandwich.

"Good day, Mr. Olsson. You don't often come into the bar so it's nice to see you," said the bartender. "Will it be the usual, sir?"

"Hi Tim. Yes the usual, please."

"And for you, sir?"

"I'll have the same."

Wolf looked around and asked what the usual was.

"Bitter Lemon," replied Karl.

"But that's so bitter. How can you drink it?

"Yes, quite bitter, indeed. It's a sipping drink. Would you like one?"

"Oh no thank you. I'll have a ginger ale and a slice of cherry cake."

"Ginger ale and cherry cake! That's so sweet," said Gerhard with a frown.

"I guess you're right." He waved his steel hand to the bartender and said, "make that a strawberry cake."

Karl said he did some thinking about how to retrieve the submarine while they were in the boat on the way back. "It brought up a question that I'd like to ask." Gerhard leaned forward. "It's about the time you went down the slope at icicle bay to look at the beams and timbers. Were any of the beams still firmly embedded in the ground?"

"Absolutely! I think they all were. I leaned on two of them to help move myself around the rubble and they were solid. Don't know how many were there. I didn't think about counting them"

"Did the beams extend from the ground enough that we could drill a hole in the end?"

"Sure, about half a meter. What's your idea?"

"The Nazis had trouble building on such a steep slope. We'd have the same trouble if we tried it. But they had a different mission. They wanted to hold something. We want to hoist something,"

Gerhard was following Karl word for word. In fact, his mind was generating engineering logic that preceded Karl's words. "And any upward pull applies a downward pressure of equal or greater force. And that requires a stable platform."

"It sure does. The side of the ground is stable, but sloped and oblique to the target."

Both men were now deeply involved in deciphering a solution to the recovery problem. It was easy to see how well they worked together.

"We need to find a platform other than the land, one in a better position to hoist, and one that offers the stability of the land, but without the slant." reasoned Gerhard. "But I don't have one."

"I think I do," said Karl.

The bartender brought the drinks and Wolf's cake. Everything was refreshing. They sipped and talked.

"I made some calls while we were on the launch to see if we could reconfigure some jobs and free up some equipment for a few days. We have several small floating derrick platforms that are on jobs now repairing docks. They are each about 10 x 10 meters. I thought about moving two of them into our little bay and positioning them along the shore and over the submarine. I could add stability to the platforms by tying them to the beam stubs that I asked you about earlier. What do you think about that as a way to start?"

"I like it. It makes sense. It could work," answered Gerhard excitedly. "Let me offer some refinements. Consider connecting the floating platforms to the buried beam ends on shore with steel beams rather than rope or wire. The stiffness would add enormous stability to the platforms."

"That would be a major improvement. I could get old 'I' beams from a lot of places, and real cheap, too."

"How were you going to position and use the platforms?"

"Hadn't thought that far ahead yet. What are your ideas?"

Gerhard took an unusually large gulp of Bitter Lemon and began.

"Put a picture of your platforms in your mind and see if they fit what I'm going to describe. I think you'd have problems if the platforms were used separately. The weight of the mass upon retrieval would be too concentrated. And that's dangerous. You'd have a better ratio of weight to mass through distribution.

"I suggest that you spread the two 10 x 10 platforms apart—say 20 meters—then connect them together with more of the rigid I beam supports. Cover the beams with thick marine grade plywood and suddenly you have a 40 meter long platform—lots of stability, lots of working space. Just lift in tandem and place the sub on the connecting 'I' beams in the middle. Will that work with your platforms?"

"Damn right it would. I think we're working a winner here."

"How are you going to catch the submarine?" asked Wolf suddenly.

Gerhard and Karl looked at each other in a questioning way as they hadn't yet reached this point in the discussion.

"Well, Wolf, I'm not sure. Guess we could gaffe it or get a rope around it somehow. Do you have an idea?"

"From the sonar pictures it seems that the front and back of the submarine are free of debris, each end just points to open water. Why not lasso each end?"

"I don't think we could lower a rope and swing it around each end—for one thing we wouldn't be able to tell where the rope was," replied Karl. "Remember, it's 200 meters down."

"Yeah, I know it's deep, but don't use regular rope. Use twisted wire cable on the low end. You know, the type that has an eye on each end. Just slip one eye through the other, and you have a lasso. Tie the wire cable to real thick rope and lower away. Get the launch out there, turn on the sonar, and watch the wire cable come down. The sonar will pick up the metal in the wire cable. Watch the screen and guide the lasso according to the picture you see on sonar. Move the lasso over an end and you've captured a submarine."

Wolf picked up his fork and finished the rest of his strawberry cake. "Damn it. I just hate it when he does this. It's simple—it's perfect. It's exactly the way we'll do it"

Karl looked menacingly at Wolf.

"We knew what to do all along."

It took only three full days for Karl to reschedule his crews, reconfigure his jobs, get supplies, and move everything to icicle bay. A truly herculean performance. Circumstances required he take both derrick platforms from the same job, a government job. The government was completely upset about the equipment pull off.

Gerhard suggested they remind the government the pull off was consistent with the terms of the contract which required the equipment be maintained in a safe condition.

"Tell them you're taking it away to test it for safety."

Karl did and the government backed off.

A similar situation arose when he filed an application to perform under sea construction work in the little bay at Oppedal. Neither Gerhard or Karl wanted anyone to know that they intended to raise Hitler's submarine. The crowds of both good guys and bad guys would be enormous.

"Let's use the same safety theme. Tell them the purpose is to clear the area of underwater debris to provide safe passage for marine vessels."

Karl did and the application was quickly approved.

He posted the Construction Permit along E 39, above the spot where the submarine lies, just as the first round of Olsson workers arrived and began to prepare the site for the arrival of supplies and equipment. Retrieving a sunken ship was no easy task, especially one that had been under water for seventy years. But retrieving Hitler's private submarine added a dimension of unknown proportions.

The work would begin the day after tomorrow.

CHAPTER 21

Interpol
Field Office
Office of the Section Director
Berlin

Gunter Geer walked around and around his tiny desk over and over again. There wasn't enough room in his small office for such robust activity. Kamza, seated on the couch opposite the director's desk, had to lift his feet every time Geer hurried past. But Geer was excited and there was much to be excited about, so Kamza didn't mind the lifting.

"We prepare, we coordinate, and we implement time and time again, only to have something screwy occur and everything disintegrates. It's enough to make one put in for retirement," announced Section Director Geer, as he rounded his desk again.

"Then something completely unexpected happens, something so marvelous that you're ready to reenlist, countered Kamza. Sounds like you're describing typical police work to me. It sure is a glamorous life, isn't it, sir?"

Kamza lifted his feet again.

Geer stopped the pacing and faced his very competent investigator. "Think of all of the time and money that we exerted to find Gerhard and Wolf, only to have some cop on vacation run into him in a bar, just by accident. It's not fair."

"Fair or not, that's how it happened, and I for one count my blessings that this lead is such a good one. First hand observation from a police officer is pretty hard to beat."

Geer picked up the electronic report from his desk and reread sections of it. "It says here that the officer and his wife were alone in the bar having a beer and a sandwich for lunch when three men came in for a drink.

"The officer didn't pay any attention to them until one of them held up his hand to get the bartender's attention. It was a metal hand. That triggered the officer's memory to an earlier bulletin that described Gerhard and Wolf. He recognized both of them and called his office when they returned to their room."

"But the report said there were three of them," questioned Kamza. "Who was the third guy? Why were they in Balestrand? It's a tiny Norwegian resort town and Gerhard isn't the resort type. Sure would like to have some answers."

"I thought you'd never ask. I'm going to telephone the Norwegian Police Service and tell them what has happened. Then I'll fly to Oslo and plan a capture with them. But I want someone on the ground at the site to provide continuous on-the-spot information about what Gerhard is doing, where he's going, who he's with. Just keep feeding it to me. Can't let this one get messed up."

He pointed directly at Kamza.

"Me?"

Geer nodded.

"I'm on my way. I feel good about this one. I think we're going to get him this time."

CHAPTER 22

The Olsson crew had to delay the start of the recovery because of an unforeseen problem. The connecting points on the beams to the shore wouldn't line up with the beams imbedded in the sloping hill side.

The lugs on the derrick platform side, however, meshed properly. It wasn't a major problem; it just took more time to resolve. And that was to be expected in a job as complicated as this one.

The on-site alteration was made to each beam. They were connected with thick bolts, and the repair worked well.

"This stiffness is going to make a world of difference in the ability of the derricks to capture the target," he told Gerhard.

That was the end of problems with the land based 'I' beams. Four more were laid in place to connect the two floating platforms together, complete with derricks, then covered with marine plywood and finally connected to the land beams. They held firmly and provided a good working surface on which to receive the recovered submarine—no drift, no sway. Everything was ready, and Karl had a brief and final meeting with the crew. The sight of him surrounded by his men reminded Gerhard of a coach and his players discussing a game plan on the field.

I bet there's very little difference between the two scenarios—they both require a leader and team work.

Gerhard noticed that there was no shouting among the men, as was so common on work sites. Karl provided each man with a new personal electronic LAN radio receiver/transmitter. Each could hear the other…each could talk to the other. Everyone knew what was going on. Complete and quiet communications. *So professional*.

The project looked good and gave the appearance of success, but that was partially a perception. The early problems with the connection of the beams should have been a warning, but rather it was just considered one of those things.

The job was far more complicated than originally thought. No one expected what was to follow.

Gerhard and Wolf rode in the skiff with Karl to the launch, which was already in position in the front of and centered on the derricks. Each tough-looking, diesel-powered derrick lowered its steel lasso into the cold clear water.

"We'll lower both lines simultaneously until they reach the sub, then we'll concentrate on working one lasso at a time," said Karl.

Wolf was glued to the sonar screen with play-by-play announcements. "I see the lassos coming down. There's the sub. The lassoes are almost at the sub. What should we do now?"

"Let's just give Karl a chance to work," suggested Gerhard.

They stepped aside and Karl positioned himself in front of the sonar. One derrick was idled while Karl and the other derrick operator began the task of capture. He studied the picture on the screen and gave instructions to the operator. They had no trouble moving the lasso right or left, but they discovered a huge problem with fore and aft. The sonar offered no depth perception of the relationship of the lasso to the sub. They couldn't tell how far back or forward to go. It was a strange feeling to have nearly perfect control of either side, but none in or out. Another unforeseen problem.

The crew leaders brainstormed, but the only idea that offered any relief was to literally bang the lasso against the end of the sub and try to drag it into position. That only resulted in another unforeseen problem. The lasso opening collapsed a little each time it was banged into the submarine. The more they banged, the smaller the opening became.

Karl halted the operation, went ashore, and conferred with his workers. Five minutes passed and he called Gerhard to join him. Karl took a piece of marking chalk and drew a diagram on the derrick floor of a trip line connected at the top of the lasso that reached back up to the platform. The crew proposed to tie the loop open until the submarine was lassoed, then the trip line would be released from above and allowed to tighten around the sub.

"What do you think?"

Gerhard looked up from the drawing and said: "You don't need the trip line. Just tie the loop open, slip the lasso around the sub, and forget about it. When it's time to lift, the weight of the sub will break the tie and the lasso will snug around the sub automatically."

Karl thought the logic was good and the crew agreed it was worth a try. They retrieved the lines from below, tied the loops open, and lowered the lines again.

It was like starting over. They banged and dragged the lasso over and over.

Suddenly the lasso slid over the end and they caught their first submarine, at least half of it. Everyone let out a cheer. Gerhard moved into position to see the sonar screen up close and then took out his iPad and began to punch buttons.

Karl told the operator to stand fast while the other derrick operator started his big diesel engine. It took a while for this operator to get the swing of things. They banged and dragged the lasso just like before and they kept missing, just like before.

Then without warning the lasso slipped around the end of the sub. They caught the other half. More cheers from the crew. Progress had not only shown up, they felt as if it was in their hip pocket. He told the operators to cinch their lines and prepare to lift, when he felt a hand on his shoulder. It was Gerhard with a concern.

"Take a look at the lassos on the sonar screen and mentally draw a line straight up from each side of the sub."

Karl looked while Gerhard talked.

"My calculations predict a high risk of failure when two independent lifting points, each separately controlled, must move an object 200 meters in perfect parallel while maintaining the object perpendicular to the lift."

Karl turned slowly from the screen and looked at Gerhard.

"What the hell does that mean?"

Gerhard searched for different words. "It means it's a long way up and we have nothing to keep the two lifting lines tight around the sub except its own weight. We need perfect balance to do it.

Theoretically, everything will be fine as long as both operators lift exactly together. But we have a good chance of failure if one of them gets a little ahead or behind of the other. The sub will tilt and the ratio of weight to lift will change. One end will tighten, the other end will loosen, and we lose our perfect balance. That could spell the end of the game."

Karl asked the crew to hold up a while.

"Why didn't you tell me this before we started?"

"Sorry. I didn't think of it. I never raised a submarine before."

Karl quickly realized that his comment was out of line. He was embarrassed and wasn't sure how to recover. The words he chose were well received.

"I must confess that I've recovered fewer than ten submarines myself. I appreciate your suggestions and I'd like to find a way to improve our odds against being tripped up by a perfect balance gone astray."

The two of them sat there thinking. A silent crew on shore watched for a signal and a legendary old submarine waited to be recovered. Gerhard tapped the image on the sonar screen.

"Do you have any more of these lassos?"

"Probably a couple."

"What if we capture the lift line? Put a lasso around it then feed one eye through the other and pull the lasso closed around the line."

Karl suddenly saw where Gerhard was going with this idea and interrupted: "Like a slip knot! And we'll do the same thing with the other lift line. Right?"

"Exactly. Then we'll tie the two loose eyes together with rope, probably double rope, and let the whole system slide down the lift lines. It'll come to rest on top of the sub and help hold the sub and the lines in place during the lift. It's not the perfect answer, but it'll improve the odds of keeping the perfect balance."

"And what shall we call this great invention of yours?" asked Karl with a devilish smile on his face.

"It has to have an engineering theme. I've got it! It'll be written as 'Sub B' and it shall be known forever as The Great Sub Bridle. But only if it works."

Karl went ashore to have The Great Sub Bridle assembled while Gerhard and Wolf stayed on board with the crew master. Gerhard used binoculars to watch the crew gather and attach the lassos and lines. He lifted the glasses to E 39 and was surprised to see little groups of people clustered along the edge of the slope watching them. He studied them closely.

Some carried shopping bags, wore denim jackets, some had head scarfs. They were locals who had heard that something was going on at the spot where the submarine sank. The bridle was attached and Karl returned to the launch. They could actually follow the bridle as it slid down the two lift lines and rested on the submarine. So far so good. He spoke to his men.

"Now I want to take up the slack on each lift line. Remember, we do this together, both derricks lift at the same time."

Both derrick operators performed as required and the short amount of slack came out easily. Both ends looked good, the submarine was straight, and the lines were proper with just the right amount of tautness.

Karl gave the "Prepare to Lift" command to get the crew's attention. It was followed by a short review of the importance of lifting slowly, in unison, with care and procession. His review included something most unusual that Gerhard hadn't expected— planned stops.

"Periodically during the lift process I'll issue the command—Prepare to Stop, which will be followed by the command—one, two, Stop. These will be stops for both technical reasons and personal ones. It will provide a time out to check our equipment and to rest a bit. This job isn't physically strenuous, but it's going to be mentally intensive."

Then he added something special.

"We had some small problems thus far during the project, but we corrected and recovered without any harm. But not now! Any mistake now could case total failure. I want to hear if anyone has a question or a problem. Let me hear….." The crew sounded back to their boss.

"No questions. Got it. I'm okay with everything. Yes sir. Ready. Ready."

They were ready.

"I say again…Prepare to Lift…………..Lift"

The recovery of Hitler's submarine was underway!

CHAPTER 23

The lift started well. Both lines were taut, but not under abnormal stress. Gerhard knew the derricks were strong enough, and hoped that the diesel engines would be too. They were. Everything seemed to go perfectly.

The lassos tightened as the submarine came off the shelf, but they couldn't tell if the tie at the top of each lasso broke during lift off as intended.

The image on the sonar screen was clear and sharp, but not clear enough to pick up such a small detail. It didn't seem to matter though, because the sub appeared to be firmly held and perpendicular to the lift. Those were the important things.

Gerhard noticed an interesting demeanor among the crew. They stood at their posts like silent sentinels, on the platforms, in the derrick houses, and scattered about the shoreline. Not a man moved. Not a word was spoken. The crew was on alert! Their eyes were on the lift lines for any sign of a tear. They listened to what the stretching sounds told them as the lines strained with the weight of the submarine. The diesel engines ran, the big drums rotated while the crew checked gauges, variable frequency drives, and an array of machinery for anything unusual.

Karl sat ramrod straight in the launch. He cast an occasional look at the shore crew, but he mostly watched the sonar screen to make sure that the sub stayed in a horizontal position.

Occasionally he would say a word or two into his epaulet microphone, such as 'it looks good guys.' But this was all in the first ten minutes. Change was already underway and unnoticed thus far.

Gerhard squinted his eyes at the sonar screen to make sure he saw it. Karl hadn't noticed it. The change was so slight that he wasn't sure. He watched and waited, then a minute later, he blinked and squinted again.

I think I see a change.

"Karl, don't suppose you have a level in the navigation drawer do you?"

"No, but I have one built in to my pen," as he pulled it from his shirt pocket and handed it to him. Karl was going to ask why he wanted a level, when Gerhard placed it across the top of the sonar.

"It's level." Then he placed it on the sonar picture and leveled it across the submarine. Both men were startled.

"It's not level," they said in unison.

"The right side is a little higher."

Karl went into action. "Operator 1. Report diesel RPM and drive turn."

"Sir, I've got 1,800 RPM and a turn of 1.7."

"Operator 2. Report diesel RPM and drive turn."

"I have the same Mr. Olsson. 1,800 RPM and a turn of 1.7."

They looked at each other.

"Both engines are lifting the sub at the same speed and both drives are retrieving at 1.7 meters per minute. How can one side of the sub move up faster than the other?"

"So far it's a very slight difference and not a big deal. Remember, we just started the lift. I think small variations like these should be considered normal throughout the lift, and on both sides, too. We can always adjust the drives, but it's a nerve wracking procedure because the whole lift format could get out of adjustment in a heartbeat. Let's tape the level on the sonar screen and sit here and watch it for a while. We really need more observation time before we do anything."

The two men watched the screen and the level closely—neither spoke until Wolf asked a question.

"What's the difference between the turning of the engines and the turning of the drives?"

Karl had the answer.

"The RPM, or revolutions per minute, relate to the effort of the engine to pull up the weight of the submarine. The drives, or variable frequency drives, relate to a device that varies the speed of the drums as they wind up the line. At the moment they're both set to wind 1.7 meters of line per minute. At that speed we'll retrieve approximately 102 meters of line in one hour. Another way to say it is that we'll lift the sub 102 meters in one hour and break surface in two hours."

Wolf seemed satisfied. Another couple of minute went by and Karl said: "The right side is pulling faster. It's clear that the sub is no longer level. What could be wrong?"

"It could be a couple of things," replied Gerhard. "I'd like to go ashore and check each lift derrick. You better shut it down so we don't increase the problem before I find out what it is."

The lift lines made some stretching noise at the stop, probably because the sub experienced a slight spring action on the long lines as it came to a halt in mid water.

Gerhard went ashore in the skiff and Karl explained to the crew that this was a technical stop as a problem had been identified and Gerhard was going to check each derrick house.

He immediately climbed into the control house of derrick number 1, talked briefly with the operator, examined several pieces of equipment, and then moved to the next derrick. He stayed only a minute and quickly hurried back on board the launch.

"You didn't stay long on derrick 2. Did you find the problem?"

"Sure did and it's not good. The retrieval drum on number 1 was virtually free of surplus line at the start of the lift, but the drum on number 2 had about 30 to 35 meters of line already wound on it when the lift began."

"Why would that matter? Both drums lift at the same speed. So what's the problem?" asked Karl in a strained voice.

"The extra line increased the circumference of the

drum shaft. Yes, both drums turn at the same speed, but the larger shaft retrieves more line with each turn." Gerhard saw a puzzled look on Wolf's face so he decided to give an example. "Take two wagon wheels—one small and one big. Put them side by side and roll each forward one revolution. The big wheel will cover more ground— or roll farther than the smaller one, even though they both turned just once."

"My God," said Karl. "We can't remove the extra line because it's under all of the line that we've already retrieved since the lift began."

"Right. Gerhard got up, moved to a window in the salon, and looked out. Wolf had seen this behavior before and knew that Gerhard was thinking, working on an idea. He was going to tell Karl, but decided it would be best to say nothing. Suddenly Gerhard asked Karl a surprising question.

"Are you a sailor?"

"No. I'm a fisherman. That's what brought me to Norway, remember. I don't have time to discuss sports with you. We've got problems."

"Hear me out. I'm taking this somewhere."

"Okay," answered Karl in a resigned manner. "I'm not a real hard line sailor, but I've sailed a bit, mostly on a ten meter sloop."

"Remember how hard it was to bring in the genoa in a stiff wind? It was impossible without the winch, right?"

"Yes. Keep going. This sounds interesting."

"Now hold on to that thought. I'm going in another direction. I noticed an equipment box behind and below the control house on derrick 1 marked, Winch. What specifically is in the box?"

"Don't know for sure. Both of these derricks and the associated equipment belong to our reclamation and dock company, which is managed by my little brother. He's the one who tossed the smoke flare under that Mercedes in Bergen."

Gerhard nodded and smiled.

"He's on the platforms with the derricks. Let's ask him."

Karl spoke into his epaulet mic.

"Little Brother, this is Big Brother. Come in please."

Karl handed Gerhard a small LAN microphone and ear piece.

"This is little brother."

"Hey. Gerhard wants to know what specifically is in those equipment boxes on the back of the derricks, marked, Winch. I'm going to put him on LAN so you can tell him and talk together."

Karl nodded to Gerhard to begin.

"What's his name?" whispered Gerhard.

"Little Brother. Everybody calls him that. You can use LB if you want."

"Hello," said Gerhard hesitantly. He didn't have to worry about the name thing because Little Brother began the conversation first.

"Hello Mr. Gerhard. Those boxes hold a built-in winch complete with lock. A button in the derrick house will send it into position automatically, below and behind the main drum. We never used it because we reclaim

274

shore line and build docks and wharfs. That's shallow water work. I know the winch is operational though, because I turned it on once or twice to see how it works."

"That's great news!" said Gerhard excitedly. "I owe you a beer."

"I don't drink, sir."

"Okay, I owe you a steak."

"I'm a vegetarian, sir."

Gerhard shook his head. "How in the world did you and Karl become brothers?"

"I've asked myself the same question, sir. He sure is weird, all right."

Gerhard turned to Karl. "I've got a way around our problem." He had Karl's total attention. "There's just one little catch."

Karl leaned closer and said sternly, "I don't like little catches. They're never little."

But he was intrigued.

"Okay, what is it?"

"We have to start over." Karl reeled backward. But Gerhard started to explain before Karl had a chance to let the idea fester.

"We're lucky as hell. It's rare that we have an opportunity to start over when were only 10 minutes into a two hour project."

Karl's interest returned.

"Here's my recommendation. We change our method of retrieval from one that rolls the line up on a drum, to one that simply winches the line in and displaces it on the platform. In other words, we'll winch in that damn submarine just like you winched in the genoa on that sailboat."

"And let the lines fall free in the cockpit, or on our derrick platform in this case!" said Karl, excitedly. "Nothing winds up, nothing piles up!"

He wasn't about to let up on Karl now, but continued to push and explain the idea.

"Of course, it's completely up to you, but I suggest that we lower the submarine back to the shelf. Remove all of the lift lines from the roll up drum, and turn the drum into the main winch. Wrap several turns of line around the main winch, then feed it down to the new winch we found in the box, which now becomes our secondary winch.

"Wrap just a couple of turns around it and feed the remainder of the line out along the platform. Keep several sailors at the winches during the lift retrieval, to watch for a snag, receive the line, and lay or coil it out of the away. We eliminate our line build up problem and the constant need to adjust the drives by changing the retrieval concept, from roll up to winch in. What do you think?"

Karl didn't have to think about it any longer.

"I don't like to go backward and start over," he said. "It's against my nature and just rubs me the wrong way. But your idea makes solid sense. If we continued with the present course, I think we'd lose more time compensating for the line build up and wrestling with drive adjustments, than if we made the change that you suggest. Let's do it. First, let me call Little Brother and run it by him. He and his crew will have to make it work."

Little Brother liked the idea. They lowered the sub to the shelf and LB and his crew changed the lines and put the new winches in position. It really didn't seem to take long before they began the lift anew. And it went well, but this time there was no lift line build up, just more screeching noise as the lines constantly tightened against the metal winches, only to wind their way off and land safely onto the platform. They kept a sharp eye on the sonar and compared the submarine's position to the little level taped to the screen. Karl used the LAN and checked regularly with his little brother. There were no problems.

They were ten minutes into the lift and Karl asked the crew if they wanted to stop for a break. Surprisingly, they all wanted to keep going.

"We've got the momentum now," they said.

They reached 50 meters after thirty minutes of lifting and Karl decided it would be wise to stop, take a break, and check the equipment.

"Prepare to Stop … one, two. Stop."

Although the crew took a break, the crew master had to stay at the wheel to keep the launch in proper position so the sonar bearing would remain constant. Wolf poured coffee for all on board while Karl took over for the crew master for a much needed break.

Gerhard took Karl's chair in front of the sonar screen to keep an eye on the level of the submarine. Little Brother reported that all equipment conditions were proper. It was a welcome report.

"We're about one quarter of the way up and things look pretty good this time around," said Karl. "I'm glad that we have this little level. It defiantly highlighted the problem of line build up and the degrading lack of load balance before it got away from us. And your sub bridle idea—it's reassuring and gives the project stability."

It was pretty obvious that Karl was feeling relaxed and good about the project. But Gerhard had discovered new problems.

He began to shake his head.

"I'm afraid we have more trouble, and it's worse than the problem we just fixed." He pointed to E 39. "See all of the people that have gathered to watch? Look to the far right. Those are cars of the Norwegian Police Service. I counted five of them. Those are federal police officers. It's interesting that they're not making a move. They're just watching us with glasses."

"Damn," said Karl. "This project seems to go from one problem to another. The police are watching because they've heard the story about Hitler's submarine, too. It's pretty obvious that we're working the spot. They think they have nothing to lose by waiting and watching. I don't think they'll do anything as long as we continue to lift. But it'll be hell when the sub breaks water. They'll descend on us like vultures. I'm not sure what to do."

"Me neither, but we're safe as long as we're lifting. I suggest that we start back up and think about our options as we lift."

Karl took a couple of minutes to explain to the crew that the police have arrived above on E 39 and that they could rush the site once the submarine surfaces. "We could retrieve Hitler's submarine from the fjord, and lose it to the state police. We'll work on a plan as we lift."

"Prepare to lift—one, two. Lift."

Gerhard sat behind Karl, watched him study the sonar, and began to reminisce.

He's a good worker and a good man. Gerhard suddenly felt remorseful. *Perhaps I should have been completely forthcoming with Karl. It was probably true that the police would indeed confiscate the submarine, but they didn't arrive on the scene for that purpose, as Karl believes. The police just stumbled on the recovery project. Hitler's submarine became a bonus for them. They're here to arrest me for the sarin gas job in the United States Capital Building. Every police officer in the world has been after me for years. I've become an Interpol oddity. It's strange—I can look over at E 39 and actually see my potential captors and I know they can see me.*

"Gerhard! Are you all right?" asked Karl.

"Sure, I'm fine. Just thinking."

"We reached 100 meters. I'm going to stop and check things. If everything looks good, I was considering going the final 100 meters without a stop until we're just below the surface. What do you think?"

"I vote for it."

Karl called for the stop and the crew checked all equipment areas. Nothing was amiss. It was almost uncanny to be so problem free after the difficulties they experienced with the first start up.

Karl queried his little brother and the crew about completing the last 100 meters without a stop and they all agreed that it would be a good idea

Karl and Gerhard talked off and on during the last five minutes of the break, especially about how well the winch idea was working. Karl looked up at E 39 and shook his head.

"It seems like the crowds are increasing up on the road."

"So are the police cars," responded Gerhard. "Two more drove up, so we have seven of them now. I've been thinking about what we should do when the lift is over. You know, the plan that we're supposed to come up with. I don't have a damn idea yet. It worries me."

"We've got an hour left. Let's lift and think."

With 100 meters of favorable lift under their belts, they began the last 100 with high hopes that it would be as good as the first half. But neither of them knew what they'd do about the police when the sub reached the top.

Conversation aboard the launch seemed to have fallen over board. The once ample space inside the boat became tight and contributed to the stuffy awkward silence. The minutes, which previously flew past in anxious anticipation of bringing Hitler's submarine to the surface, now dragged on with concern and fear of what would happen when it appeared.

Gerhard, of course, had an additional fear. He became increasingly despondent about the sure trap that awaited him in less than an hour. Suddenly he was resigned to the reality of being caught. *What would prison be like*, he wondered. He found himself talking out loud without realizing he was doing it. Karl listened with interest—Wolf listened with concern.

"I'm very disappointed that I won't be able to explore the submarine. There's something on board that's waiting for me—something the monks felt sure I'd find for them. It's part of the explanation about why the ancient books were desecrated. And if I don't find it, the questions at the abbey will have no answers. Neither will the church. Hell, I don't even know what I'd be looking for."

Karl motioned to Wolf.

"There's some Irish whiskey in the foot locker. Heat it up and serve it to everyone."

Wolf had it ready and served in only a few minutes. The hot drink slid down worried throats smoothly.

Time moved on and the steady lift continued unblemished by problems. The submarine was now only 40 meters from the surface.

"We're getting close to the top. There's increasing natural light around the sub," observed Karl.

Gerhard put the binoculars to his eyes and scanned the ridge along E 39.

"My God! I guess I should have expected it, but I just didn't. There's that same old dented Mercedes parked way over on the left of the spectators. I see three burly men leaning on the car watching us."

"Only three?" smirked Karl. "How interesting! I wonder what happened to the other two? I doubt that they'll be a problem for us with the federal police all around the place."

The lift continued. Less than 20 meters to the top. Karl issued some crew instructions.

"We're closing in on 10 meters. I'm going to call a

stop when we reach that point so we can change lift masters and do a final review. I'll have some words for everyone, too."

"12 meters."

"11 meters."

"Prepare to Stop.......one, two. Stop."

The crowd of spectators along E 39 held their breath and watched like children waiting for a surprise birthday party as the long dark unmistakable outline of a submarine came slowly into view, then stopped and hovered just below the surface. Ripples and little fountains of water gurgled up, pushed from the rising mass below, then fell back and formed widening circles on the water's surface.

"We did it," said Karl.

"Well done," said Gerhard.

They both thanked the crew master for his many hours of steady splendid work. Karl looked out the window of the launch and watched the crew for a few seconds as they scurried about the task of checking equipment. He knew they could hear him as they worked so he began a short rambling speech.

"Little Brother, crew, many thanks for a job well done. Less than a week ago you were scattered over southern Norway, scraping shore sides and pounding piling. You dropped what you were doing and joined me here because I needed you. This time you reclaimed not land, but a unique piece of history ... something no one else had ever done. Hitler's submarine is ready to come ashore. We don't need the sonar anymore, so the rest of the journey is in your hands, Little Brother. I suggest that you pick her straight up, use one derrick and swing the bow in between the platforms and line her up with the other derrick. Then, with both derricks, slowly bring her over the work space between the two platforms and gently put her down. The submarine sank with her hatches and vents open for ventilation so she's full of water. Consider putting her on her side for a few minutes until the water runs out, than right her.

"There's something else. I don't know what's inside this special sub. It's surely crammed with historical artifacts, but we may never get inside to find out. I want every man who hears my voice to pay attention to these next words. Do not turn around. Continue to look in my direction while I tell you something important. I'm sure you've noticed that E 39 behind you is full of local people who have watched us with great interest and great excitement. I want to remind you that a bunch of Norwegian Police Service cars are there too, probably waiting for us to raise the sub so they can seize it. There's also an old Mercedes parked on E 39 with three terrorists inside waiting to do harm to either people or the submarine. They're from the same group that tried to kill my friends Gerhard and Wolf a few days ago. Be careful of both groups. Don't get in their way, but don't be too helpful either.

"One final word and I'll stop talking so you can bring the sub ashore. We may have a chance to get inside the sub. It's a remote chance with the police around, but it's a chance. I want you to keep your eyes open for something if we do. Here is where the mystery deepens. There's an object in the submarine that belongs to my friend Gerhard, but he has never seen it. It has religious overtones and it led Gerhard to this site from the famous Benedictine monastery of Melk Abbey in Austria. Gerhard doesn't know what the object looks like so one could truly say that it is without description. But I want you to look for it. I feel it will resemble the solid look of fearful Nazi Germany.

"Okay Little Brother, Hitler's submarine is all yours."

Little Brother spoke briefly to his crew, then they took their positions as Karl, Gerhard, and Wolf left the pilot house and walked outside to the bow of the launch to watch. The derrick diesels came alive for the final lift and the drums of the steel winches screeched with the pressure of the tight lines.

The submarine left its grave and broke through the surface of the water. It felt air and light for the first time in over seventy years. The derricks positioned the sub just as Karl suggested, then slowly moved it over the working space between the two platforms.

Suddenly the back quarter of the submarine folded like a tin can. The perfect balance was gone. The sub slipped from the safe grip of the lassos and the entire vessel collapsed onto the platform workspace. The back quarter of the sub hit the edge of the platform, cracked apart, and plunged back into the deep fjord.

The remaining section smashed onto the platform with such force that the entire submarine split open like a banana in a banana split. Water gushed out and emptied from the sub in seconds. Hitler's submarine, its innards exposed, looked like a gutted fish. The quickness of it all left everyone, local observers and recovery crew, in a state of shock. Even the federal police watched spellbound at the sight.

It took only a few seconds for the crew to process the event and realize that an opportunity had unfolded before them. They immediately swarmed over the wreckage like bees. They pulled open doors that had buckled during the drop, and hurriedly combed the debris for anything that looked salvageable. Karl realized what the crew was doing and motioned to the crew master to quickly motor to the platform. They just reached the side of the platform and were about to tie up when Little Brother raced up to the launch and handed Gerhard a stainless steel cylinder with a swastika embossed on the side.

"I found this wedged between a bulkhead."

It was what Gerhard came for.

It was like magic the way Karl assessed the situation, assumed control, and began to issue instructions. He told Gerhard and Wolf to go below and motioned for the crew master to motor to the crew boat. Karl held the two boats together when they arrived as the crew master jumped from the launch to the crew boat.

"No time to explain," he told the crew master. "Just follow me, keep your radio on, and stay close."

Karl went into the pilot house of the launch and sped away from the recovery site at a noticeably high rate of speed toward the hook at the entrance to icicle bay. The crew boat was right behind. White spray flew everywhere. He handed the binoculars to Wolf.

"Tell me what the federal police are doing."

"Some are trying to get down the side of the cliff to the sub and the rest are getting into their cars."

"Perfect! Their force is split. They don't know which is most important, reaching the submarine or catching us. I haven't had this much fun since I was a kid."

Gerhard and Wolf exchanged glances. They didn't see any fun in being chased by the police.

Karl didn't slow down as the launch approached the hook—a violation of procedure when a vessel enters or leaves a harbor. Rather, he pushed the throttles forward and increased his speed. The crew boat followed suite.

"Aren't we attracting the attention of the police with this speed?" asked Wolf.

"I sure as hell hope so!" he said, as he nudged the throttles forward even more. Both vessels sent out sheets of spray as they passed through the rocky harbor entrance.

Gerhard noticed a smile on Karl's face. *He must have a plan. God I hope he does.*

Then Gerhard saw it. The big ferry was approaching the Oppedal Ferry Terminal.

Please, please, no more problems.

"Damn! Now the ferry's in our way!"

"It's not in our way," answered Karl. "It *is* our way."

The smile was still on his face as both boats raced toward the big ferry.

"My friend Captain John is running the ferry today." He picked up the marine radio, switched to the ship-to-ship frequency, and called him.

"Captain John this is Karl Olsson. Come in please. I need your help."

"This is Captain John. I see your boats down there, Karl. What do you need?"

"I want to come around behind you—out of sight of land— and put two special passengers on board the ferry through your rear quarter service door. Just slow down a little please, but don't stop. I want to do this on the run."

There was a moment of pause. "The service door is open. Come ahead."

"Get your stuff together and prepare to jump onto the ferry when I come along side," yelled Karl over the noise of the speeding launch. '"The ferry deck crew will be there to help you."

"But the ferry is going back to Oppedal," pleaded Gerhard. "That's where the police are."

"Yah, I know. Isn't this the greatest idea yet? I made sure that the police saw you leave in the launch. They won't even imagine that you came back. Little Brother will meet you with his truck when you get off the ferry. Got to run now. Have a chase to lead."

The launch passed behind the stern of the ship, then came along the far side. The quarter service door was open. Two sailors stood braced in the opening, ready to grab.

"JUMP NOW," yelled Karl.

They did. The service door closed. Karl radioed the crew master to take off for the city harbor at the Knudsvig Hotel. He did. Karl pushed the throttles to full forward.

Anyone on shore who watched the two boats pass

momentarily behind the big ferry now saw them reappear in a spray of white water—the fast launch that once carried Gerhard and Wolf now screamed west on the Sognefjord toward the open Atlantic. The crew boat sped east toward the deep water of the fjord. Karl was playing a shell game with two boats and a ferry.

Fifteen minutes had passed since Karl sped away from the ferry. As CEO of several corporations he never had any time to go boating, until now. He scanned the horizon and saw nothing. The launch felt good under him. The twin diesels purred. He knew that diesel engines benefited from regular full load operation and he was giving them a good workout.

A federal police helicopter, its blue lights flashing, dropped from the sky 300 meters in front of the launch. It pivoted toward the launch, then hovered menacingly in midair just above the water and waited for the launch to arrive. He had expected something like this. He brought the launch close to the helicopter, then slowed to a stop a safe distance from the whirling blades.

"Prepare to be boarded!" came the threatening voice from a bull horn.

The helicopter landed on its pontoons and the rotors were immediately shut down. An officer motioned for the launch to proceed to the helicopter. Two armed and determined looking officers, wearing bullet proof vests, dropped onto the launch.

Karl was ordered below, handcuffed, and told to sit while the boat was searched. The search ended quickly.

"Where are the other people?" demanded the officers.

"I'm the only one on board."

"We were told that you took off from Oppedal like a bat out of hell with several people on board."

"That's most interesting," replied Karl.

Suddenly he decided to borrow an idea from Gerhard.

"This is a company boat and I'm conducting some engine tests under the Government of Norway's Safe Engine Operating Guide. I wouldn't have spectators on board during full RPM safety tests. Rules, you know. Who did I have on board? What did they look like? Maybe they were trying to disrupt the tests. Perhaps I should file a complaint with your office."

The officers looked confused. Even uncomfortable. *I wonder if it would be wise to try a second idea? Hell yes! Gerhard would be proud of me.*

"I believe I know what happened. Another boat was nearby when I started my safety tests. It moved east out of Oppedal at a high rate of speed. I bet that's your boat."

One officer said to the other…"Call in and check it out."

He stepped out on the deck and made a radio call, then came back inside.

"It's confirmed," he said to his partner. "Headquarters verified there was another boat that left Oppedal at the same time this gentleman did. We're very sorry to have troubled you, sir."

They un-cuffed Karl. Then they climbed back into the helicopter, lifted off in a roar of engine noise, and headed in the other direction.

Karl radioed the crew master and told him to turn around and head back to Oppedal at a slow rate of speed.

"A police helicopter may stop you. Be polite. Just tell them that you're returning to a work site."

Then, Karl took out the last bottle of Irish whiskey from the foot locker, started his diesels, and motored casually back to Oppedal. His mission was over.

Gerhard and Wolf disembarked from the ferry and were met by LB and his white pickup truck. It joined the other cars and trucks in the exit line from the ferry and they all headed the same way on E 39, toward Bergen. Every ferry arrival discharged scores of vehicles.

It was a normal, expected, and congested event. At this particular arrival time, a large number of federal police were in the area. They saw the line of traffic coming from the ferry and routinely cleared the road and waved the vehicles through.

CHAPTER 24

The ride back to Bergen was quiet. The day spent recovering Hitler's submarine, with all of the changes in the lifting technique, the fall and breakup of the sub, then the challenges of eluding the police, had been unusually stressful. The truck became a respite. The riders sat alone with their thoughts as the white pickup kept up with the other traffic on E 39.

Little Brother decided there was nothing he could do to retrieve his platforms and derricks until someone decided what to do with the submarine that rested on top of it all. Gerhard couldn't keep his mind off of Hitler's cylinder.

The lucky happen-stance of how it was discovered among the debris and what might be inside kept his thought waves pounding. He was glad that Wolf picked up the newspaper from an empty seat on the Oppedal ferry. It was the perfect size to wrap around the cylinder to hide it from prying eyes. Wolf on the other hand had a more personal concern. He wondered how they were going to get their luggage. It was back at the Knudsvig Hotel.

"Big Brother reminded me about your duffels when he told me to meet you at the Ferry Terminal," he asked LB. "I called a fishing buddy of mine who lives in Balestrand and told him to get your bags and bring them to Bergen. He said he'd tie each one to his Yamaha and would probably be in Bergen about the time we got there."

After a couple of hours on the road, the white pickup truck entered Bergen and drove directly to the Skoltegrunnskaien ferry pier. There in the parking lot was a tall skinny guy sitting on a Yamaha with two duffel bags strapped to the rear fender. Wolf was pleased. They collected their luggage and promptly boarded the overnight ferry to Amsterdam.

Wolf skipped supper and went immediately to his cabin for the night. Gerhard was too wound up to sleep. He leaned on the rail of the departing ferry and watched the elegant city of Bergen disappear into the sunset. He twice bought a glass of wine from the roving hostess and relaxed in a deck chair with his thoughts for over an hour. The events of the day drifted repeatedly through his memory, but his mind constantly produced images of the cylinder.

Perhaps it held the pages of Hitler's diary or directions to a secret location where he intended to hide out. Probably just a list of his officers. Maybe important battle field plans were inside. Then he started to laugh. *It's probably instructions on how to operate the submarine.*

Weariness caught up with him. He returned to his cabin, climbed into his bunk, and fell asleep.

The ship arrived in Amsterdam sometime around mid-morning. They were unsure of the exact time because they were both still asleep, awakened only by the sharp rap of boney knuckles on their cabin door and the hurried voice of a frazzled stewardess who announced,

"All ashore please! We have arrived in Amsterdam! All ashore please!"

They made their way off the ship and into the baggage area of the terminal. Gerhard held the newspaper wrapped cylinder tightly under his arm, next to Wolf. They walked past the line of waiting taxies, to the street where Gerhard hailed a passing cab for the ride to the railroad switching yard. He always felt it was safer to skip the line of cabs waiting for customers and instead pick one at random that was passing by.

The ride to the railroad yard seemed to take a long time. Gerhard felt it was because he was anxious to get there and open the cylinder. Wolf felt it was because the railroad yard was far away from the sea. They arrived around noon and went directly to the yardmaster's office to check in and then a switchman walked them to the side track in the yard where the car was stored. It was good to see it waiting for them.

Wolf quickly thawed some slices of prime rib and made a couple of sandwiches. Gerhard unwrapped the cylinder and placed it gently in the center of the table in the drawing room. Then he poured two glasses of wine and waited for Wolf. He wanted to savor the moment so they sipped the wine, took only a bite of the sandwiches, and talked for a minute or two.

"What do you think is inside?" asked Gerhard.

"Money! A stash of jewels! How about you? What do you think we'll find?"

"Whatever it is, I think it was something very important to Hitler's Germany. I've been carrying the cylinder with me under my arm and it's not heavy. Nothing rattles inside. It's either packed well or destroyed by decades of being under water."

"I think you should open it now."

He picked it up and placed it directly in front of Gerhard.

Gerhard looked at the stainless steel cylinder and wondered if he should disturb the sleeping beast. Perhaps all things would be better if the cylinder was left unopened.

"Go ahead," said Wolf.

Gerhard noticed that the once shiny stainless steel was now black from years under the sea water of the fjord. He rubbed the embossed swastika with his finger. It seemed to be made of a different metal.

"I think you should open it," said Wolf again.

He picked up the cylinder, studied it closely, and found that it was made of a single piece of stainless—the sides and bottom were all one. Engineers referred to such construction as 'unibody.' The top was separate; it fit like a cup over the rest.

"I mean you should open it sometime today, preferably now," pleaded Wolf.

Gerhard put his hand over the cupped top, but he couldn't move it. The top was too tight—surely from the years of being submerged. Wolf came over, took the cylinder and put his steel hand on the top, energized it, twisted, and the top moved. He moved the top a bit more, just to make sure, and then handed the cylinder back to Gerhard.

He turned the top seven revolutions before it came loose, then he removed the top, looked inside, and saw spirals of something. Spiral sheets of metal. Wolf held the cylinder while Gerhard grasped the edge of the sheets and slowly turned them and pulled them out of the cylinder all in one continuous motion.

Whatever they were, they were in perfect condition, just black in color. He carefully removed one sheet from the spiral group. It had German writing on it, etched into the metal sheet. And just as carefully he began to unroll the spiral, to flatten it with his handkerchief wrapped around the palm of his hand, with care not to smudge the etching. They removed a total of six sheets and carefully flattened each one.

Now it was easy to see that the sheets of metal were actually very thin sheets of foil, like aluminum foil except these were stainless steel foil, and each one was numbered. Gerhard spread the foil sheets on the table in numerical order.

"Gosh, a little German newspaper." Wolf was disappointed. He got up and walked to the window. His hope of finding a treasure of diamonds and rubies was dashed.

"Let's just see what's in our newspaper today," as Gerhard picked up a foil sheet and began to read.

Up to this point both Gerhard and Wolf engaged each other in whimsical expectations over the contents of the cylinder. Secretly, both hoped for something special. Wolf counted on actual treasure that registered somewhere in the extra high to sensational range, while Gerhard felt confident that they'd find something historically interesting. Neither expected a mundane bunch of foil sheets. However, the writing was the real treasure.

It was hard to read the etching. The light cast shadows on the marks and played tricks with his eyes. He had to constantly move both the foil sheets and adjust his position relative to the light, but he could read the words. Gerhard read for about ten minutes. Wolf noticed that the more he read the more uncomfortable he became and the more he twisted in his chair.

"What does it say? Is it some type of secret message?"

Gerhard strained to choose his words carefully. Surprisingly, they were just ordinary words, but strange ones. "No. It's more of an answer to a problem."

Wolf was confused.

He read for several more minutes, then slowly put the foil down and looked again at Wolf. He didn't say anything at first. The daunted look as the color drained from his face said it all—he was shocked by what he read. Wolf had seen this happen before with Gerhard and it never ended well. He moved back to the table and took a

296

chair next to Gerhard—to steady him if necessary, but mostly to insure that he heard every word Gerhard was about to say.

"This is a highly technical engineering report."

Gerhard's speech continued to be unusually slow and deliberate. "It details the solution to a new form of manufacturing that Hitler planned to begin after he won the war." Now his speech dropped to a whisper. "It was to be the new Nazi industrial revolution."

Wolf listened intently as Gerhard stared into space and continued his observations in a sluggish cadence.

"It describes the procedures necessary for a country to move from die casting, molds, and traditional metal stamped manufacturing to additive manufacturing where parts and equipment would be made with 3-dimensional printing that used thousands of layers of metal or fiber powder as the construction process."

Wolf leaned forward, closer to Gerhard.

"The report proposes that Hitler employ just a few skilled workers to operate thousands of machines that would print or manufacture a large variety of equipment, and do so with profound quality."

Gerhard became more comfortable with the words now, less shocked by what he read—his voice steadier, but no less filled with surprises. He continued.

"His idea would neutralize the low-cost labor advantages offered by developing countries and dry up their jobs and their money. Nazi Germany would become the richest country in the world."

Wolf shifted in his chair. He was uneasy.

"I don't know much about 3-dimensional printing, but I've heard about it. It isn't new and I don't see how it would work for Hitler, so how could it be so important?"

"Put it in perspective and you'll see the importance. Hitler's report was prepared during the Second World War, early in the 1940's. American engineers first started to use additive manufacturing in the late 1980's. Hitler was more than 40 years ahead of the United States in this idea. But it wasn't just his knowledge that eclipsed the Americans; it was his intent as well. This type of manufacturing had growing problems—the printers were expensive, small, and only small things could be made with them."

"What kind of things?" asked Wolf.

"Like a torque converter for a car transmission, a toy, a sport trophy, a prosthetic finger, a stove burner."

"Yeh, those little things couldn't make a country very rich. So what made Hitler's plan better?"

"The report explains how to make cheap printers and manufacture very big and robust equipment units."

"Like what?" asked Wolf as he got up to pour more wine.

"Like energy turbines and rocket engines."

Wolf quickly sat down without pouring the wine.

"This is pretty major and serious stuff that we found in the cylinder." Gerhard watched as Wolf slowly reached out with his hand and moved his finger along the top edge of his wine glass. Around and around the edge. Faster. It made a high-pitched sound. He continued ringing the top with his finger. The sound screeched higher. He was deep in thought.   Then he stopped, looked up, and made the most profound statement of the evening. "It seems that the writing on the foil was more of a treasure than the diamonds and rubies."

Gerhard wasn't sure how to continue.

Perhaps I shouldn't tell him the rest. It might upset him too much. Just let him think about what he's heard so far. Without thinking about his actions he picked up the bottle and poured more wine for both of them. *I have to tell him.*

He spoke in a slow and deliberate manner, careful not to confuse Wolf.

"The most startling, awesome and gruesome revelation of Hitler's intentions is written in the second part of this report." Wolf didn't move. He was listening hard to Gerhard.   "It combines DNA with additive manufacturing."

"I've heard of DNA. It's a new thing that the police use to catch criminals," injected Wolf.

"It's so much more than that and Hitler was ready to implement it all. It started in 1868, when a young Swiss doctor discovered something no one had ever seen before—the nucleus of cells—or nucleic acid. It's the 'NA' in DNA or Deoxyribo-Nucleic-Acid.   But the unbelievably complex structure of DNA eluded understanding for almost a century until 1962, when Doctors Watson and Crick where awarded the Nobel Prize for unlocking its secret."

"Sure they found the secret. That's great. So what's the big deal?" asked Wolf.

That secret is revealed here, in Hitler's report, written twenty years before Watson and Crick discovered it."

Wolf got up from the table and walked around the drawing room. The culmination of all of the information that Gerhard had imparted was taking its toll on him. Gerhard watched as he moved from one window to another, thinking. Although Gerhard was stressed when he first read the words on the foil sheets, it was now Wolf's turn to unravel. Suddenly he turned and faced Gerhard squarely.

"I don't see how this DNA thing fits into 3-D printing.

"Hitler always wanted the master race, and this report details how to accomplish it. The individuals would all have blond hair and blue eyes. A DNA nucleic from a select intelligent blond haired, blue eyed person mixed with a BioAssembly computerized 3-diminsensional additive manufacture process would produce hundreds, perhaps thousands of identical master units—all within a day. And Hitler lost the war. Think what would have happened if he won?"

"I still don't understand. What were they going to manufacture?"

"People,"……..answered Gerhard, simply.

Wolf's wine glass shattered.

EPILOGUE

The Cylinder

Wilhelm Gerhard requested the Eversoll Family of Zurich, and The André L. Beau Company of Lucerne, to form a limited partnership and conduct a private auction of Hitler's cylinder. Notice was sent to a highly restricted list of qualified bidders from around the world. No public announcements were made. Two days before the auction, Gerhard received an "Offer to Purchase," which was so superior that he agreed to the cylinder's immediate sale and the auction was canceled.

Two months after the cylinder was sold, a large donation was received by the Abbot of the Monastery at Melk Abbey, Austria. The donation was specific. The funds were to be used first to cover medical expenses of the Abbot's fight against cancer. Second, they were to pay the costs associated with the repair of all damaged books in the abbey's library. The balance to be used for the benefit of the monastery.

It should be noted that as word spread of the stainless steel box that the Nazis hid in the secret chamber in the old ventilation shaft of the Great Library, so did the number of tourists who wanted to see it.

The monastery used part of the donation to purchase a new wheeled library ladder that was permanently stationed in the Great Library so tourists could climb the ladder, see Reference Volume Number 45.326/7, and the little box in the once secret space behind it. (Those who wish to view the items and use the ladder should make a request to the library staff.)

A check was given to Wolf to use as he saw fit, but especially for cornea replacement operations for his parents. His mother was afraid of the surgery and did not have the operation. His father decided under the circumstances, it was best to stay as he was.

One year later, an unknown donor bequeathed Hitler's cylinder and its contents to the European Molecular Biology Laboratory at the University Medical School of the University of Heidelberg, Germany's most prestigious medical school and the oldest university in Germany. The donation stipulated that the cylinder was to be put on display for all future generations of doctors to see.

The Submarine

The Federal Republic of Germany insisted that the submarine was government property and demanded that it be returned to Germany. Norway said no. Actually, the submarine belonged to Karl Olsson. The purpose of the Olsson Company Construction Permit application to begin work in icicle bay was to clear the area of underwater debris to provide safe passage for marine vessels. Gerhard wisely added a sentence to the application that "the underwater debris would become the property of the applicant and said applicant would be responsible for its safe disposal."

The government approved the application.

Later, after the submarine was raised, Karl claimed ownership of it, but the government quickly challenged his claim. The courts ruled in favor of the Olsson Company. After a brief review, Norway awarded a contract to Karl for the removal and transport of the submarine to a government site deep in the Sognefjord.

Here Norwegian scholars examined the submarine and collected artifacts prior to its complete restoration and display. Other government contracts were also awarded to the Olsson Company over the years, including wharf construction in various cities and physical maintenance of the gigantic Kollsnes gas pumping station.

Funds were received by Mrs. Knudsvig of the Knudsvig Hotel in Balestrand, Norway for the installation of a tasteful brass plaque in the dining room used by the seniors when they met with Gerhard and told their stories about Hitler's submarine.

The plaque was to be engraved with the words … In Honor of our Seniors. A portion of the funds were earmarked for two glasses of wine and one cup of tea or coffee per senior at each monthly meeting for the next three years.

Other

André Beau's client from Qatar decided to purchase one of Gerhard's Gutenberg Bibles for the price of 35 million euros.

Nicole Eversoll and Gerhard were married, but divorced amicably one year later. There were no children.

THE END